The Peach Seed

J. Wesley Gold

J. Wesley Gold

J. Wesley Gold

Return to old watering holes for more

than water; friends

and dreams are there to meet you.

---African Proverb

J. Wesley Gold

Dedication

Some people don't know their parents and most didn't know mine. Thank God, I knew them; they were the heroes in my life. This book is dedicated to my dad Booker T., the one who taught me to be a man. And to my mother Bernice, the one who taught me to be a better man.

.

J. Wesley Gold

ACKNOWLEDGEMENTS

Special thanks to Louis Jones "Uncle Louie" my friend and mentor.

TABLE OF CONTENTS

1 THE PREMONITION

Adelia Wade was an extraordinary mother and devoted wife. A petite beauty at thirty-three with naturally curling hair, smooth dark skin, and freckles sprinkled around cinnamon colored eyes. Since childhood, she knew a clairvoyant gift was something inherited from her mother. One of God's creatures by her own admission, probably would have been a soothsayer had not God saved her.

She walked across the cracked linoleum on her kitchen floor and glanced at what once was her grandmothers' clock. Sitting on the windowsill with its twisted hands and fractured face. It was almost noon, dinner time in the South. Her family would be home soon, and food was on the table. Hot oil spattered out of her cast iron skillet as she started frying hot water cornbread.[1]

Moving towards an open window, she looked out, stepped away and untied her apron, placing a safety pin where her dress had been torn, sewn together, and torn again. Grabbing her apron she tied it around her waist and uttered a prayer, "God, please, don't let me die, not today." Something was wrong, and she didn't know what. Was it a premonition or an ominous feeling caused by the light?

---

[1] Cornbread made with plain meal and hot water

The familiar sound of a wooden screen door closing signaled her family's arrival. Along with her dad Pap and husband Ed were six sons, thirteen year old Edward Jr. (EJ), twins Bobby and Bennie, Jason, Tommy, and Chris. Bobby and Bennie were a year younger than EJ, and the last three were about two years apart. Adelia lived in a world of men. Chris came in and ran out with a piece of homemade Lye soap. Made in a three-legged cast iron pot, used by many generations for multiple purposes, from frying fish and cracklings[2] to washing laundry. The others were busy scrubbing their hands as Tommy turned a rusty crank, pumping water from an underground well. Adelia picked up a hand towel from a laundry basket, called Jason and tossed it to him.

The two men came inside with the boys following close behind, the last to take their seats around their kitchen table. A table bought second hand, with money Adelia earned from the sale of hand-stitched patchwork quilts. Once it could have been described as a piece of art, designed with a white laminated top, chrome plated steel framing and elegantly curved legs. Steel chairs with black padded seats and back cushions completed the set. These chairs were reserved for guests and special occasions. For everyday use, there were wooden ones with wicker bottoms.

Everyone sat silently in those wooden chairs as Ed gave thanks to God and the cook for a wonderful meal. Family meals were a unique part of life; everyone young and old joined in the mealtime conversations. Big ceramic bowls and platters filled with corn bread, buttery mashed potatoes, cabbage, white beans and neck-bones covered the table. Pitchers of Southern sweet tea were passed around. For dessert, there was Pap's favorite, pudding and sauce

---

[2] Fried pieces of pork fat with a small amount of skin attached

(homemade cake and sauce). Pap and Ed settled into wooden rocking chairs with quilted covers. It was time for an after dinner nap. Nap time in a room that served as a living room by day and bedroom by night. The boys stretched out on the floor as Bennie switched on the television set and adjusted the "Rabbit Ears."[3] He tuned into an episode of a black comedy, filled with racist stereotypes named "Amos and Andy."[4] The show was adapted from radio and written by whites. It showcased blacks in a despicable light. However, it was one of only a few shows that allowed black actors to be seen in roles other than menial servants, the primary reason millions of blacks watched it.   Nonetheless, the NAACP critical of any show portraying blacks as "idiotic buffoons," launched a formal protest against it. It ran in syndication until 1966 and was then pulled from TV under pressure from the NAACP and a growing civil rights movement. The show had its humorous moments although sleep usually prevented Pap and Ed from viewing an entire episode.

Some hours of the day seem shorter than others, twelve to one felt like the shortest hour of the day; dinner was over, and work was calling. Ed climbed onto a red Farmall tractor with a sickle bar mower and steered it towards the hay field. Pap and the boys ambled towards the tobacco patch. Pap lumbered along the road, watching Bennie's bare feet as he carried a one gallon Mason jar wrapped in burlap, and filled with ice water. The three older boys would make several return trips for water during the afternoon.

Alvie Campbell (aka Pap) moved slowly, plagued with arthritis, and sore muscles compounded by years of hard work. Sixty-eight years old, six-feet-four, two-hundred and fifty pounds, he was quite an imposing figure, but not the man he once was. He took off his

---

[3] A type of TV antenna
[4] http://wikipedia.org/wiki/Amos_'n'_Andy

straw hat and used a checkered handkerchief to wipe the sweat from his brow. All the while looking at his scarred, knotted hands, and the gray hairs covering them. He walked off the shoulder of the road, sat down on a mound of dirt, removed his shoe and adjusted the cardboard insert covering a hole worn into his sole. Pap grew up under a philosophy of "waste not want not." His family had been extremely poor and believed in getting the most out of everything. Pap didn't wear the new shoes Ed bought him because he thought there was a little more wear in the old ones. As a child, he was taught using his resources wisely would keep him out of the "Poorhouse."

Yes! There really was such a thing as a Poorhouse![5] It was not just something his parents made up, like a boogeyman, to frighten him into saving his money and spending carefully. Nor was it intended to discourage him from making excessive, greedy demands on his family. Before Social Security, there were County Poorhouses located throughout the United States.

Hunched over as he walked, he looked like so many other farmers working the land on just another hot-as-hell day in the South. The only relief from the blazing sun came from the shade of a tree, cool drink of water, or the occasional cloud passing over. Today there was cloud cover. Pap walked along the roadway his eyes drifting towards an old red barn with a rusty tin roof, leaning from age, "See Rock City" painted on its side. That's me he thought an old barn leaning from age. Barn Swallows[6] seemed to be playing a game of tag flying in and out of the barn's loft. A rattlesnake with black irregular shaped rings around its body darted from the grass. It quickly slithered across the road in front of him, the hot asphalt burning its belly. Normally, Pap would have warned the boys to stay

---

[5] http://www.poorhouse.com/
[6] Small birds that inhabit barns and other buildings

clear of such a deadly snake. Now he watched it with an unseeing eye; he was in another place daydreaming and wondering how time moved so swiftly. As a young man with small children and a loving wife, he never saw this day coming. Hard work was his creed, and once he enjoyed the fruits of his labor living on his own farm. For years, he had raised animals and grew crops that provided for his family. He thought about the treachery, and deception used by white farmers to take his property. His livelihood was stolen, and there was no fighting back. In February of 1953, he was scheduled to make the last payment on his 120 acre farm.

He didn't know his white neighbors were envious of his success, wanted his land and put a scheme in play to get it. Pap was thrilled at the idea of paying off his mortgage, until his banker told him there was something wrong with his account. When he asked what was wrong, Mr. Parker told him not to worry everything would be worked out. He would be contacted after his account was put in order.

After several weeks of waiting Pap's patience ran out, he decided to pay a visit to his bank. Mr. Parker whom he usually dealt with was no longer a bank employee. He spoke to a Mr. Harrison, who judging by the size of his stomach, obviously loved food, beer, or both. Alvie he said, (never Mister Campbell) you've defaulted on your mortgage agreement, and the bank intends to foreclose. Pap said Mr. Harrison I've tried to make my last payment and can make it now. I'm sorry, Alvie it's out of our hands. Pap was escorted out of the bank by a guard as though he were a common criminal instead of a long term customer. Never being allowed to make the final payment, his farm went into foreclosure. His neighbors bought it at auction for a fraction of its worth, adding his property to theirs. He sought relief through the courts and was told everything was done within the law. Due to his failure to honor his mortgage agreement his property was foreclosed and legally auctioned off. There was no lawful avenue available to him to correct a wrong. The old adage of picking oneself up by your bootstraps only applied to certain people. Blacks were not allowed to lift themselves beyond a set level. It was okay to have a house or corn crop better than your black neighbor, but not your white one. This and other unethical tactics were regularly used to keep blacks at a certain level.

In America the land of opportunity this should have been an aberration, but unfortunately it wasn't. Blacks couldn't live the American Dream, only parts of it. Their dream came with restrictions in place preventing advancement beyond a pre-designated point. To put it in the vernacular of the day, your dream couldn't allow you to become "too uppity" or act "too white" by owning more than a limited amount of land and property. Moving beyond a set boundary, as Pap had done, meant your dreams could be shattered. Ironically he lost the farm by being too successful. His property was taken by legal means with the aid of corrupt bankers and attorneys. Other blacks lost their land through illegal means used by Klansmen and night riders. One injustice was no different from the other. The legal justice system gave innocent victims no recourse and no appeal. Too often the so-called purveyors of justice aided in the theft.

Most of his adult life was spent working towards the goal of paying off his mortgage, and now there was no farm. At fifty-eight, he had neither the desire nor resources to purchase another one. Although Adelia adored him, and Ed treated him like a father he never knew, Pap hated the situation he found himself in. Like the biblical character Lazarus,[7] he felt like a beggar living in a strange land. Adelia pleaded with him to stop working the fields, but retirement was not an option. He felt accepting charity would kill him and didn't think hard work ever would. He smiled at his

---

[7] Lazarus from the parable of Lazarus and Dives

grandsons trailing behind and started to swell with pride. They were the happiness in his life. What would their future hold he wondered; could their dreams ever become reality? Every man wants the satisfaction of accomplishing a goal in life, Pap was no exception. He wanted a taste of the silver spoon; he wanted the "mister" in front of his name. Just a small measure of success and a larger measure of respect. Prosperity had been too elusive, though it was once within his reach he wasn't allowed to grasp it. Death took his wife, and greed took his farm. Nevertheless he refused to give up. After losing his farm, he became what his father was, what he loathed, a sharecropper,[8] and at the end of every year the payoff was less.

A year's work equated to little more than a new pair of dress shoes, a pair of brown khaki trousers and a small amount of money for his "coffee can." He no longer trusted banks. Failure can be more than a bitter pill to swallow, especially when that failure is due to no fault of your own. It can be the catalyst that stifles ambition, kills determination, and fractures hope. Pap felt it was the death nail that sealed his coffin. He came to live with his daughter and Ed, after suffering a stroke that temporarily paralyzed him. Adelia nursed him back to health and after months of recuperation, he was back at work. His vision of a better life had faded, he knew for him there would be no second chance.

His grandsons were playing along the side of the road, he stopped and waited for them to catch up. He, heard the call of a "Bobwhite,"[9] looked towards the heavens and wondered if rain were coming. The boys knew when they reached the field, work would be the order of the day and the old man would be leading the way. He would pull

---

[8] People that farmed land belonging to someone else, providing all the labor to plant and harvest crops for a share of the profits from crop sales

[9] A popular game bird of the South that some believe can predict rain with a characteristic call of "bob-white"

out a flat metal file from a pocket of his overalls and sharpen weeding hoes for another afternoon of chopping grass from endless rows of tobacco. Another day of blistered hands and aching backs. They reached the field; Pap casually walked over to a massive Red Oak, stretched out on the ground under its shade and called his grandsons over. As he gazed at clouds migrating overhead, he said nothing and began to hum a song he remembered from long ago. His mother taught it to him. Finally, he looked at the boys. Go over to the hay field he said, find your dad and tell him to come see me; I've got something for him.

Which one of us, asked Tommy? All of you, and take your time, it's hot. EJ looked at him and said all of us Pap? Yeah, all of you. Walking off EJ kept looking back to see what Pap was doing. They didn't know what was happening and rushed off to find Ed. Pap stood alone and watched as his grandsons hurried off. Watching them allowed him to forget about the bitterness in his heart if only for a moment. He loved those six little boys that would always carry a small piece of him. Vicariously he would live through them hoping their good works, and accomplishments would compensate for his disappointments and failures.

He heard thunder overhead and knew the call of the "Bobwhite" was true; rain was coming. Reaching into the bib pocket of his overalls, he pulled out a shoestring connected to a gold pocket watch and looked at the time. One thirty-five on a hot and humid day in August. A treasured possession that held both material and sentimental value, an old watch his father gave him. A gold pocket watch with a built in alarm, adorned with ornate hand carvings, and an engraved cover that snapped over the face. Ed would cherish it as much as he had from the time it was given to him on his eighteenth birthday. His father gave it to him as he was leaving home. Something he could sell if he ever needed money to get back, his dad told him. He would never have sold it and made up his mind long ago never to part with it. He placed it back into his watch pocket and out of another pocket took out a lighter and red tin of Prince Albert tobacco. He removed a sheet of paper, sifted in tobacco and rolled a cigarette. Now his senses were heightened; he felt young and alive. He smelled the rain in the air and the dirt underneath his feet. The aroma of tobacco in his tin, and the perfumed smell of honey suckle growing along a nearby fence row. A change was taking place; he felt no fear, no bitterness, and for the first time in his life felt totally free.

Perspiration combined with stifling heat moved like waves over his body. He looked closely at his "Zippo"[10] and ran his fingers over the engraved name of James Campbell, his only son. James, who had been a Navy Steward, was killed during World War II. He turned the lighter over in his hand studying every nick and scratch before he lit his cigarette. Slowly he took a few easy pulls from it and tossed it to the ground. Again he took out his watch and held it in his hand. He cursed under his breath after a lifetime of work all he had to give Ed, was something given to him. There was nothing to leave his daughter and grandsons except fond memories and a few dollars in a tin can.

Sadness was an emotion he seldom displayed. He always told his grandsons "never cry," that tears were for women, and a man should give them a shoulder to cry on. His heart was heavy; he had worked hard and played by the rules with nothing to show for it. He broke his own rule and shed a tear; his chariot was coming; he could see it just beyond the horizon. It would pick him up and take him down the road to eternity. He saw a grayish-brown Mourning Dove with dull red legs and black spots on its wings. It perched on a nearby fence post with an air of anonymity and locked into his gaze. Rain

---

[10] A metal encased brand of cigarette lighter

began to fall as he held steadfast to the post. The dove, a symbol of peace which represented the triumph of life over death. It flipped water off its head and stared at Pap through the rain. Each one probing the other and both knowing today life would not triumph. Rain fell on Pap's head as he took off his hat and placed it on the ground beside him. He slipped off his shoes and stretched his legs out on the grass, thinking today he should have worn his new shoes. He closed his eyes and went to sleep. It was the summer of sixty-three, and Alvie Campbell was dead at sixty-eight.

Bobby is my name. Bobby Wade, Pap's grandson. The end of his story is the beginning of mine. I was twelve when he died, my first encounter with the death of a loved one. Life is hard and even harder when you lose someone you love. Pap was the anchor in my life the only grandfather I would ever know. How could I live without him? A grandfather who showed me how to make whistles from the stems of squash plants, and slingshots from inner tubes and leather shoe tongues. Always my teacher, he taught me a man's word was his bond, encouraged me to work hard and believe that anything was possible.

As I pulled out drawers from my shared dresser, looking for something decent to wear for Pap's funeral, I wondered how much worse it could get. I had one pair of hand-me-down dress shoes (a gift from my uncle), shoes too big and made to fit by stuffing pieces of newspaper into the toes. My so-called "good shirt" was too small, and my Sunday pants worn slick and shiny were so thin one could see through them. Mom lost her mother years earlier, now her dad was gone, and she had a hard time dealing with it. A couple of days before Pap's funeral mom's pastor Reverend Winters came to pay us a visit. He pulled into our driveway and parked his new Cadillac Coupe Deville with its glistening blue paint and sparkling chrome. Reverend Winters was a short, portly, bald headed man who loved red suspenders. Wearing a blue silk and wool suit with diamond rings on his fingers and black Stacy Adam shoes on his feet, he rolled his well-fed body out of his car. He went inside not bothering to speak to the kids gathered outside, purposely stepping around them. He was in and out within fifteen minutes. Someone from my neighborhood wearing tailored clothing and driving a Cadillac was a person to be admired, not someone to be resented. As a minister, I didn't think he should wear old clothes and drive a beat up Chevy like the one my parents owned. But, I thought maybe having a new car, and tailored clothing could have caused him to misplace his priorities.

Many churches and ministers who started out praising and loving God almighty had succumbed to the temptations of material gain, lost their way and wound up praising and loving the almighty dollar. I remembered verse 19:24 from the book of Matthew: "And again I say unto you, it is easier for a camel to go through the eye of a needle than for a rich man to enter into the kingdom of God." Sometimes diamond rings, new cars, and a full stomach made one forget they were servants of God. I didn't care if he spoke to us although I wondered what comforting and consoling words he could have given mom in such a short time.

How could he consider my grandfather's death such an insignificant event? To make matters worse, he told mom since Pap was not a member of his church he could not perform the eulogy. Never would I have guessed a eulogy had to be bought and paid for. True Pap was no saint, wasn't a member of the church and rarely attended services. Only Pap knew what type of relationship he had with God. He was my mother's father and my grandfather, nothing else mattered. The father of a woman who dedicated her life to the church and her pastor. Someone who gladly sacrificed her own welfare and the welfare of her family for the benefit of the church. Religion had always been something of a mystery to me; this experience provided me with a bit of clarity. I now saw it as a tool used by some to control and manipulate others, using God for personal gain. Why else would Jesus Christ who came from a region of the world populated by black and brown men be portrayed as a white man? The so called religious slave masters taught their slaves to love God and be good Christians. Yet they had no problem raping their female slaves and felt no remorse when they murdered male slaves for not picking enough cotton. This pastor in my book was no better. I didn't know what more he should have done, but felt my mother deserved more than fifteen minutes.

I felt betrayed and angry mom deserved better and so did Pap. I felt there was no longer a place for the church and religious practitioners in my life. When I talked to mom about it, she told me only God is perfect; I should learn to forgive and forget. Mom was a wonderful woman, deeply religious and devout. I loved her more than life but for the first time in my years there was a significant difference between us. I was angry and wanted her to be angry too. I thought as a people we had always been too quick to forgive and forget. Blacks were too trusting, too humble, and too eager to offer allegiance and appeasement to a people and country that excluded and exploited them.

The author and poet Maya Angelou[11] said if you don't like something change it, if you can't change it, change your attitude, and don't complain. Attempting to change something I couldn't control was useless. I decided to change my viewpoint. I could not accept our pastors' actions and decided for the rest of my life I would need no church or pastor. In my view man was too flawed to show me the path to the kingdom, only God could. I had a great deal of faith

---

[11] Brainy Quotes (2010) Maya Angelou, Retrieved Dec 10, 2010, http://www.brainyquote.com/quotes/m/maya_andelou_2.html

in religion, but no confidence in the people that taught it and pretended to practice it. Christians have a beautiful ideology of how to live one's life and treat their fellow man, lofty goals that, in fact, may be beyond the reach of many. My experience with many so called Christians (and not necessarily the radical factions such as the Christian Knights of the KKK) showed me a great void between their principles and practice. It was a complex paradox, and I had no reassurance in someone telling me "I'm a Christian." I hated the total hypocrisy of it all and wondered if any of them had read Titus 1:16: "They profess they know God; but in works they deny him, being abominable, and disobedient, and unto every good work reprobate."

I had known true Christians in my life and knew the sacrifices they made. I was only twelve not willing to make those sacrifices and not willing to risk God's damnation as others had by calling myself a Christian. God himself had written the Ten Commandments, and I could follow them without doubt or distrust. Until I learned otherwise, those Ten Commandments would become my bible. I saw no need to read or adhere to the sacred writings of other men. As blasphemous as it sounds I would need no intermediary between God and me.

The pain raged within me as I thought about seeing Pap in an open field stretched out beneath an Oak Tree, soaked from rain. Lifting him up, placing him on an old farm wagon and covering him with a canvas sheet used to cover loads of sawdust from the mill. Chris holding his grandfather's hat and cradling his shoes on the way home. Trying to keep him dry as his body turned cold. The hurt was so powerful I felt a tear forming but my anger would not allow it to fall. Pap taught me crying was for women, and it was a man's responsibility to give them a shoulder to cry on. At the age of twelve, I chose to be a man no matter what.

J. Wesley Gold

.

2 THE WAY WE WERE

I awoke around 5:00 a.m. one morning to the sound of mom's voice calling me. It was January with snow on the ground and ice on the windows; the house felt like a tomb. The fire inside our coal stove went out overnight and had to be rekindled every morning. We lived in what was called a "shotgun"[12] house with no insulation or storm windows. Cold air came in from every crack and crevice even through knotholes in the floor boards. The temperature inside the house was about the same as the temperature outside. I did not feel like getting out of bed.

Each child took their turn getting the morning fire started, and today was my turn. I slowly moved away from my brother and a warm bed, stepping onto an icy floor fumbling for my shoes and socks. Placed behind the coal stove in the living room was an old bucket called a scuttle, filled with coal, and another one filled with wood chips. After clearing out ashes, I placed newspapers inside, threw in wood chips and started the fire. Sometimes kerosene was needed to ignite the kindling before coal was thrown in. In a short time, the stove turned red from the fire within; the house warmed up, and everyone started their day. Mom and dad never waited for

---

[12] A narrow rectangular house common in the south with doors at each end, "shotgun" comes from the fact one could shoot a shotgun through the front door and out the back without hitting a wall.

the fire to warm the house, getting up at the same time I did. Cooking breakfast on a cold winter day was no easy task. The pot-bellied stove used for heating was in the living room, heating the kitchen meant turning on the electric range and opening the oven door. Dad placed pots of water on each heating element, hot water for washing dishes and cooking food. A bucket of drinking water left in the kitchen overnight had to be thawed before the dipper could be removed.

Every morning there was homemade biscuits or hot cakes (pancakes), buttery sweet rice or oatmeal, bacon, sausage or fatback. Whatever meat was available from the smokehouse and eggs from the henhouse. Using the toilet required a trip outside with a newspaper, napkin, paper towel, or if you were lucky, toilet tissue. When faces were washed, and teeth brushed everyone took a seat at the table, the food was blessed, and we ate. Picky eaters were rare and within our family there were no obese kids. We gladly ate what we had. When there was no more, we scraped our plates, stacked them for washing and thanked God for having something to eat. School clothes meant flannel shirts, patched denim jeans and a pair of hard leather shoes, polished even if there were holes worn in the soles.

Pap's death affected each family member differently. Dad no longer had the ambition or the desire to be a farmer, especially a sharecropper. He was much smaller than Pap, stricken with polio as a child. Polio was a traumatic disease that left him with a slight limp. He never got any pleasure from the hard life of a farmer. This would be our last year on the farm. In a few days when crops were sold, we would take our portion of the profits and leave. My parents purchased a small home of our own. Pap's death forged a new beginning for the ones left behind. If this looks like the picture of a hard pressed family living a grim life, it's not. Living a deprived life should never be confused with living an unhappy, miserable life. Happiness is rarely found in one's bank account. There was love, and happiness seldom seen in the richest of households. With no fear of losing money, material gain, or status in life, incongruously it gave us the freedom to live our lives without pretense. We were raised with strict rules and old fashioned values with plenty of love, discipline, and the knowledge that each of us was our brothers' keeper. All of us were taught the golden rule though later I learned it is "he who has the gold that makes the rules." In the sixties when I heard the words "old fashioned values" I felt a sense of family and belonging. Those words have been so overused when I hear them today in the year 2010 I feel a cringe, knowing they have turned into a politician's tool reduced to words without meaning.

It had been three years since we moved away from the farm. Since that time I had the luxury of being able to attend school every day, no more days lost to planting, cultivating and harvesting tobacco or other crops. No more scrambling to catch up with other kids in the class. Our house was equipped with indoor plumbing, with hot water that didn't have to be heated on the stove.

For the first time in my life, I was not living on a farm and loved it. I had summer and after school jobs and replaced my patched jeans with new ones. Now I bought shoes that actually fit. I could afford to give mom a few dollars to buy things for my younger brothers and her. My fraternal twin Bennie and I were now fifteen and loved making summer cash, even if it meant going back to the farm for work. Working on the farm was a far cry from living on one. Summer cash sometimes meant working for the Castleberry's. As many times as the stories have been told, what some people love and hate about the South is its people. For blacks especially it's a love/hate relationship. For copious reasons, black and white relationships will always characterize the South. In America, we're all defined by race a fact far too many people refuse to believe. In the

South during segregation that definition took on a new meaning. Life for blacks in the South came with daily reminders of their perceived inferiority.   One method of re-enforcing that "inferiority" and keeping blacks in their place was the "back door policy." Whenever a black person entered a white person's house it had to be via the back door. Coming through the front door was a privilege only whites could enjoy. Black parents complied with the policy primarily because they seldom had an option; their children were taught to comply as a means of survival.

Contrary to many perceived assumptions there have always been good and decent people in the South, both black and white. Good people who actually followed the golden rule of doing unto others. I believe they were the majority; conditions for blacks could not have changed without them. Unfortunately in far too many situations and for far too many years when a voice for justice was crucial, they were the silent majority. Because they never spoke out, their complacency was interpreted as complicity.

The Castleberry's, however, were a white Southern couple that could best be described as "a white couple living in the South." Frank Castleberry had been an Army Sergeant Major originally from Ceeville; his wife Marjorie was a California native. They met and married while he was stationed at the Presidio, a foreign language teaching and resource center in Monterey, California. After retiring from the Army, Frank and Marjorie settled in Ceeville, on a farm Frank inherited from his grandfather. They had no kids. Bennie and I loved working for them. They knew little about farming; we gave them the benefit of our years of experience. The Castleberry's gave us simple dignity and respect, treating us like everyone wanted to be treated. Working for them at times could be confusing, though they were not the cause of the confusion. On a hot summer afternoon, Bennie was working in their front yard and Mrs. Castleberry, who often bought us gifts, called him to the front door. Before he got there, the telephone rang, she answered it and started carrying on a conversation. When she hung up the phone, she looked for Bennie, who wasn't at the front door. She heard a knock on the back door; there was Bennie.

Weren't you in the front yard? Yes ma'am. Both of them stood there looking at each other with a befuddled look on their face. Frank, coming into the room holding a cigar and calling cadence, disrupted their attention. Marjorie said, please don't march in here and put that nasty cigar down. She turned her attention back to Bennie. Were you in the front yard? Yes ma'am. Then why in the world did you go all around the house to the back door? She could not figure out why he went to the back door; he could not imagine why she expected him to go to the front door. Bennie didn't have an answer and finally Frank broke the impasse by asking Marjorie why she called him. Oh, she said and immediately went to find the new shirts she bought us. Bennie thanked her and hurried out the house.

Why in the world would he do that, Marjorie asked Frank? Do what? Come to the back door when he was already at the front door. This is the South, said Frank. And that explains it she asked? Frank explained the backdoor policy and Marjorie was outraged. Her hazel eyes were locked on Frank; she tossed her long red hair to one side, strode to the front door and called Bennie back into the house directing him to come through the front door. He grudgingly walked in, feeling he had done something wrong. As long as I have a house you can enter it through the front door or the back door. Do you hear me Bennie? Yes, ma'am, he said, glancing at Frank. Frank, pulling up a chair, said, sit down Bennie; I know why you went to the back door that's a policy we don't practice here. I'm not telling you to stop doing it at other places; I'm saying you don't have to do it here. Do you understand Bennie? Yes sir. We recently started to work for the Castleberry's, and Bennie wondered if we could continue working for them. How could we work for any white couple wanting us to enter their house through the front door? Incredibly insanity can be turned into something resembling sagacity. How anyone could be taught to accept a practice that made something as common as walking through the front door seem odd and out of the ordinary was simply amazing.

We did go back to work for the Castleberry's, and we felt a closeness we never experienced with anyone outside of the family. Marjorie met mom, and they became close friends. Mom taught her the art of quilting and how to make a delicious sweet potato cobbler. Marjorie taught her to use a sewing machine. They loved listening to each other's stories and learning how their lives were intertwined. Of course, some of their neighbors frowned on their relationship but in the words of Mrs. Castleberry, "who cares about what they think." She always smiled after saying it, Tommy loved the way her cheeks dimpled.

Mom and Marjorie both possessed the same giving and sometimes defiant nature, never afraid to speak their mind, never afraid of the consequences. I loved both of them for never having to seek society's permission to be the people God made them to be. Dad and Frank, on the other hand, never developed a relationship and didn't bother crossing that invisible line separating black from white. Although neither one, discouraged the relationship between mom and Marjorie. They were alone sitting in our living room one day when a salesman drove up, a shyster called the "L. B. Price man." He sold pots and pans door-to-door on the installment plan. He probably made a hundred dollars from junk that cost him ten bucks. Marjorie watched him pull into our yard, mom went out to meet him. As he stepped out of his car, mom said, "I don't have any money for you today." Let's see, you did not have any money for me last week and now you don't have any today, what's the problem? The problem is I don't have any money. Well, if you don't have any money next week the only choice I'll have is to send my supervisor out. Mom looked into his tanned face and asked, "Is he a bear?" Puzzled with an "aw shit" look on his face, he stuttered. "No, no he's not a bear." Well if he's not a bear I'll tell him the same thing I just told you. The guy decided it was time to move on. Mom went back into the house; Marjorie had fallen onto the floor with tears streaming out of her eyes, she could not stop laughing. Mom was a little woman with a lot of spunk. I loved the way she added humor and courage to sincerity.

I may have enjoyed working with the Castleberry's, though it was hard for me to give them one hundred percent of my trust as Bennie had. I remembered the guy we worked for prior to the Castleberry's. A hairy, rotund fellow named Tim Caldwell who had the biggest feet I had ever seen. "Big foot Tim" was what the workers on his farm called him whenever he was not around. He owned two farms, one locally where we usually worked and another about thirty miles from Ceeville. It was on that second farm that I decided never to work for him again.

We were picking up bales of hay from the field and carrying them to a flatbed wagon where they were loaded and stacked for transport to the barn. An elderly black man named Ebb who lived on the farm was working with us. Ebb was seventy-two and weighed about a hundred and forty pounds. He had the look of worn leather with patches of hair on an otherwise bald head. Ebb was an amazingly hard worker though, at times, he tired. Bennie and I would help him get his bales on the wagon. The owners' daughter lived in a house on the farm. Ebb lived in her basement. When we broke for dinner, he took us into his living area. What I thought was a basement was nothing more than a cellar[13] with a dirt floor and no access to the upper level of the house. The place was musty and damp with a chimney on one wall and the pipe from a coal stove lodged into it. His clothes were hung on a wire line supported by metal braces and running the length of one wall. Electricity for his television and small refrigerator was provided by a single electrical outlet. He couldn't use more than two appliances without an extension cord.

Wooden shelves with concrete blocks between them served as his kitchen pantry which held cans and jars of fruits and vegetables. Wooden pallets with boards nailed across the top were placed in one corner of the room supporting a small iron bed. Buckets of coal and pieces of wood were stored in another corner. It was the middle of summer; I could imagine what this place was like in the middle of winter. Ebb worked on this farm for forty years, and this was how he was expected to live.

No running water or indoor plumbing not even a wooden floor to protect his feet in winter. A small window provided the only natural light except for light shining around and through the cellar door. Ebb was born in Cartersville, Georgia in 1894, before the turn of the century. He never learned to read or write, having worked on a farm from the age of five. I could only imagine the indignities he had experienced fighting his entire life for the simple right to be called a man.

My economic status in life was nowhere near middle class, but it was far better than this. It hurt me to see anyone having to live under these conditions. The worst part of the situation was I could do nothing for him. There were occasions earlier in my life when I

---

[13] A room or enclosed space under a building usually used for storage.

lived under similar circumstances, but I was a young man starting my life and he was an old man nearing the twilight of his. I had been taught to respect my elders no matter who they were or where they came from. I felt angry, acrimonious and completely helpless. I didn't utter two words all afternoon, worried about Ebb, not knowing what I could do to help him. When "Bigfoot" took us home, we asked for our pay and told him we would no longer work for him. When he asked why, my first inclination was to say nothing, even though there were a thousand things I wanted to say. I felt his sense of decency should have told him what was wrong. I realized he had no decency or conscience; I could not just walk away.

I needed to voice my contempt for his treatment of Ebb, telling him what I thought about Ebb's living conditions and how a person of his age should be treated better. He gave me a strange look but didn't defend his actions. Ebb was a good and decent human being with very little but shared all. In the short time, we knew him he had invited us into his home, shared his knowledge, his stories of life and his homemade blackberry jam. He was someone you liked from the start, someone you wanted to fight for even though you had nothing to fight with.

Caldwell drove off, and I thought it was the end of the story, what I told him had fallen on deaf ears. We told mom what happened; we weren't going to work for anyone that would treat another person with such indifference. She didn't say what she usually said when we had a disagreement with an employer, telling us we needed a job. She smiled and told us we did the right thing by sticking to our principles. Months later mom received a letter addressed to Bennie and me, inside were photos showing the exterior and interior of a small wood frame house. There was a neat bedroom with a beautiful quilt spread over an iron bed, bathroom with folded towels and a small kitchen with new appliances. The last picture was one I kept to this day. Standing outside in front of the house holding a sign that read "its' for me" was Ebb, all smiles and wearing a suit. Not satisfied with pictures, dad took Bennie and me to see Ebb at his new home. He was overjoyed to see me and Bennie and meet our dad. He had a thousand things to tell us. He now worked around the house where he used to live, no longer working the fields. He was getting a small Social Security check which paid for his utilities. The thing he seemed most excited about was Caldwell's granddaughter teaching him to read and write. I could tell from the look in his eyes this was one of the few times in his life when he was happy.

I couldn't have been more grateful for what Caldwell did. Although I could not figure out why he hadn't done it earlier. I wondered if he were seeking praise for doing the right thing. He called himself a Christian. I felt a true Christian would have felt a moral obligation to do the Christian thing without outside influence. I knew Ebb would probably never own the house he was now living in, but for the rest of his days he would have a decent place to stay. Caldwell did something wonderful for whatever reason. I believed Bennie, and I played a small role in it. We sent him a letter thanking him for being his brothers' keeper, although I wondered if he truly were.

Factory work gave us a much better life, and dad wondered why he spent so many years sharecropping. Working in a factory making and assembling air conditioner parts had a definite advantage over growing tobacco. Eight hours a day was a far cry from the sunup to sundown hours worked on the farm. Dad had more time for mom, for us, and our homework problems, girl problems and all the other problems growing boys encounter. Most of all it gave him a chance to know each of us individually. He learned more about our likes and dislikes, our strong and weak points, our goals and dreams. He was a small child when his father died too young to remember him. Every time he looked at the watch Pap gave him he thought about how Pap became the father he never had. He missed his dad, his companionship and knew mom sometimes cried because he was no longer there. The night before Pap died an eerie light appeared on their bedroom wall, mom, woke up dad to show him. Do you see it she asked? What, I don't see anything, what does it look like? The light on the wall can't you see it? No, I don't see it. It's a weird light, and it's not a projection, it's a light emanating from within itself. I'm sorry, honey I don't see it. He didn't want her to think he was dismissive, but he was tired, turned over and went back to sleep. Mom watched it until it faded from sight. Mom's gift sometimes frightened her because it was difficult to understand. Her mother had willingly accepted her gift and used it as a medium and fortune teller. It was a gift that felt natural to her mother, but never felt normal to her. Her first thought was death was coming for her; instead it foretold the death of her father.

Dad loved Pap but did not share his idea of success. For him, success meant six healthy sons and a loving wife. Knowing how hard Pap worked, the injustices he experienced and his sense of disappointment before his death, Ed understood how unfair life could be. He believed placing less emphasis on material gain and more emphasis on family was the right move to make. He had the drive and ambition to succeed but did not need the elusive "silver spoon" Pap searched for.

We lived in a small Tennessee town called Ceeville on a street named Drakes Alley, located in a "colored" part of town called East End. Just beyond the alley was a self-contained city within a city everything we needed was only a short distance away. There was Robin High School that educated black kids from grades 7 through 12. Mr. C's barbershop where a haircut cost seventy-five cents and a shoeshine could be purchased for a quarter. A numbers runner hooked you up for a dime, and the latest news of the day, came for free. The "Pit," where young folks could get a hamburger, fries, and the chance to learn a new dance. Miss Pearl's where old folks could get a plate of fried fish, white beans, coleslaw and a bottle of beer. Miss Elsie's house of prostitution for those who felt like sinning and Mount Nebo church of God for those who wanted to confess those sins. Cobb's Cleaners where your Saturday night stepping out clothes and your Sunday go to church clothes were cleaned to perfection.

Catching a movie required traveling to the "Roxy," a white owned theater where people of color were restricted to the balcony. Whites felt no obligation to provide blacks with the same services provided other whites; however they were willing to take your money and provide you with substandard or limited service. As luck would have it, we preferred the privacy of the balcony.

For me, the biggest thrill of all was having neighbors nearby. Neighbors we could talk to from the front yard, something we never could do up to that point in my life. Our neighbors always lived a couple of miles away. East End took on a carnival like atmosphere on Saturdays when farm hands came to town and got together with city folk. They gathered at New York City imitators called the Savoy Club or Harlem Cafe for good food and drink. Women had the opportunity to show off buxom figures in new dresses, gorgeous hats and spectacular patent leather shoes. Men smoked big cigars, wore starched white shirts with cuffs turned up, and hats tilted to one side. These were people who faced numerous unnamed obstacles during the week. People who learned to deal with their troubles unwind and relax on the weekends. For a brief period, they forgot their cares and totally unwound, something I felt whites could never do; formality was too much a part of their lives and "getting loose" wasn't part of their vocabulary.

Friends and neighbors helped to shape our lives, colorful characters called "Silver Legs" and "Cottonmouth." Reverend Winters, the pastor of Mount Nebo and Mr. Bell, the principal at Robin High. Blues men like "Irvin Backus," a master of the harmonica and "Billy Hicks," a sax player like no other. Or "Big Lucy," who belted out vocals at the "300" club. East End was more than a neighborhood it was a village, a community of black faces, doctors, teachers, preachers, businessmen and entertainers. Each one played a part, sometimes good, sometimes not so good, in raising the children of the village.

It was a community of modest homes with freshly cut lawns and whitewashed fences. A place where neighbors looked out for neighbors. Segregation was a lousy, degrading system of apartheid but had its good points. It helped to keep the village alive and well by enjoining everyone with the same shared goals of betterment, opportunity, education and advancement. Things far too many of us failed to seek after integration.

On a temperate Saturday in May of 1968, EJ awoke to a long awaited day in his life. It was graduation day, and he was graduating from Robin High School. He had bought a dark blue suit with a light blue ruffled shirt and black bow tie for the occasion. EJ was a perfectionist who spent a week finding the perfect pair, of thick-and-thin socks and spit shining his shoes. Working at a local college for the last two years busing tables and washing dishes, he was a bit envious of privileged kids, getting a college education with no appreciation for the opportunity they were being given. He wanted something no one in his family had: a college education. He knew there were no rich parents to provide it; he could only get one through his own devices. The guidance counselor at Robin High gave his attention only to certain students. Those were the ones who received the scholarships. If you were too dark skinned, had hair too kinky, were too militant or your parents didn't belong to a particular section of the black community; you were out of luck. No matter how good your grades were. Blacks discriminated against other blacks just as whites did. I hated them for doing it just as much as I hated whites for doing it. On the day of graduation EJ told his family he was joining the military. I was confused, and angry this was nineteen sixty-eight. For me, the military represented the so-called establishment power structure and as a young African American male I wanted no part of it. There were better career choices available and other ways to get a college education. Why would any black man join the military and move from second class citizenship to third class?

I felt EJ was joining to validate his citizenship. He, his parents, grandparents, and great grandparents were U.S. citizens born in the United States. Why did he have to prove he belonged here? His lineage led all the way back to his slave ancestors. Ancestors who suffered unmentionable atrocities ensuring their white countrymen enjoyed a way of life denied them. There were certain segments of society that would never accept him for what he was, a man. It was that simple; there was no need to prove anything. I was at a crossroads, confused and angry, when I got EJ alone I tried to explain my disappointment in his decision. Why should we be defined by other people? Why can't we live our lives by our own rules and realize our own goals and dreams?

We will never live up to the expectations of some people and I for one say, "Fuck them," let's live our lives for us without any false hopes. "Freedom, justice for all, and equal opportunity" was a propaganda package the U.S. gave to the rest of the world. For us, it was nothing more than a nefarious prevarication. The more I talked, the more furious I became. All the while EJ seemed to be looking

32

beyond me and never attempted to explain the reasons for his decision which angered me the most. Bennie told me to leave him alone; he said EJ knows what he's doing. No, he doesn't and neither do you. Ordinarily after a remark like that Bennie and I would be throwing hands, or locked in a death grip. But they knew I wasn't angry at them. It was the system I was showing contempt for. Mom took it all in stride when she learned EJ was enlisting in the military, giving him a hug and wishing him well. Dad called him aside for a father-son talk and gave him a four leaf clover carved from a peach seed, something to carry with him. A "talisman"[14] to bring him good luck and guide him back home.

EJ wanted to see the Castleberry's before he left, the reaction he got from Marjorie Castleberry was a revelation. Why in hell would you want to join the military she screamed? Don't you have enough problems here without going off to some foreign country to fight? Fighting for a country that does not give a damn about you! For God's sake can't you find something better to do with your life? Think about it please; please think about what you're doing. Talk to him, Frank, talk to him. He's nothing but a baby. Frank tried to console her she would have none of it. Her response caught EJ totally off guard. She couldn't stop the tears, at a loss for words she hugged him tightly and kissed his cheek. She studied his face for what seemed like a long time then went into her bedroom and closed the door.

EJ wasn't the only one caught off guard. She told him what I believed about my country though I wasn't sure I believed it until that moment, and truth be told it wasn't something I wanted to hear. It was like having a wicked step mother who gave her kids everything and gave you what they didn't want. And although you

---

[14] An object believed to confer on its bearer supernatural powers or protection

never expected to hear the "I love you" she told her own kids, you hoped she would never blatantly say she didn't give a damn about you. Frank was a hard core disciplined veteran proud of his country, though I sensed a bit of shame before he reached out and shook EJ's hand. I'm proud of you EJ; don't worry about Marjorie, one day she will understand. You guys are like her own sons she loves you and wants to protect you. Take care of yourself, keep your nose clean, and drop me a card now and then. I thought about what he said and totally agreed with him, Marjorie loved EJ, but her words gave me an uneasy feeling. I felt like a man without a country.

Two weeks after graduation EJ enlisted in the military, I hated his decision. EJ wanted a challenge and a college education; joining the Marine Corps would provide a challenge and the opportunity. Before he left Bennie, and I took him to the "Pit" for his going away party. Sitting at one of the small booths' listening to James Browns' "Say it Loud" and watching people on the dance floor, it dawned on me EJ was actually leaving. Although only a year older, he was a guy I looked up to, someone who guided me and always had my back. EJ was the one who carried the older brother responsibility of keeping the rest of us in line. The one who paid the price not only for his screw ups but ours as well, the guy who took the heat. Now those duties would be shared by Bennie and me. It was a job that carried plenty of responsibilities but few rewards. Maybe that's the reason EJ was eager to leave and become independent of the rest of us.

He was someone with an outgoing personality and had a knack for making friends. He loved school, sports, motorcycles and most of all girls. Girls, he had plenty of girls and even shared one with me, without her knowing it of course.

Mom and dad were off visiting relatives, and we had the house to ourselves. There would be no wild parties, just a chance to sneak a few girls into the house without the neighbors getting wind of it. Our parents always asked the Anderson's next door to keep an eye on us when they were gone. Asking wasn't necessary; they kept an eye on us even when our parents were home. After making sure Jason, Tommy and Chris were asleep; we cut all the lights out except for a small lamp and brought three girls in through the back door. We took the girls upstairs and broke out bottles of the favorite wines of most teenagers in the neighborhood, MD 20/20 a.k.a. Mad Dog. Mad Dog and another cheap wine made by the Gallo Brothers called Thunderbird, mixed with grapefruit juice to make what was called a "shake-em-up." Believe me when I say it "shook-em-up" it didn't take long before EJ had two girls in the mood for love.

I wanted one of them though she wasn't that eager to get with me. EJ decided to help me out. He got the girl I wanted out of her clothes and into bed. When he got up to use the restroom I moved in; the rest is history. Later word got back to her of the switch; we both denied it ever happened. I thought about fights with EJ, how I could never get the best of him. Dad taught us all to defend ourselves. Fights were pretty common from the youngest to the oldest; we would fight each other one day and fight someone else the next. Sometimes dad broke us up, and other times he stopped mom from intervening to see what the outcome would be. His rule was if someone had your brother bleeding you should be bleeding too.

I knew I might never have the chance to talk to my older brother again. I felt uncomfortable even bringing it up, but I had to say something. I did not like the choice he had made, the more I thought about it, the more it pissed me off. EJ was eating a burger and mopping up ketchup with his fries. You know what, when I get back I'm going to get a new Plymouth Roadrunner or a Dodge Charger, but whatever I get you guys can drive it. I said yeah, if you get back. Why would you say something like that asked Bennie? I hated saying it, but I thought it might be a last ditch tactic to change EJ's mind. It didn't work. I got over my anger; I tried my best to change his mind with no success. Now the matter was settled. I decided my selfish opinions and ideas may not be EJ's. My goal now was to have the best time possible with EJ and Bennie, exactly what they wanted. I forgot about my wants and with Bennie, and some female friends gave EJ the sendoff he deserved.

EJ completed basic training at the Marine Corps Recruit Depot located at Parris Island, South Carolina and advanced infantry training at Camp Geiger on the Marine Corps Base at Camp Lejeune, North Carolina. He adjusted well to military life, making new friends, meeting new girls and enjoying life in the military. EJ was having fun but regretfully not for long. In a few months, he had finished his military schools, took a few days leave, and found himself in the Republic of South Vietnam. For six months, his letters home gave me a glimpse of a strange new world. Never did he say he made a mistake, he simply made the best of a terrible situation. He told me about a world that was completely foreign to me, one of Hooches (shelter), Benjo ditches (open ditch used for toilet), and Jing (change or money).

He used terms like Boo-Coo (much or many), Assholes and Elbows (in a hurry), Pogey Bait (candy, sweets) and Skivvie House (whorehouse). EJ was no longer in my world and went out of his way to describe military terms and Vietnamese phrases to bring me into his world. I wondered about him sometimes when the mood in his letters changed. He would become angry talking about Chuck's

36

(White Marines') and the Crotch (Marine Corps) or Dinks (Vietnamese). In my letters, I always tried to give him good news mixed with funny stories. He was becoming darker, and I never wanted him to be anything other than the EJ I knew. In October of 1969, the last letter I wrote EJ was returned as undeliverable. Returned in a Department of the Navy letter that told me what I already knew. On September 10th, 1969, EJ was killed in action. We were notified earlier of EJ's death, but this letter sent me into a rage. I hated this country filled with bigotry and hatred, I was consumed with the same bigotry and hatred. I cursed my country for sending EJ to fight in a senseless war. He should never have fallen prey to lying politicians and policy makers who created the patriotic illusion that caused him to join.

I lived in a country where I could never feel totally free, regardless of the sacrifices I made for it. EJ was gone there was nothing I could do, but accept it. Never again would I have an older brother to give me advice and keep me pointed in the right direction. I often read and re-read his letters and knew the pain and suffering he tried to hide. I kept all of his letters and wanted to hear his voice once more. I pulled out the last letter he wrote me dated four days before he was killed by enemy combatants:

6 Sep 1969

Hey Bro,

What's happening your way, still riding your

old bike or have you traded it for a new one?

I'm hanging in there and doing ok. I got hit

by shrapnel and had a heat stroke.

They released me from the hospital yesterday.

Send me some pictures so I'll know what's going

on in the real world. I don't have a lot to say we've been

getting a lot of rain here lately. This is the first time in about

two weeks that we've gotten mail. So keep the letters

coming. Hopefully we'll get pulled out in time to be home

for Christmas.

Be cool dig you later your soul brother in Nam EJ.

P. S. Send more Kool Aide (grape and orange)

Hospitalized for shrapnel wounds and heat stroke, he took it all in stride with the hope of getting home by Christmas. I was becoming a different person hardened and cold. Paranoid or not I would carefully choose the people and things I placed my trust in, never letting my guard down. Mom said, "He's not dead, not my son; he's not dead." She would not believe it when a uniformed officer notified her of EJ's death, and she would not accept it now. While everyone knew the obvious, he was dead, no one made any attempt to counter her claim. Privately everyone thought the loss was too painful, too much for her to handle. Maybe the thin line between sanity and madness had been crossed, no one said anything, not a murmur, not a word.

Months later I got the courage to ask mom if EJ wasn't dead why she cried at the funeral. She told me her tears were not for her son but another mothers' son. We had a closed casket funeral for EJ. I wondered if it was him inside or someone else, obviously I would never know.

3 EARNING THE EMBLEM

Life is weird and unpredictable; we never know the path fate will choose for us to follow. A year after Bennie and I graduated, we joined the Marines. Our reasons for joining were more personal than patriotic. At eighteen, I married what I thought was a wonderful girl and planned to spend the rest of my life with her. Planning is not always a good thing, my plan would never see the light of day. I was excited about the possibility of getting a new job, searching everywhere for a copy of my high school diploma. Looking through dresser drawers, I found letters addressed to my wife, not something I was looking for.

Not a diploma, but love letters from my wife's boyfriend. I had been a complete fool, totally trusting, totally blindsided. Reading those letters was something that would tear at my psyche for years to come. As I read her letters there was disbelief, followed by disillusionment and the raging emotion of anger. I thought about unleashing my rage, striking her down and placing my hands around her neck. Choking her until she gasped for her last breath. Anger was overtaking me, then unexpectedly I felt the gentle calming of acceptance. Betrayal can be gut-wrenching and hard to accept but sometimes shit just happens. I was taught to play the cards dealt me.

There would be no self-pity, no self-analysis trying to figure out what went wrong. I accepted her betrayal as a matter of fact; why she did it was of no consequence. For me it was over, there would be no asking why, no arguing, no forgiveness, no second chances, just an opportunity to move on. She took my love and gave me deceit and bitterness in return. She broke my heart though I still loved her. It was the only thing stopping me from killing her. I packed my bags; when my wife got home, I showed her the letters and left. I never said a word to her and have not spoken to her since. My mistake was lowering my guard and allowing myself to trust her. We had no kids, and she did not contest the divorce; I sent her a copy of the final divorce decree and that chapter in my life ended.

Now, I just needed to get away. Bennie joined because he saw an opportunity to meet new women and be a hard ass. Words can't explain why I joined the military. Knowing how I felt about it and the misery and suffering it caused EJ before his death. It wasn't for revenge or any type of retaliation and certainly not to prove my citizenship. The reasons why we do some things defy common sense. Marines are a distinct breed. Unless you've earned the title, it's hard to relate to the experience of arriving at Parris Island during the early morning hours on a hot and muggy South Carolina night. Earlier in the day we picked up orders and airline tickets from a Marine recruiter. He drove us to the airport in Nashville and gave us a thumb up as he left the airport. For some unknown reason I felt he had not been totally honest with us, there was something he was holding back.

After a flight to Charleston, we took a bus to Parris Island and arrived at the front gate at approximately 2:45 a.m., or as we would later learn 0245. Driving through the front gate the place looked deserted. We moved along a dimly lit highway with palm trees and swampy marshlands on each side. Later buildings began to appear and soon we could see bodies walking around. The driver parked in front of an old wooden building I assumed was a barracks. Our odyssey began here. Drill Instructors boarded the bus yelling, screaming and pushing recruits off. No movie you have ever seen or book you have ever read about Parris Island Marines will give you the feeling of standing on painted yellow footprints at 0300 in the morning. Every recruit stood on a pair which placed him in a position of attention and placed everyone in a formation. Here a DI gave you the "yellow footprint speech":[15] You are now aboard Marine Corps Recruit Depot, Parris Island, South Carolina and you have taken the first step towards becoming a member of the world's finest fighting force - the United States Marine Corps. You should be standing at the position of attention; that means your heels are together; feet spread apart at a 45 degree angle; thumbs along the trouser seam; palms rolled inboard; fingers in their natural curl; head and eyes straight to the front; and your mouth is shut. I'll say again your mouth is shut. This is the only position from which you will speak to any Marine, sailor, or civilian personnel during your stay on Parris Island.

You are now subject to the Uniform Code of Military Justice. Be familiar with three important articles - each punishable at Commanding Officer's Non Judicial Punishment or Court Martial.

Article 86. Unauthorized Absence - you will be where you are supposed to be at the proper time in proper uniform.

Article 91. Disrespect - you will be respectful to all Marines, sailors, and civilians aboard the Depot. Disrespect can be through words, facial expressions, or gestures, and it will not be tolerated.

Article 92. Disobedience of a lawful order - do what you are told to do, when you are told to do it, without question. Our indoctrination had begun. For the next thirteen weeks, we would cease being an individual person. We would become a turd, maggot,

---

[15] Excerpt from DepO P1513.6 Depot Training Order SOP for recruit training

pig, slime bucket, reeeeeeeecruit; shit bird or shit head take your pick. I was disappointed to find out the first week was not considered training. It was a week of forming, and we had started Forming Day 1 (FD-1). Recruits were held in forming until there were enough of them to form a series which consisted of four different platoons. Usually it took about seventy-five recruits to make up a platoon. I agreed to twelve weeks of training. I had no intention of giving them any freebies. I wondered if this were a breach of my contract.

Our scuzzy civilian clothing worn to the island was packed up and put in storage along with any contraband (non-military items) we brought in. Bennie and I joined under the "buddy program" which meant we would be assigned to the same platoon for recruit training. We were placed in a forming barracks that contained about twenty racks for 80 recruits. Most of us slept on hard wooden floors. Meals at the mess hall were served on steel prison-style trays. For breakfast, we had two pieces of toast,ice cream scoop of powdered green eggs, a strip of bacon and all the milk we wanted. Talking and eyeballing was not an option. We side stepped through the chow line all the while being urged by second or third phase recruits on the serving line to "keep the line moving Private."

There was a rumor circulating that something was added to the milk to reduce our sex drive. Seventy-five horny creatures in a platoon might be a little hard to control. So maybe there was some truth to it. A couple of vending machines placed inside our barracks dispensed candy and sodas. Those machines were designated off limits and by no means could we use them. Of course, there has to be at least one recruit willing to test the waters. Bennie saw Private Moore buy a candy bar when he thought no one was watching. What an idiot, he barely got his illegal purchase into his pocket when he and five other recruits were called out by a Drill Instructor. Of course, the five other recruits had nothing to do with it. The Drill

Instructor did not want to give the impression he was singling anyone out. He had them move in front of an empty table as if this was a routine procedure and told everyone to empty their pockets. Here is where a small act of defiance became a major production. The Drill Instructor who witnessed the illegal purchase upon discovering the ill-gotten gain called other Drill Instructors to serve as jurors in deciding punishment for the crime. Their verdict was swift and unanimous. They all agreed by failing to obey a lawful order, the recruit violated the Uniform Code of Military Justice (UCMJ). They all agreed any recruit, who could enjoy a candy bar knowing all other recruits were not allowed the privilege, was lacking in character. They all agreed such an individual was lower than snake shit; they all agreed; punishment must be swift.

They escorted the hapless recruit into a small side room, and the humiliations continued behind closed doors. Drill Instructors were doing a number on him. When the beating was over we could hear a stern lecture being administered. He was later brought out battered and bleeding. MP's were called; they came in grabbed the recruit and cuffed him. After bouncing him off the walls a couple of times, they dropped him to the deck and dragged him out. He was placed in the MP's vehicle, and they drove off. There was absolute silence throughout the barracks. This may have been staged to give us some "shock and awe" but at the time there was nothing to debate.

A Drill Instructor walked out into the middle of the room and said the next one of you Motherfuckers who decide to break the rules should think twice before you act. Your fellow recruit decided he was an individual and not part of the team. Now he has to pay the price for being an individual. He will be spending the next thirty days in a red line brig on bread and water. If you want to join him, "fuck up." He glanced toward my direction and said I know some of you recruits witnessed this violation of the code. You chose to look the other way as your fellow recruit placed himself and you in jeopardy. Now you too must pay the price, get on your face, bends, and thrusts[16] until your heart stops. After countless bends, we were allowed to stand up and assume the position of attention. He said, you turds will learn we work as a team, we live as a team, and we die as a team. I wasn't ready for the dying part. Without giving it a second thought, the Drill Instructors went back to what they were doing. What simultaneously went through the minds of every recruit was, "what the fuck have I gotten myself into." There was one thing I knew; I was a man and would not be taking any beatings without a fight, not from a recruit and not from a Drill Instructor.

After what seemed like the longest week on record we were picked up from recruit receiving by our Drill Instructors. Gathering all our gear, which included a sea bag filled with uniforms, our 782 Gear (Cartridge belt, shelter half, canteen, magazine pouch etc.) and a galvanized bucket. I figured the bucket was thrown in just to make carrying the load more awkward. We were now ready for the infamous sea-bag-drag from recruit receiving to the barracks that would become our home for the next twelve weeks.

Boot Camp was just how EJ described it, hell, pure and simple. Before leaving for Parris Island, our recruiter told us we would hate his guts before we got back; he was right. I could have killed the bastard for getting me into this shit. Hazing was nonstop; stress both mental and physical was part of the daily lesson plan. It was enough

---

[16] Bends and thrusts one of the exercises used by the Marine Corps to comprise the daily seven regimen of exercises that included side straddle hops, bend and reach, rowing exercise, squat benders, Marine Corps pushups and body twists.

to make you say "to hell with this shit." But there was something that made you want to stay, something that made you want to say, "I made it." Something that made you want to pin on that eagle, globe and anchor that is the Marine Corps Emblem and be called a Marine. After four weeks of fun and games the effect was evident. Having to ask permission to speak, ask a question or even take a crap was enough to try one's nerves as well as patience. At this point, everyone wanted to be someplace else, any place other than Parris Island. This was a perfect opportunity for the Drill Instructors; they seized upon it. We were locked and cocked standing at attention on the red line drawn on the deck (floor) in front of rows of racks[17] on the port side (left) and starboard side (right), we got the command "eyeballs."

The command "Eyeballs" caused our head and eyeballs to turn in the direction of the voice while, at the same time, the rest of your body remained at the position of attention. A Drill Instructor walked to the center of the squad bay all head and eyeballs followed him. Each platoon has three Drill Instructors, usually two Sergeants and a Staff Sergeant. Although each one plays the role of asshole, there was another part played by each. The Senior Drill Instructor, usually a Staff Sergeant, is "Big Daddy," his role is the fatherly figure, the one to go to when you have a problem. Supposedly you can tell him anything.

The more experienced Sergeant is called the Heavy Aide. His role is to provide the majority of training and discipline which he cherishes especially the discipline part. The less experienced Sergeant is the Junior Aide, usually fresh out of DI School. He may be working his first platoon as a Drill Instructor.

---

[17] Beds used by Marine Recruits are called racks or bunks.

He is learning along with the recruits but tries his best not to let them know he's new meat. He makes up for his lack of experience with added yelling and screaming. Our Junior Aide was Sergeant Byrd, a tall, lanky, light green Marine who was in a word, a maniac. He always seemed hyper and on the verge of losing it. If this were his first platoon, I didn't see how he could survive two years as a DI. His military appearance didn't fall into the outstanding category, but his energy level was off the charts.

Sergeant Jones, a light green Marine, was the Heavy Aide, short in stature but a giant in everything else. His knowledge of Marine Corps training and techniques was unquestioned though, at times; he was a bit on the morbid side. The other DI's had a routine practice each night before lights out. They would recite a quote from some heroic Marine or describe some legendary Marine battle. Not so with Sergeant Jones, who told gory filled stories of mutilated bodies and severed heads. If you ever felt like making an escape from the Island, his stories made you think sticking around, and graduating was the route to take.

We were lying in our racks at the position of attention prior to lights out. Sergeant Jones was walking back and forth the length of the squad bay. He carried no pencil or paper all of the stories he relayed to us were from memory. He breathed heavily and started talking: On June 26, 1924, three recruits deserted by wading across a shallow creek onto an adjacent island (Horse Island). The next day two of them surfaced alive on the shores of Port Royal Island. The third one showed up a couple days later in a marsh by Horse Island—without a head. After a systematic search, the head of Private Aaron Frederickson was found in the bushes. According to articles in the Beaufort Gazette at the time it had been severed from

his body. Sergeant Jones didn't finish the story leaving us to
contemplate the how and why. He spun on his heels and said for all
you rats thinking about jumping ship I suggest you think again. With
that, he exited the squad bay. I don't know where he dug up those
stories or if they were even true, but he told them with such
conviction I believed him. Another one of his stories was "the
Ribbon Creek Incident." If you haven't heard the story, here is how
it goes:

"On April 8, 1956, at 8 p.m., Staff

Sergeant   Matthew McKeon

a combat decorated veteran of World

War II and the Korean War led Platoon

71, his assigned platoon of 74 recruits

on an extra exercise to an area called

Ribbon Creek as a disciplinary

measure. McKeon led the platoon

towards the swampy tidal creek on Parris

Island and upon arrival 45 minutes

later, McKeon jumped into the creek

and ordered the platoon to follow.

From that point forward, the platoon

marched along the creek bed. However,

some of the recruits could not swim

47

when the platoon marched into deep water.

Recruits suddenly started to yell and panic followed by a mad

dash for the shore. After a short while, it was noticed some

recruits were missing; six had drowned.

Sergeant Jones commented about DI's having the power of life and death. He affirmed his admiration and respect for Staff Sergeant McKeon, describing him as a Marine Corps legend who went on to retire from the Corps with honor. He backed his story up with pictures of the six dead recruits pulled from the swamp. All of them shown with bloated bellies and swollen limbs. Some had hollow eye sockets, their eyeballs having been eaten out by crabs or other creatures. Others had large holes in their stomach with crabs coming out.

Among our three DI's, I think Sergeant Jones was the one who enjoyed being a Drill Instructor the most. Our Senior Drill Instructor was a dark green Marine by the name of Staff Sergeant Wright. Wright was a seasoned Vietnam veteran who always presented an impeccable appearance in uniform. He had mastered that distinctive DI voice and combined it with an extraordinary drill cadence. He was a bit calmer than the other two but certainly didn't fall into the category of "drinking buddy."

The Drill Instructor who gave us the command "eyeballs" was the Heavy Aide. Sergeant Jones commenced to walk the squad bay, every step he took was followed by seventy five sets of eyeballs. I know a lot of you pussies hate my guts and don't want to be here. I know a lot of you miss mommy and want to get back to that tit. I know some of you pot heads can't wait to have a joint stuck in your mouths, and I know some of you pigs wish you had joined the Army.

Well for all you shitheads that fall into that last boat, I've got some good news. We have a new program called an inter-service transfer. Personally I don't think any of you dipshits should go anywhere. But I'm not the guy calling the shots and the senior Drill Instructor has agreed to let anybody who wants to apply for the program do so. So if there are any of you non-hackers that want to transfer to the Army for unlimited coffee, donuts and pussy every weekend, take one step forward. Roughly a third of the platoon stepped forward. My bunkie Private Brinkley stepped forward and quickly stepped back. As much as he wanted to leave the island he knew this wasn't the route to take. Sergeant Jones stepped out with a wicked grin on his face, all right he said all you turds transferring out, get your trash ready. Leave your 782 gear, it'll be turned in for you; just pack your sea bags and stand in front of your rack when you're done.

I never saw recruits move faster, in a flash they were all standing in front of their racks with sea bags in hand. A cattle car pulled up in front of the barracks, Sergeant Jones said all right head out. They were loaded up, and the cattle car drove off. Here is where Brinkley started to doubt his decision to remain behind, although he was still skeptical. Sergeant Jones, sensing his indecision, was immediately in his face. What's wrong turd, did you miss the boat? No sir! Do you want me to call that cattle car back? No Sir! All right then get into my "rose garden" and start those "bends" for looking like you wanted to leave.

The cattle car with the transferring recruits drove off at 0700 and returned with those recruits at 1600. One by one they came running in dragging their gear back into the barracks. They looked nothing like the recruits that left, covered with mud from head to toe you couldn't distinguish the black ones from the white ones. When everyone was standing on the red line at the position of attention, the Senior Drill Instructor came into the squad bay with a stern look on his face. I'm disappointed; I'm really disappointed, some of you worms tried to leave my Corps. You would rather turn your back on the Corps and be a slime bag in the Army than follow the time honored traditions of the Corps. I cannot allow that; you signed on to be Marines, and it's my job to make you Marines whether you like it or not. You deserted your fellow recruits for an undisciplined life of bar room brawls and pig-fucking in the Army. You recruits are low down scum who would sell out your mother for a six-pack; you've got the balls of a cockroach. I accepted a huge responsibility, and that responsibility was to train you. I will not shirk on that responsibility, and unlike you have not lost my motivation to ensure you become Marines, even if it kills you. Better a dead Marine than a lousy low down pig-fucker in the Army drinking beer every night and sleeping with a fat whore every weekend. I thought about his last statement. Maybe, being one of those low down pig-fuckers in the Army wasn't so bad.

It wasn't until lights out that we found out what happened to those recruits. They were taken to a place called "Motivation Platoon." Shortly after arrival they were told why they were there. It was because anyone wanting to leave the Corps for the Army was not motivated enough towards being a Marine. Motivation was a key element in becoming a Marine and "Motivation Platoon" was a place designed to give them that motivation.

They were marched to an area where there was a long ditch filled with mud, stagnant water and who knows what. Each recruit was marched to the front of the ditch and ordered to jump in, to the amusement of several Drill Instructors. One Drill Instructor ordered them to roll over while another ordered them to "do the Miss Piggy" and squeal, another one liked having them oink and rub their nose in the mud. Their entire day consisted of fun in the ditch and numerous physical training (PT) sessions. Their only break came when they were marched to CCP (correctional custody platoon). Reaching motivation was like reaching Nirvana and for those who went to Motivation Platoon and failed to obtain the proper motivation, the next step towards achieving Nirvana was an extended stay at CCP. Here you were issued a painted helmet liner (chrome dome) worn everywhere. You were taught to hike around the island all day with rocks in your pack and how to eat by the numbers. Eating by the numbers was a real trip. Recruits moved through the chow line and once their tray was full they stood at a dining table until there were enough recruits to fill the table. The Drill Instructor blew his whistle and all of them assumed a seated position. Forks were picked up, and the entire meal was eaten in conjunction with the Drill Instructors whistle, one blow of the whistle for each movement of hand and arms. Whistle pick up a fork, whistle, stick fork into food, whistle, bring fork up, whistle, fork into mouth, whistle, and fork out of mouth and don't even look like you're not enjoying your meal.

Getting off Parris Island was simple: run everywhere, scream at the top of your lungs and do what you were told when you were told. The rest of the time keep your mouth shut. Recruit training at Parris Island was a twelve week quest to become a Marine. Along the way, you were made to feel like a maggot in a shit pile.

All good things come to an end and sometimes bad things do too. Our day of graduation was finally approaching, after hours of harassment, drill, PT, rifle range training, swimming instruction, mess duty, essential subjects training and more. To ensure we were competent in every area we were force marched to an area called "Elliot's Beach" and tested on every subject. Failure in any subject could mean being recycled to another platoon farther behind in training. Passing Elliot's Beach meant you were ready for your final Command Inspection. Pass it and you graduated.

The day before graduation, we were given our orders and found out what our Military Occupational Specialty (MOS) would be. I would be assigned to Personnel and Administration School as a basic 0100. Something my Drill Instructor disgustingly called an "office pogue." Bennie was going to the school of infantry at Camp Lejeune being assigned as a basic 0300, what everyone enthusiastically referred to as a "Grunt," his number one pick.

For me, the worst part was the thought of returning to Parris Island for MOS training. I hated the idea but first there were ten days of leave to look forward to. Graduation day finally arrived and for the first time we were allowed to pin on the Marine Emblem. The first time we were called Marines, a title bestowed upon us for the rest of our lives both in and out of the Corps. After graduation Bennie and I didn't wait around to congratulate other recruits, kiss any DI's ass or visit any of the base facilities. We were not concerned with that. Once we were given the command "dismissed" we wanted off the island.

After a tumultuous period in our life, we were on a Greyhound bus pulling out of the Station at Beaufort, South Carolina. Beaufort looked like a nice quiet little Southern town; too bad I never had a chance to see it. We slipped a six-pack of beer on the bus and after no alcohol for weeks it only took a couple to knock us out. The ride home was incredibly peaceful, being able to do whatever we wanted without having to ask permission and have someone scream in your face for not asking loud enough.

Jason, Tommy and Chris picked us up from the bus station in Nashville and wanted to know all about Parris Island. We told them about our thirteen week sabbatical on the way home. After thirteen weeks, we were back in Ceeville, back in East End and headed for Drakes Alley. I had a third phase recruit haircut that looked like crap

and got out at Mr. C's to have it trimmed and lined. Bennie wanted
to go home, he could tell them the rest of the Parris Island saga. East
End was the same, although I did expect it to change a little in the
weeks I was gone. I left Mr. C's started home and ran into Uncle
Otis, dad's younger brother. Uncle Otis resembled dad in many
ways: they both were around a hundred and ninety pounds and stood
about six feet. Both had outgoing personalities with deep resonant
voices. The difference was dad was a family man and Uncle Otis was
a self-described ladies' man. Accompanying him was his friend
Irving. Irving stood about six two, weighed around one hundred and
seventy five pounds, best described as long and lean. He considered
himself an official "Blues Man;" both of them loved the streets.
Confirmed bachelors they worked the graveyard shift at the same
factory where dad worked. Both of them enjoyed what they called
high fashion and prided themselves on always "looking sharp."
Irving asked where I was going. I'm on my way home. Where have
you been in the war? No, I just graduated from boot camp.

They were riding in a red and white 57 Chevy convertible with
the Jackson Five's "I'll be There" playing on its AM radio. They
insisted I accompany them. Uncle Otis asked if I wanted to drive; he
got out of the front seat and moved into the back.   It seemed like
ages since I had driven a car. I headed for a juke ran by a sweet little
lady named Miss Pearl. I loved the smells that came from her place
and not just from the kitchen.

There was the ever-present smell of cigars and cigarettes coming
from the side room where a game of craps was always in session.
The sweet smell of freshly cut flowers placed on her dining tables and
the smell of perfumes worn by Short Barbara, Miss Pearl and female
patrons. Miss Pearl was what Irving called "pleasingly plump" with
an attitude. She hugged me tight enough to feel her breast pressing
against my chest. I wanted my first meal from home, but the turnip
greens, fried corn, pot roast, mashed potatoes and blackberry cobbler

were too good to pass up. I felt like a stuffed pepper seated at the table with Irving and Uncle Otis. They started telling me about their adventures in the Army. Irving said the ladies on one of the islands he visited ran around naked. He was laughing about how he could never get any work done because he couldn't keep his mule down. Irving stopped laughing long enough to lean over and ask me, "boy are you getting any?" Not lately I've been gone for thirteen weeks. What kind of shit is that? Did you hear that Otis?

After thirteen weeks, I would be so horny I'd ask a sand crab for some. What's wrong with young guys these days don't you know that stuff is going out of style you have to get it whenever you can. I and your uncle stopped by Miss Elsie's before we picked you up, didn't we Otis? Yeah, and you talk about a sweet piece, that little honey I had would make you fight your daddy for some. I figured it was time to go; the saltpeter[18] or whatever they put in my food for the last thirteen weeks was wearing off. For a young man thirteen weeks can be a long time without sex.

Uncle Otis asked if I wanted to see Pinkie one of his favorite girls at Miss Elsie's. She'll treat you real nice he said; even give you something special for an extra five. No thanks, I'm going to head home and check out mom and dad. Someone said don't go now; I looked up, it was my dad. He came up to me shook my hand and welcomed me home; don't go he said. I want you to help me spank some ass in 5-Up. Uncle Otis said all shit, its' on now, sit down Irving, and don't screw up this time." Hell, it wasn't me screwing up you were the one who kept getting his jacks caught. "Five Up" was a

---

[18] There was an unsubstantiated rumor the military put Saltpeter (Potassium Nitrate) in the food of recruits to keep a certain joint from getting stiff.

card game played primarily in the South. It was a fast and sometimes furious game, and all the old schoolers took it seriously. If you couldn't play don't make the mistake of sitting at the table. Dad taught me the game and now felt I was good enough to be his partner. When I say the game was fast I mean fast. One round and you could be eliminated. Two players made up a team, and there were several teams in waiting. Each team took their turn at the table in a series tagged "rise and fly." As long as you won you stayed at the table, but if you lost you were replaced by the next team which put you in the rotation. It's one of the few card games I have played that allowed talking between team mates. Talking was allowed but with these old heads it took a lot of strategies to win.

The object of the game was to be the first to acquire five points, get five points and your opponents would get up. I'll try to explain the game and how it was played. Five points meant you were going for high, low, two jacks and the game. Every game was played with two teams, with two players each. The dealer dealt cards in multiples of three, six cards to each player. Once each player was dealt six cards a card was turned up, this became the trump card. From the deal off, only the dealer and first person dealt could look at their cards. Cards for the other two players remained on the table if they peeped at those cards they would be penalized a point. Once six cards were dealt the first person dealt would look at his hand, if he had several trump cards he would "play," which meant the game began.

If he had no trump cards or ones he didn't like, he had the choice of "begging." Once he begged, the dealer would look into his hand. If he had several trump cards he would "give" one point to the person begging, and the game started. No trump cards or not the ones the dealer wanted forced the dealer to deal out three more cards to each person and turn up another trump card. Another trump card in the same suit meant dealing out three more cards to each player. If the same trump card turned up again, he would run out the deck and earn one point. When a Jack or Joker was turned up as a trump card, he earned another point. If a trump card in another suit turned up the first person dealt had no choice but to "play" and the game began. Earning a point for high meant you had the ace or the highest trump card played. Low meant you had the deuce or the lowest trump card played. Jack meant you had a Joker or Jack and made it without your opponents stealing it from you. If they stole it, they earned a point.

The last point was for game, for game purposes the ten was the most valuable card in the deck worth ten points. Aces were worth 4 points, Kings 3, Queens 2, Jacks or Jokers 1. No points could be earned from any other card in the deck. If after two rounds of play both teams had earned five points, the order of precedence was high, low, Jacks and game. It's a highly charged game; bluffing and lying were a big part of it along with trying to develop a strategy that would fool and outwit your opponent. After knocking out five teams with dad, I retired a winner and headed home. Uncle Otis told Irving he was fired; he was taking dad as his partner.

I got home and for the first time in my life felt I had a home somewhere else. Mom hugged and kissed me; I stood there not knowing how to respond. I could not remember her hugging me for a long time. She asked me about boot camp. I gave her the censored version. Although having been married and living away from home before, I never felt confident enough to make some decisions in my life. Now, I didn't need anyone's input to make my decisions.

Ten days at home came and went, soon I was headed back to Parris Island. Bennie was headed to Advanced Infantry Training School at North Carolina. Returning to the Island was different this time. I no longer was required to say 'yes sir' to enlisted personnel and didn't have to worry about Drill Instructors. I was returning as a fully-fledged Marine wearing PFC (Private First Class) stripes no longer the bottom of the barrel recruit from a few weeks earlier. The strangest part of my return trip was not having Bennie with me.

I got there on a Friday checked in to Schools Battalion and was assigned to a barracks. The duty NCO told me to get a rack, store my gear and be ready for formation on Monday morning. Until Monday, I could do whatever I wanted with no one watching or telling me what to do. The Corporal on duty hooked me up with a horse blanket,[19] linen and temporary meal card.[20] Once I made my rack and stored my gear, I decided to see what the island really looked like. Another Marine checked in about the same time and together we visited the bowling alley, Post Exchange (PX) and Enlisted (E) Club.

Monday morning rolled around, and I found out though I was not in boot camp there was still a structured routine and hierarchy to the military. Every morning reveille went at 0500, field day (cleaning) of the barrack, chow, morning formation and then off to class. No longer a recruit meant you could have "liberty"[21] or "libo" as it was called. Of course, liberty was a privilege and could be cancelled at any time. At the end of the day when classes were over, you were on your own until reveille the next day. After school, we spent time at evening chow, studying for class and finally a trip to the "E" Club. On my second trip, I was sitting at a table with a couple of guys I met in class, drinking beer and giving our best impression of our Drill

---

[19] Heavy green colored wool blanket issued to Marines for personal use

[20] A card that allowed the user to eat in the Mess Hall without paying for meals

[21] A "pass" (called "liberty" in the Navy, Coast Guard, and Marine Corps) is time off, not chargeable as leave.

Instructors. Probably a mistake on my part was sitting next to a couple of guys shooting pool. One of them knocked the cue ball off the table grazing me. My warning to keep the ball on the table didn't seem to register.   On the next break, he knocked the ball off the table, and it connected with my head. I was on him before he could even lower his cue stick. This was the perfect opportunity to try out my newly acquired combat skills.   I gave him what my uncle Otis called a "horse whipping" as his partners watched. It was one-on-one; everyone else stayed out of the fight edging it on. Finally, the club manager broke up the fight and ejected us from the club.

I drew first blood and felt good about it until the next morning when I found myself in the First Sergeant's office explaining what happened. I made sure he knew the fight wasn't started by me, thinking it might give me an edge. It did not; he didn't give a damn how it started and told me just that. For using my battle skills I received 7 days restriction to the base, 7 days extra duty and oh yeah, the club was now off limits. The 1stSgt told us he was doing us fuck-heads a favor by keeping this out of our records and not giving us "Office Hours."[22]

I won the fight; it was the only thing out of the entire scenario worth mentioning. We had one month of school and after that I could depart the area forever, making Parris Island a distant memory. When the class began, I remembered one of the instructors telling us the top ten percent of the class would get a choice of duty station. Since I could no longer visit the club, I hit the books and came out number eight in a class of eighty-seven.   I did not have a clue as to where I wanted to go. Some guys in the PX told me Camp Lejeune

---

22 Article 15. - punishment under the UCMJ that does not require a Courts Martial [25] Commander in Chief, Atlantic Command

sucked, so I didn't want to go there. I sought the help of Staff
Sergeant Allen, one of my class instructors. He said Camp Elmore in
Norfolk, VA was the ideal base; you could look through the front
gate and look out the back gate. Sounded like a shotgun house. He
said nearly everyone stationed there supports CINCLANT Fleet
Headquarters.[23] I had the slightest idea what that meant, so I took
his advice. Hell, I only enlisted for two years anyway, with eighteen
months left I really didn't care where they sent me. I was issued PCS
(permanent change of station) orders and with proceed; (time
authorized certain members to arrange personal affairs while, en
route to a new duty station) delay and travel, I had about forty days
to kill before reporting in to my new duty station. This meant a few
days back in Ceeville.

I got home and the first person I ran into was "Silver Legs" who
spent most of his days inebriated. He was wearing an old army field
jacket with a "Silver Star' Medal"[24] pinned to it. At the time, I didn't
know what the medal was, or if it were his. He said boy, I thought
you were in the military; every time I turn around I see your ass back
home. Arguing with him was useless, besides there were more
important things on my mind than screwing around with this drunk.
Later dad told me, not only had he earned the medal, he had been a
highly decorated soldier in Uncle Sam's Army.

One should never judge too quickly. I wondered what tragedy in
his life forced him to become an outcast from society. I went home,
spent a few hours with my folks and decided it was time to go
looking for some of that pussy my Drill Instructors had spoken of
with such repugnance. Who knows, maybe Irving was right, maybe

---

[23] Commander in Chief, Atlantic Command
[24] The Silver Star third-highest military decoration awarded to a
member of any branch of the United States armed forces for valor in
the face of the enemy.

sex was going out of style, if it were true I wanted to get my share before it went anywhere. I left the alley and went over to Tenth Street, another section of East End" full of dives, juke joints, good old fashioned hole-in-the-wall clubs and places of ill repute. I was sure to get sex here even if it meant buying it, which thanks to my uncle and his friends I had done from time to time. Call it a weakness. The closest joint was Big George's place and what do you know, how lucky could I be, there was Uncle Otis and Irving. Uncle Otis and Irving were both in their thirties, this time they were joined by an older guy a notorious sexaholic called Smitty. They always had something new to tell me; it was always good seeing them. There was a couple of ladies seated at their table; they caught sight of me as soon as I walked through the door.

I went over to their table; Irving introduced me to the ladies, who were a little young for them, but that's how they liked it. Uncle Otis grabbed me a chair, and one of the ladies pulled it next to her. How's the war going, asked Irving? I don't know I'm not in the war. Aw hell boy, you know what I'm talking about are we winning or losing? My uncle broke in and said who gives a shit about the war we've got other things to talk about.

The lady who pulled my seat next to her asked, is that an army uniform? No, it's a Marine uniform. Well, you look good in it honey; sit down and drink a beer with me. We need some young blood at the table. Irving motioned for the waitress to bring me a beer. I picked up my beer, took a few swallows and the Temptations "Just my Imagination" started playing on the jukebox. My new found lady friend pulled me onto the dance floor and held me tight; she smelled good and felt incredible. It had been too long since I held a woman. Inhaling her intoxicating fragrance and feeling her body pressed against mine caused an unexpected response. I moved away from her; she looked down and said well isn't that sweet. That's okay honey; I'll take care of that later if you want me too. Embarrassed I let her go back to the table, grabbed my beer and headed for the bar. Irving came over and said Pinkie told me you got a little horny out there; that's okay; we'll get you some of that sweet stuff. That's just great I thought. Now everyone in the place knows I'm a horny bastard. I'm okay I said, by this time Smitty had joined us at the bar.

Talking loud enough for everyone in the club to hear, Smitty said Pinkie told me you got a little excited out there. That's nothing to be ashamed of, hell a young man has got to have sex; it's what drives him and keeps him alive. Don't be ashamed of it, you should be proud you can get a stiff one just by rubbing against a hairy cat. Yeah, said Irving, one day you'll be like old Smitty and carry a string in your pocket to get it up. That's a lie I'll never have to use a fucking string! I'm still hitting it like I was twenty-one. If you think, I'm lying ask Pinkie. Irving winked and said Pinkie will say anything if you're paying.   What they were saying was pretty funny, and there may have been some truth to it, but I knew better than talking about sex around this sex-obsessed duo. When they finished embarrassing me, Smitty and Irving joined Uncle Otis and the ladies.

When I sat down at the bar to finish my beer, there was someone giggling at the other end of the bar. I turned around to see Vanessa smiling. In high school, Vanessa was a lovely little bud that had blossomed into a lovely rose. Where have you been? I joined the Marines. So what are you doing here? I'm here because I had a few days to kill before I head off to Vietnam. Are you going to Vietnam? In thirty days. Before graduating from Boot Camp, our Drill Instructors told us we would all be in Vietnam within six months, so even though I wasn't actually telling the truth, perhaps, I wasn't lying. Are you going to spend any more time with your uncle and his lady friends? No, I think I'll let them stay over there and enjoy the ladies. It's good to see you. I can't believe you joined the military. So where are you going when you leave the club? I don't have any plans; my schedule is open. I get off in thirty minutes. How about going over to the Pink Poodle; they've got a band there tonight. That's just what I was going to ask you. She looked at me and said don't start lying like your uncle and his friends.

Compared to Big George's place the Pink Poodle was an upscale version catering to a somewhat younger crowd. Like nearly all the joints in East End, it had a long bar with the kitchen located behind it. Colorful posters of Ike and Tina Turner, Al Green, James Brown and some locals lined the walls, high-lighting upcoming attractions. There was a framed picture of Jimi Hendrix and the King Kasuals, a group that played there a few years back. Old wooden floors were cleaned with sawdust mixed with a small amount of scented linseed oil. The Poodle had a little something different. All the table tops, chair backs, and bottoms were pink which gave it some uniqueness and a touch of class. Customers had the option of buying a gigantic frankfurter sandwich, home style gangster burger, fish sandwich or a full course meal. Beer was sold over the counter; seal and bootleg whiskey could be purchased from the back room. Irving told me this was where he played harmonica with Jimmy Hendrix and his band among others. Sure enough when I looked at the picture on the wall there he was posing with the group.

I wondered why he hadn't vacated the streets long enough to pursue a well-paid musical career. Then I remembered him telling me he didn't care about fortune or fame, he just wanted to be Irving. I had to admire him for that if nothing else he had character. We got a booth, ordered a coke for Vanessa and a beer for me. I took a second look at her; she was stunning. The skinny little twig of a girl I knew in high school turned into a beautiful young woman. She had filled out in all the right or should I say tight places, and I wasn't thinking with my little head. Her squeaky high school voice had changed into one that was sultry and sexy. Standing about five eight she had a gorgeous face with the statuesque figure of a model.

How long have you been in the military? I've just been in a few months. Army? No, Marines. Aren't they all about the same? Not even close, we're America's first line of defense; the army is our backup. She laughed, I told you about lying. So how are you and Rudi Johnson doing? We don't talk anymore; didn't you have a baby by him? No, I did get pregnant but I lost the baby. Sorry. That's okay, maybe it was for the best. I don't think having a baby is the best thing for me right now. I'm working at Big George's and going to school; that's all I can handle for the time being.

So who's the lady in your life? I don't have a girl. That wasn't your girl you were dancing with earlier? Real funny, I bet you got a good laugh out of what Smitty and Irving were saying. I didn't hear them. Yeah right! Was it true? She was holding you pretty tight. Now what do you want to know that for? Just curious that's all. You know you really do look fantastic, good enough to dance with, she asked. We danced to "Still Water" by the Four Tops; I loved the song, and I loved the feel of her soft body in between my arms. It took some effort, but this time I was able to control my hormones and enjoy the dance. Seated back at the table, she said I guess you don't like me as much as the last girl you were dancing with. She had always made me laugh. I had forgotten about the good times I had in high school with this former cheerleader. We had a good time that brought back old memories, when I took her home she gave me a long sensual good night kiss. I wanted to go inside, but her mother was waiting, call me she whispered. I went to bed smelling her sweet fragrance on my body; I slept with her for the rest of the night.

Bennie got home on leave a week after I arrived. It was if I hadn't seen him in years, he told me outrageous stories about North Carolina women. "Any man can get sex by buying a woman a bucket of fried chicken and a Nehi[25] grape soda." He told me about a club called "The Wash Out," located off in the woods that closed every time there was a hard rain, because the dirt road leading to it washed out. If there were any good looking women in the club, Bennie told them he was going to pick up a bucket of fried chicken. I knew he was lying, but it was good to have him home telling me some new lies.

We got up early the next morning and ate breakfast. My dad had the day off, so we hung around with him for a few hours. Later we decided to go down to the basketball court for a pickup game of twenty-one. We played three games and took a break; someone fired up a joint and started passing it around. When it got to me, I passed it on to a buck-toothed guy named Flipper. You can't have a few puffs with us anymore. I've never had a few puffs I don't smoke and never have smoked that shit; you have a puff for me. So you're hot shit since you joined the Marines. No, I just don't smoke that shit, what's the big deal? Sounds like you're turning into a fairy.

There always has to be at least one, and Flipper was it, the birdbrain who had to be the center of attention. The crap he was instigating wasn't about me, it was about being that center of attention. I knew arguing with this dumb shit was a waste of time, but I could not let him get away with what he said. I picked up a

---

[25] Nehi pronounced "knee high" is a flavored soft drink introduced in 1924. In 1955, after the fruit flavored sodas became popular the company changed its name to Royal Crown Company, after its RC Cola brand.

basketball and with all my strength fired it directly into his face. It hit him with such force it knocked him off his bench, busted his lip and broke his nose. He wasn't prepared for that fastball, blood was gushing from his broken beak. Who's the fairy now bitch? He didn't answer; he was busy trying to stop the bleeding.

He could have saved himself the embarrassment and pain of a basketball flying into his face simply by keeping his mouth shut. I don't know what the dumb bastard was thinking; I kicked his ass in high school for having the same smart ass mouth. Bennie said you dumb ass never talk shit unless you can back it up. I spent a lot of my leave time with Vanessa. The day before I was scheduled to leave I went over to her house and her mom told me she was at her sister's house. When I got there, I found out she was filling in for the babysitter. She had the night off and decided to help her sister out and get in some studying time. I said it's nice of you to help out, I was thinking screw that. I had other plans; now those plans would have to be changed.

Even though I wanted to hit and run, Vanessa was someone special, whether I scored with her or not she was definitely somebody to spend time with. She got me a cold brew from the fridge. After four more brews, my horny meter was up and running. I was ready to go on the hunt, somewhere out there lurking in the shadows was a willing partner. I saw a serious look in her eyes, she said are you going to Vietnam? As much as I wanted to tell her the truth, it was easier to stick with the lie, so I said, yeah, I am. She went into the bedroom and came out wearing a set of silk pajamas and sat next to me on the sofa. Seeing her naked form under those pajamas was worse than having Pinkie pressing against me. She slid onto my lap and started kissing me; this was it, no turning back. Don't tease me Vanessa, she kept kissing me.

My hands were everywhere pressing against her breast and massaging her inner thigh. I felt her nude body underneath her pajamas overflowing with heat and passion. She definitely brought the heat. I could have stayed there coupled with her forever. Leaving her and walking down the street, I thought about what she said. She had been my friend for a long time and what she did was as much for her as it was for me. If I did not make it back she wanted to have a lasting memory of me and tried to give me a wonderful memory of her, then she kissed me goodnight. She gave me her most precious possession and asked for nothing in return no promises, no commitments.

I felt like a cretin lying to her; why couldn't I have gone to see Pinkie and let her take care of business? Vanessa was a sweet girl; the last thing I wanted was to fuck her over. I packed my bags and headed for the bus station knowing my piece of shit car probably would not make the trip. I could not face Vanessa; I intentionally avoided her, said goodbye to my folks and headed for Norfolk, VA.

4 THE BIG DECISION

Having a conscience is not always such a good thing, mine was bothering me. It was a long trip, plenty of time to catch up on my sleep and think about Vanessa. I wanted Vanessa to be a part of my life. Although I knew, it would take more time before I could commit to her. My former wife had left me distrusting with too many bad memories of a failed marriage.

Always check into a new duty station on the weekend, a tip given to me by senior Marines. That way only a few people know you're there, and you don't get stuck with some lousy detail right off the bat. I checked in with the duty NCO and was assigned to a barrack. It was a typical World War II leftover. Wooden barracks with steam radiators for heating, open windows for cooling, dull drab interiors and cockroaches big enough to do battle. I wasn't an NCO and did not rate a single room, for me it was a rack, a small desk, wall and foot lockers located in an open squad bay. But what the hell at least there was no rent to pay, and no one coming to see my wife when I left home.

I unpacked my gear and put my uniforms and civilian gear into a wall locker, the rest went into a footlocker. I checked out a pillow, horse blanket and clean linen from Supply. Once my gear was stored, and my rack made; I got a couple hours of sleep and decided to check out the local area. Camp Elmore was just as my class instructor had described it. You actually could look through the front gate and look out the back gate. This had to be the smallest base in the country. Following my Drill Instructor's advice about using the buddy system, I found another Marine checking in named Keno, an Arkansas native. This was the first permanent duty station for both of us. Keno had a car; we decided to tour the area. Norfolk was definitely a military town. Along with the adjoining cities of Little Creek, Portsmouth, Virginia Beach and Chesapeake. They were populated with military types from jarheads, and doggies to squids and fly boys. We rode over to the Naval Amphibious Base and checked out the huge ships in port. It was my first time seeing a carrier class ship; there was one in port called the Forrestal. I was amazed that something that size could actually float.

We talked to some guys on the pier and later hit on a few women at an amusement park in Oceana. From Oceana, we traveled to Portsmouth and ended up near the Naval Ship Yard. There was a long concrete wall along one side of the base; we noticed what looked like women walking down the sidewalk. We started to stop but, drove pass them instead to get a better look. Keno, were those women? I don't know let's stop and let them get closer. We pulled over, and the women started walking faster towards our car. The closer they got, the more we questioned whether they were females or female impersonators. Once they got in range Keno yelled out, "man they're a bunch of fags."   They heard him and started to curse at us like the sailors they probably were.

We picked up gravel along the sidewalk and began pelting them. For a short time, they kept coming, but those rocks were coming hard and fast, I heard one cry out as I nailed his ass. They called us everything but a child of God and decided to retreat. As they walked the other way, they continued to call us names with voices that sounded like Bluto.[26] The ugly bitches had completely forgotten

---

[26] "Bluto the Terrible" nemesis of Popeye the sailor

about their feminine side. That episode was the highlight of our day; we rode around a while longer and eventually landed at Camp Elmore's "E" Club. I was broken down from the ride to Norfolk. After a couple of beers, we left and headed back to the barracks. The next day was Sunday; I got up, caught brunch at the mess hall and spent most of the day watching TV and lying in the rack. This would probably be the only day I'd have nothing to do.

Reveille went at 0500 the next morning. After a shit, shower and shave, cleaning the barracks and catching morning chow, I checked into the Company's S-1 Office and was told to see the First Sergeant. First Sergeant Ibarra was a small, gaunt looking Marine with a booming voice that seemed out of place with his less-than-masculine physique. He gave me a welcome aboard speech, told me the do's and don'ts and what was expected of me. If I did my job and kept my nose clean, I would have no problem with him. He warned me to stay away from Church Street, gave me a list of establishments in town placed off limits and told me to see a clerk. The Unit Diary clerk gave me a check-in sheet with the location of each shop. I was issued 782 gear[27] from supply, tennis shoes and sweat gear from special services, assigned a rifle at the armory and given a shot at sickbay. One day was given to check-in; I started work the next day.

Gunnery Sergeant Branson was the Administrative Chief for the Force Human Affairs Section. During my in-brief, he told me I would be working for Lieutenant Colonel (Ltcol) Santel. The staff also included two Majors, a female 2nd Lieutenant, Master Sergeant, Gunnery Sergeant and a Corporal. After my brief with him was over, Corporal Henson covered the work schedule with me. He walked me through the compound to familiarize me with the location of every

---

[27] Equipment owned by a unit and issued to a Marine while assigned to that unit to include shelter half, cartridge belt, poncho, helmet, canteen, first aid kit and other equipment.

shop. Henson was a spit and polish Corporal. I looked forward to him giving me the low down on everything, on and off base. The first thing I wanted to know was "what's happening on Church Street?" He told me we would check it out after work. The Force Human Affairs Section encompassed Special Services, Drug and Alcohol and Human Relations Training. I and Corporal Henson were there to provide admin support for all the sections.

This was my first permanent duty assignment; I had never been this far away from home. I loved my family but felt no pangs of homesickness and set about the business of learning my job in the military. During this period, the military like society in general was experiencing a great deal of racial turmoil, although, in the military, it was less publicized and to a greater extent contained. The Marine Corps put a vigorous human relations training program in place that included phase I and II training. Two phases incorporating eighty-hours of annual training, mandatory for every Marine. Whenever a racial incident occurred, units were required to submit a racial incident report. These reports were compiled and monitored by the officers in my section.

Human Relations training sessions were conducted by a Staff NCO or junior officer, usually a First Lieutenant or Captain. Supposedly rank played no part in the discussions. If there were something you didn't like, you were encouraged to bring it up. We were told to lay it out on the table. Even so, the possibility of backlash kept you from saying what you thought, unless you were a short-timer. Short-timers were Marines coming to the end of their enlistment who voluntary or involuntarily were not going to re-enlist. If you wanted unfettered feedback ask these guys, they held nothing back. They complained about everything from shitty details and antiquated barracks to lousy chow, sometimes they were worth listening too. During a round table discussion, a white Sergeant from

Georgia was explaining how he perceived blacks as being inferior to whites. This was his perception until some black guys saved his ass in Vietnam, which changed his opinion significantly. A black Corporal (short-timer) challenged him on this. He wanted to know if he felt that way about all blacks or just the ones that saved his ass. The conversation carried on after class and ended with a fistfight. Clearly those two needed additional training.

Military life was different from the "ho-hum" existence of civilian life. I would not say I bought the Navy crap about it being an adventure, but it was certainly different and sometimes different is good. I was the youngest guy in the office and the older guys taught me the ropes and treated me with respect – at least most of them did. They helped me make the right decisions and do things to further my career. They took me into their confidence; it was great having a career instead of a job. We were a family both on and off the clock, though technically in the military you're never off the clock. I worked directly for Gunny Branson, who in his own words was "hard but fair," and he proved to be just that. He freely shared his experience teaching me how to be a Marine and how to do my job. He told me as long as I worked for him, there would only be two things to keep me from getting promoted, something I did or didn't do.

If I screwed up of course, I wouldn't get promoted, and if I didn't make myself competitive I wouldn't get promoted. He encouraged me to be competitive, following his advice got me a meritorious promotion to Corporal. I made Corporal and was so disgusted with living conditions in the barracks that I complained to him about it. I told him about what some people called water bugs, which to me was nothing more than big ass cockroaches that ruled the barracks. I would go to sleep at night and feel tiny little legs crawling over my neck. After a few times of feeling those little legs, I would get up and turn my lamp on. Once the lights came on I could see several of them scurrying for cover. It had gotten to the point where I had to ignore the "lights out after ten rule" and keep a light on to get any sleep. Gunny got me permission to live in an apartment off base (required for E-4, and below) with an added housing and rations allowance. I found a nice one bedroom furnished apartment in Portsmouth. Now I had a place where I could get a good night's sleep without the lights being on. Having my own apartment meant I could entertain women without having to shell out money for a motel room. I had a girl, not a regular girl, one that I occasionally got together with.

My apartment quickly became a favorite place for guys to stop by with their girls. When it was time for me to hit the rack, I showed them the door. I wasn't about to let them turn my apartment into a motel. There were only a few people that I called friends, and it was just the way I wanted it. My dad told me too many friends spelled trouble; I chose them wisely. My friend "Bumpy" lived across the street in an apartment directly in front of mine. Bumpy was from a little town in North Carolina called Kingston. He was a Sergeant stationed at the Naval Base in Portsmouth. In the Marines, you were taught you didn't have friends, only military acquaintances. Friends were the ones that got you killed.

Bumpy was my partner (and not in the sense it's used today) a guy who would give you his last dollar, and I would give him mine. I met him when I was standing on my balcony looking for girls wearing short shorts. I saw him pushing his car down the street and ran down to give him a hand. We became good friends. He was the only person in the apartment complex I trusted. We hung out at the base gym on Saturday's and a local watering hole after work. If we had nothing better to do, we stayed home, grilled out and drank beer.

I usually called home on Saturday morning to find out how things were going. Mom always told me who got married, who died, who had a baby and who went to jail. It was all part of my routine; everyone should have a good connection with their family. I wanted to call Vanessa but figured she might be pissed at me and decided not to. I just wanted to enjoy my life, it was a splendid time to be young, single and free. I lived only a few miles from Gunny Branson, which I thought was a good idea on my part. I could always get a ride to work with him if I needed one. His wife Helen called me shortly after I had called home. Both actions were unusual, having his wife call me and being called on a Saturday. He wanted me to come over to his house.

I wondered why he didn't call me or tell me what he wanted. I knocked on his door; Helen opened it with a peculiar smile on her face. Gunny is in the bedroom go on in, strange she should call him Gunny. Perhaps it was the "Old South" thing being put in play, a wife telling me Mr. Charlie (her husband) was in the bedroom. I wondered if she knew every Gunnery Sergeant in the Marine Corps was called Gunny. I found him in his bedroom fully clothed with a blanket wrapped around his waist. I need you to take me to the base hospital "Champ" (his name for everybody). My wife is too embarrassed to take me. I wondered how taking Gunny to the hospital would embarrass her.

Gunny Branson prided himself on being what he called a "stud puppy," someone whose services were in high demand. He often talked about providing those services to any female who needed them, not just his wife. He told me there was nothing more uplifting than seeing a beautiful girl naked as the day she was born. On this occasion, he must have overextended those services, thank God he was with his wife. I was taking him to the hospital because the guy had a "woody" that would not break from the position of attention, giving him a considerable amount of discomfort. Helen didn't want to take him to the hospital with his "Johnson" sticking out. What would the neighbors think? Or maybe she didn't want anyone to know what her involvement was. On the way to the hospital, Gunny joked about putting a sock on it and letting it hang out the window to say hi to the ladies we passed. Wishful thinking on his part. I got him to the hospital waiting room where he chose to stand with his hand under his blanket. A short time later a Corpsman called him in to see a doc, who hooked him up with something to relax his "love Jones."

On the way back to his house (his, woody down) he picked up on a familiar theme and started telling me about one of his sexual adventures. Are you sure you want to talk about that Gunny? Oh yeah, I'm okay, the doc said it won't be anything happening down there today, now tomorrow that's a different story. By the way, I heard about that little game you and Bumpy played. I thought about that game and decided to tell him about it. For one month Bumpy and I played a game of numbers.

The object was to have sex with as many women as you could in one month, one point per woman. Nailing the same woman more than once would not give you extra credit. We were dealing on the honor system, but each woman's name had to be entered into your log. Numbers would be tallied on the first day of the next month. Our numbers were running pretty close when Bumpy ran into a snag with one of his ladies. She kept coming back for repeat performances, preventing Bumpy from getting his numbers up. She had even chased a few prospects away from his apartment. Finally, Bumpy decided it was time to have a heart to heart talk with her. He said Cheri', you're a wonderful girl, but you know we date other people.

She didn't like that arrangement and told him she didn't want to date anyone else. Thirty minutes later he realized he wasn't getting through to her. Nothing he said had convinced her to stay away. Bumpy had enough. Listen baby you're a beautiful girl, but you should stop and think about your reputation. What's wrong with my reputation? Well nothing right now, but you're headed for disaster. She asked what he meant. He sighed and said well one of the worse things that could happen to a young girl is; she gets a reputation as being a, well you know a "dick hog." What she screamed, a dick hog, well isn't that some shit, a dick hog. Just because I like sex now I'm a dick hog, you bastard. You can kiss my ass you'll never have to worry about seeing this dick hog again.

I saw her storm out of his door and could not wait to find out what happened. He told me the story; I laughed until I couldn't stand up. Bumpy opened up two beers and said man, I told you; we're only in it for the nookie. Gunny said shit I've got a million stories I could tell you. Hell you've probably got a million stories to tell me. You keep a pretty low profile around the shop, but I know you're hitting something. Most motherfuckers need help getting it up; I bet I'm the only one you know who needed help getting it down. It was true; Viagra was years away. Don't tell the Colonel, he'll want to know my secret, after that we both had a good laugh.

I thought about Uncle Otis, Irving and Old Smitty; my experiences in Norfolk told me they weren't the only ones preoccupied with sex. I planned to do a two year hitch in the Corps and get out. Now I wasn't sure I would follow through on my plans. The Marine Corps was starting to feel like home. I kept telling myself two years in the suck, and you're out. But each day I felt the pride of being a Marine in the Corps. My recruiter told me once I became part of the Marine Corps; the Marine Corps would become part of me. He was speaking the truth, and I didn't believe him; I thought he was just giving me some recruiting bullshit.

Thinking we were the only two in the shop I and Corporal Henson were discussing being black in America. We're never going to get the respect a white guy does I said; it's just the way things are. You've got to be twice as good to get half the credit. Gunny Branson who overheard the conversation stepped through the door. Okay, you have to work twice as hard for half the recognition, so what? You have to work twice as hard for half the respect, so what? I'm a white guy and know your words have some truth to them, but don't use that as an excuse for not doing your best, not with me. Give me one hundred percent effort and I'll back you one hundred percent.

I'll give you as much recognition and respect as I give any other Marine. Have we got a deal? Henson spoke up and said we've got a deal. Gunny Branson was a rough edged son of a bitch who loved sex, but had a way of earning your respect. He was a man of his word and proved it many times over. My time at Camp Elmore went quickly, in eighteen months I went from an E-2, (Private First Class) to an E-5, (Sergeant). Now it was time to re-enlist, I wasn't sure if I would, of course I was in constant contact with Bennie, if he got out so would I. Everyone in my section and Company was encouraging me to re-enlist.

Gunny Branson told me it was time to shit or get off the pot. He said don't take this decision lightly I'm giving you a "96"[28] to make up your mind. Write down a list of all your pros and cons go with the one that leans in your favor. Let me know what you're going to do when you get back. When I put it all on paper, the pros won out. As a first termer, I could get a regular re-enlistment bonus, an MOS bonus, pay for unused leave and a choice of duty station. It also meant a trip back home before reporting to my new duty

---

[28] Ninety-six hour (four day) pass.

station. I contacted Bennie and told him of my plans. We used our re-enlistment option to select the 6th Marine Corps District as our next duty assignment. Our decision to stay in the Corps had been made. Georgia would be our next home. I was going to train Reserves in Atlanta and Bennie was going to the Marine Corps Detachment in Augusta. Both places a few hours' drive from Ceeville. I previously bought a used Volkswagen for two hundred and fifty bucks, a real rusted out bucket of bolts, temperamental as hell. One cool morning after pushing it off and straining my back, the damn thing failed to start. Frustrated I kicked the front fender and my foot went all the way through. I never bothered to fix it and rode around with a huge hole in it.

It wasn't a safety violation. I could get on and off base. Most of the time it got me where I needed to go and the ladies who rode with me didn't seem to care. It served its purpose now I needed to get rid of this rust bucket and buy something decent for my trip home. No one had to know I stood on the lowest rung of the economic ladder. I started looking for a new road machine and after trying out a few vehicles, settled for a 1973 VW Super Beetle only about a year old.

It ran good and looked great, with gas rationing in effect I could forget the "even" and "odd" days and run forever on a tank of gas.[29] I packed in all my military and civilian gear, and prepared to head home with a few extra bucks in my pocket. Following Gunny Branson's advice, I opened a saving's account with a local credit union and left the majority of my money in safe-keeping. I wanted to have fun, but had no intention of having so much fun I couldn't rent an apartment at my new duty station. I made a few last minute

---

[29] Depending on their license plate number people could purchase gas every other day during the rationing period.

rounds with my p's and checked out all the ladies I had met, choosing not to tell them I was leaving. If there were some things I didn't know, I didn't want to find out about them now. I knew sometimes the kid's father was the one with a regular paycheck. My friend Reggie and I were in court for a paternity suit; he pleaded with the judge saying there was no blood test completed, and the baby didn't even look like him. The judge said that's okay, pay child support long enough and he'll start to look like you. She thought that shit was funny. I sure as hell didn't. On my last night in Virginia, my friends took me to a club called Anchor Inn on the Naval Air Station in Norfolk.

Two of my friends had pooled their resources and bought an older model Cadillac limousine. With a lot of effort put in at the hobby shop on base, they had brought it back to a pristine condition complete with a custom paint job. They would wash and wax it during the week, on weekends they alternated chauffeuring duties, one driving while the other played the tycoon riding in the back with the ladies. Tonight I was getting the royal treatment. They were picking me up at my apartment and giving me a chauffeur driven limo ride to the club. I had never ridden in a limo before; I have to admit these guys spent their money well in restoring it. Their bar was stocked; Henson and I had a drink on the way to the club.

Anchor Inn was a local watering hole usually packed with sailors, Marines and civilian women. We got there on a Wednesday "Go-go night,"[30] where ladies strutted their stuff and showcased their ample assets. A rowdy crowd with lots of women, just the way

---

[30] Go-go Girls- scantily clad female dancers

Marines liked it. We were having a great time; after three or four beers I left for a head call. I got back to our table, and two young ladies had joined Henson. The other guys had moved to another table with other women. Henson knew both the ladies; they were his girl Pat and her friend Marilyn. They came from Elizabeth City, North Click[31] to share my last night. Every time I finished a drink there was another one waiting for me and the ladies. I was starting to get a buzz; Marilyn kept me on the dance floor. Elton John had recently released an album titled "Goodbye Yellow Brick Road" - our favorite cut from the album was a song called "Bennie and the Jets." It started to play, I guided Marilyn onto the dance floor.

My friends black and white loved this song, and there were some real cut-ups among the bunch. They all came on the floor, and Bumpy literally turned it out. He started a "Soul Train" line, everyone in the club joined in. I knew some good dancers, but Bumpy a guy from a small town in North Click was the best dancer I had ever seen. The girl with him matched him step for step. We stayed there until the place closed; I wished I could have stayed longer.

On my day of detachment, I checked out of my unit at 0800 and by 0815 was on the road home, having loaded in all my belongings the day before. It was a twelve hour drive home which would put me into Ceeville between 2000 and 2100. I picked up a Lance Corporal Adair from "swoop circle"[32] thumbing a ride home to

---

[31] North Carolina
[32] Swoop Circle the place to hitch a ride with other Marines going your way. Rides were available nearly every weekend.

Nashville. Nashville was on my way, having him ride with me took some of the boredom out of the trip. He had bought a bus ticket and was glad he could cash it in. I told him about my last night at Elmore and the sendoff my friends gave me. He was new to the area, so I gave him the full rundown on places where the ladies loved to hang out. I told him about Bumpy and some of my friends, told him to look them up.

Having someone to talk to made the trip home quick and pleasant. Adair helped with the driving and chipped in on the gas. Our conversation covered a lot of topics, when we got around to sports he told me his high school basketball team beat Robin High School in the state tournament. I couldn't remember it. Maybe that was the year some of our best players were suspended.

Soon I was dropping him off and heading for the alley. I wanted to see Vanessa but after one of mom's big meals I fell asleep and didn't wake up until the next morning. Which was just as good, I probably needed the rest. I got out of bed early and surprised mom by helping her clean the house. When I finished it was still too early to creep around to Vanessa's house, so I decided to roam the neighborhood. It was a mild November day, around 0900 I put on a Marine sweatshirt and headed for Mr. C's for a quick trim. I always got the same questions from Mr. C's patrons. Where have you been, how many kids have you got? These guys were worse than my uncle and his friends; they thought sex was everything, and who knows maybe it was. Shit, who am I fooling, it was number one on my list too.

I didn't' see Vanessa on this trip. She was out of town, which was okay because I received a telegram from my new unit ordering me to report in two weeks early. Vanessa being out of town saved me from having to answer some tough questions from her. Why hadn't she heard from me in almost two years? Why did I feel the need to lie about going to Vietnam? Did I lie to get her in bed?

As I was leaving Mr. C's someone yelled out "hey boy," I turned in the direction of the voice, it was Silver Legs. I need you to take me down to the liquor store. I took him to the store about two miles away. He bought a couple of bottles and asked if I would give him a ride home. We got to his house; he invited me in; not having anything else to do I went in. Do you want a drink? No thanks I'm okay. I got inside and was outdone; his home looked like a modest house on the outside. On the inside, it was immaculate. There was beautiful furniture from different countries, with crystal vases and unusually odd-looking knick knacks. Polished hardwood floors and shelves of wood carvings from exotic islands in the Pacific, Thailand, and the Philippines. Exquisite china from England and Korea, things I had never seen and not one thing seemed to be out of place, not a speck of dust to be found anywhere.

All of his beds were made; his towels were folded, and his dishes washed. One wall of his living room was lined with military medals, awards and commendations. I bet you didn't think my house looked this way did you? No, I didn't it looks great. Well I may be a drunk but my mother told me "never live like a pig," and I always remembered that. My parents taught me the right way. I didn't do things wild ass kids do today. I looked at all the perfectly aligned pictures on his wall; he started to tell me about each one. He described every piece he brought home from a foreign country and what he paid for it. I haven't always been a drunk; I've done some good things with my life. Did you know I spent twenty-seven years in the Army? I helped to defend this country I fought in World War

II and Korea. With some effort to steady his hand, he managed to pour out almost half his bottle into a glass with no chaser. Sure you don't want a hit? No, I'm good. How about a coke then? I'll take a coke. He told me usually he didn't invite any young people into his house, but he knew my mom and dad, and they were good people. He talked to me for almost an hour; I was impressed with his range of knowledge.

He answered every question I asked him in detail. I figured he had a cast iron stomach that allowed him to drink alcohol at such a rapid pace. Before I could finish my coke, he was refilling his glass. He started to get sleepy, his yawning was making me sleepy. I saw him slumping in his chair and told him I was going home to catch a nap. He said boy don't you ever go to war; it does strange things to you. Those people I killed, I never really killed them. They always come back, and they never let me rest. I guess each of us has his or her own demons; we deal with them in different ways; alcohol was how Silver Legs dealt with his. He fell into a deep sleep. I locked his door and walked out

Sleep was what I needed. When I woke up, I decided to visit my cousin Tiki, who lived a few blocks away from the alley. I got to her house around three in the afternoon on a windy day with warm swirling winds; being nosey we sat on her front porch. This way we could see everyone coming down the street. In between talking to people walking down the street, we discussed the events happening in East End. Tiki was one of my favorite cousins who felt like a sister. She always had the 411 on everything and everybody, even Vanessa. Later her husband Leon came home after work and fixed us a drink. Crown was his drink of choice, but most of the time he drank moonshine, not because of taste but affordability. Anyway after the first couple of drinks no one seemed to care what they were drinking.

Around five o'clock, some friends showed up in an old Ford Galaxy 500, two guys and a lady asleep in the back seat. The two men got out, "Wimpy and Chili Bean." I can't recall their real names we never used them. They were drinking from a jug of moonshine and wanted to share it with me and Leon. I'm definitely not a fan of moonshine but mixed with Kool Aid it wasn't bad. We had a great time drinking and joking when Tiki asked Wimpy about his wife and daughter; they're asleep in the back seat. Tiki told him they shouldn't be sleeping in the car and went to get them out. When she looked in the back seat, she saw Mildred, but not her daughter Cari, who was around thirteen months. She reached into pull Mildred out and discovered her daughter underneath her. She was not breathing; Tiki began yelling for help.

We got Mildred out and placed the girl on the ground. I was taught CPR; this was the first opportunity I had to use it. When I touched her, I knew it was too late, this beautiful little child was dead. In the heat of the day, she had an icy touch that unnerved me. I tried my best to revive her, nothing worked. She was dead; there was no bringing her back. I picked her up, started to place her on the porch and saw the look on Tiki's face. She was spooked,[33] if I placed the child on her porch she would see her every night. I asked her for something to cover the child and placed her in the front seat of the vehicle.

Wimpy lost it and began brutally beating Mildred swearing and cursing. Leon and Chili Bean tried to calm him down and get him to listen to reason. Finally, Chili Bean punched him and when he dropped to the ground it brought him back to his senses. Mildred went from a state of drunkenness to a state of agony. How could she have allowed this to happen? The tragic and senseless taking of her daughter's life, killed by the one person who loved her most.

---

[33] Spooked – to make frightened or frantic.

By the time the mortician came for the child, Mildred was crying and asking God to kill her. How could she have made such a horrible mistake? She killed her daughter and would be eternally damned. She left with the mortician; the other two followed close behind. I reached for a shot of moonshine; I needed a stiff drink didn't care what it was. Tiki was visibly shaken, though she seldom took a drink Leon made one for her. A good day of drinking, joking, and getting the 411 on everyone had turned into a disaster. I stood on Tiki's porch looked into the sky and saw a rainbow. I don't know if it were a strange occurrence or some kind of sign. There was a rainbow in the sky though we had no rain. I had a few drinks, thought about what happened and decided to leave the next day and check into my new unit.

Two months later Jason told me Mildred died in an accident. She lived in a second story apartment and had fallen down the steps leading to the ground level. Wimpy said the steps were snow covered, and she had been drinking. The rumor being circulated implicated him as the one who pushed her down those steps. Driving home for her funeral, I wondered what we would face in the next life, surely it had to be better than this one. I was lost in a maze of conflicting thoughts; this trip to Ceeville would not be a pleasant one.

A sea of umbrellas lined the parking lot as people ushered into the church on a dark, drab and somber day with a gentle rain and whispering winds. As I entered the church, there it was, a bright red casket contrasting and defying a dull and melancholy day. Mildred brought a little sunshine to every day and here she was doing it again on her last day. For some cultures, funerals consist of little more than a stoic ceremony with controlled emotions. Not so in the Black world, where attending a funeral is a ritual witnessed with great joy and pain. A true celebration of life and death, where

84

emotions are allowed to run the entire emotional gamut. Mount Nebo Church of God was a small wooden church with a brick front. Its' stained glass windows, wood floors and pews bore witness to such occasions for countless souls over countless years. When I entered all pews on the right and left sides were filled. The back pews of the center section had open seats while the front section was reserved for the family. I noticed Wimpy, his older daughter Anchelle and other relatives coming into the church and being seated. What struck me as peculiar about the family seating was that empty pew separating Mildred's family from Wimpey's family. The families were seated; the choir opened with mom's favorite song, "Oh Happy Day."

Seated in the pulpit were the church pastor and other invited ministers. The pastor stood, opened with a scripture, introduced the guest ministers present and followed with a prayer, igniting the celebration. The tempo starts slow and with each stage of the celebration builds until a crescendo is reached. In reality, the ministers do become somewhat animated, although it's totally different from the comedic portrayals of Flip Wilson and Cedric the Entertainer. It's not unusual for people to become filled with the Holy Spirit and start speaking in tongues.

I would describe the scene as sacred and solemn yet spirited and free. One of the musical selections was "God is," sung by Mildred's younger sister Evelyn, a euphonious songbird. She started the song in Acappella fashion. Her voice needed no accompaniment; however, a pianist soon joined in and before the song ended the entire choir was accompanying her. I attended church regularly before Pap's death this musical genre was no mystery to me. Since Pap's death, I conveniently had places to go other than church. This day I was reminded why my parents, grandparents and my ancestors before them found such solace in the church. If anyone ever sung a song that made me believe in heaven and an afterlife, this was it. She sang it with such fervor; I could feel her soul crying out like a wounded nightingale crying for its mate. It made me aware of a valuable asset that was uniquely ours. The "Black Church" our sanctuary. This was the village glue that held everything else in place. In troubled times, we could always bring our problems to God, solving them with his help. Too many of us had abandoned our faith and the trusted ways our parents and elders taught us.   Trusted methods that served us well for hundreds of years. We began to listen to the so-called experts, who told us our children needed drugs not recess and time outs not discipline. Experts who told us children had rights but failed to mention along with rights come responsibilities.

They told parents discipline was child abuse and denied them the right to raise their children, yet parents were the ones punished when things went awry. Proverbs 13:24 told us he who spares the rod hates his son, but he that loves him is careful to discipline him. Now our children are getting their counseling and discipline behind prison walls. Hours of therapy, numerous time outs, and drugs cannot replace a hardwood paddle that taught discipline, courtesy, and respect for other people's property. I had not given up on or abandoned those ways, although admittedly I had abandoned the church. My faith in religion was there; I had to rebuild my confidence in the ones that taught it. Thankfully my faith in God had not changed. I believed one day he would show me the path to follow.

Jason attended Mildred's funeral with me, after it was over we stopped by Miss Pearl's to see who was there and grab a quick snack. Short Barbara was serving tables and kissed us both on the lips when we came in. Short Barbara was the one who introduced me to my first sexual experience. There would always be a special place reserved in my memory just for her. Of course, I knew I wasn't the only young guy whose cherry she had busted. Miss Pearl was behind the bar talking to Short Barbara and another lady. I'm just saying, I don't give a damn about what the white man thinks. They would be glad if all of us were dead. It's not the fifties, and this isn't Whisper Alley. If you know, someone has committed a crime don't be afraid to tell somebody. Shout it out if you have too that young girl deserves better, and so does her mother. They didn't call any names, but we knew they were talking about Anchelle and Wimpy. Jason motioned for us to move to a table. As soon as we were seated he asked me. Man, do you think Wimpy killed her? I heard he pushed her down those stairs and killed her. Hell I don't know, he's not in jail.

Yeah, but you know that if a black kills another black that doesn't mean shit if you work for the right person. Remember how Smoky shot that guy in Mr. C's and didn't do any time. He worked for old man Pressler, who got him off without doing a day. If someone did see him push Mildred off those steps who would tell? No one trusts the cops. You're right, maybe one day that shit will change; this is the seventies. Jason smiled and said man that shit will never change. One thing is for sure it won't change on its own we'll have to change it. What worried me most about everything was how Anchell would see Wimpy from here on. What would it be like living with a father who may have killed your mother? Anchell was about twelve I hoped she would never have to experience that dilemma. If Anchelle ever felt uncomfortable living with Wimpy, I'm sure Evelyn would take her in.

On the way back to Atlanta, I was listening to Earth Wind and Fire's "Shining Star" and "Ain't Understanding Mellow," a slow jam by Jerry Butler and Brenda Lee Edgar. Two of Tommy's favorite songs. Humming along with the tape was better than trying to sing, knowing I wasn't the greatest at carrying a tune. I was tired, but it was only a five hour trip and driving a VW Beetle meant I didn't have to stop for gas. I had made it to Marietta with only a short distance to go. I thought about Mildred, who was now with her lost child whose name I couldn't remember. I thought about the rainbow I saw when her daughter died. Many people have mentioned an uncanny feeling. Or seeing some kind of sign which affirmed their deceased family member or friend had survived physical death, and continued to live in another dimension of existence. Sometimes it was an eerie chill that went through your body (what Pap told me was someone stepping on my grave). At other times, it was a macabre feeling that left you wondering. Was that why I saw a rainbow? I wondered if Wimpy could kill someone especially his wife. Dad often said anyone could kill under the right circumstances. God truly does work in mysterious ways.

I yawned, stretched and saw flashing lights in my rearview mirror. I wasn't speeding so why in the hell was this guy stopping me. I pulled over and waited for the cop to get out. He took his time coming to my driver side window, I rolled it down. He asked for my driver's license and looked it over, what's the problem? What do you mean? Well you kept hitting the shoulder of the road. I was tired and not on my best how-to-talk-to-a-cop behavior. When did that become illegal? It's not illegal just a sign of someone who may be impaired.

Well I'm not impaired. That's for me to determine, step out of the vehicle. Where are you going? Atlanta. Is that where you live? Yes, it is. Why do you have a Tennessee driver's license, Tennessee plates and live in Georgia? I'm in the military and Tennessee is my home of record. So why don't you have Georgia tags? I have the option to purchase tags from my home state or the state I'm living in. I was sure this jack ass knew that. Tennessee tags are cheaper. Where are you coming from? Tennessee, is that a problem? Just hold on I'm asking the questions. Don't you think if you had spent a little more money and gotten Georgia tags it would have lessened your chances of getting pulled over? I think you would pull me over with whatever tags I have on my car. Would you step back behind your vehicle? He pulled out a pen and said without turning your head follow this pen with your eyes which I did. Now recite your ABC's from Q to X, which I did. I did what he asked and began to get irritated. He knew I wasn't impaired in any way, why was this dumb shit detaining me? Why did you pull me over? You were weaving across the lanes. I thought it was because I was running onto the shoulder. He didn't reply and said without looking at your watch what time is it? Ten thirty I said. He looked at his watch and said no; it's eleven fifteen. So why didn't you tell me that without looking at your watch? Are you being a smart ass?

No, I'm just asking a simple question you're asking me to do something you can't do. When did a dumb ass question like that become part of the field sobriety test? Please place your hands behind your back. He snapped on the cuffs. What the fuck are you doing? I'm taking your black ass to jail. You're the type of egotistical son of a bitch who could make someone bust a cap in your ass. Well you won't be doing it tonight will you? I'm not drunk. It doesn't matter if you blow into the Breathalyzer I'm going to make sure you're over the limit. If you don't, I'm going to stick it to you for failure to consent to a sobriety test. What could I do my civil rights had just been successfully violated by this bigoted bastard.

On the way to the station, the ignoramus had the gall to strike up a conversation. I didn't utter a word. As luck would have it, the Neanderthal was looking at me in the rear view mirror and ran a stop sign. Some guy driving a farm truck hit us broadside and pushed us into a ditch nose first. The cop was pinned between the twisted dash and seat. I was thrown into the steel cage separating me from the cop. My wrists were burning from the cuffs, but there was one thing I had to do before help arrived. I drew my legs in as tight as I could and got them through my arms. With my hands now in front of me I inched along the steel cage and aligned myself directly above the cop in front of me. He was bitching about his legs and never noticed me. I knew there was a brief window to accomplish something heroic. Working my hands down to my pants zipper, I unzipped, took out my sprinkler and stuck it through a hole in the cage. I was holding back a piss when the bastard pulled me over and now he could have it all. I started pissing through the cage, when he figured out it was hot piss raining down on him he started cursing like a short changed whore. Thank God help arrived before he could get out, or my story may have ended that night. I was taken to a Marietta hospital in one ambulance; the pissy cop rode in another one. I was treated for my injuries and stayed in the hospital overnight, no one bothered to give me a blood test.

When I went to court the arresting officer never showed and the judge dismissed my case. Probably the reason I hated cops so much was because I never had a positive encounter with one. I felt they existed only to protect whites and the property of whites. All of them were power hungry. They would go out of their way to humiliate and belittle someone. They knew whatever they did would be justified by a criminal justice system that always tilted in their favor. Ironically I credited this experience as a positive one. Remembering how that cop looked when he saw me pissing all over him gave me a newly found respect for the job he did.

5 THE VISION

My new duty station was considered independent duty with no base or barracks. Permanent personnel had the option of renting a civilian apartment with a subsidized government lease or purchasing a home. When the unit's Administrative Chief found out I was being assigned to his unit, he assigned me a sponsor. Someone responsible for finding me a place to live. That task fell to Sergeant Gutierrez who wasted no time finding an apartment in an area called College Park. It was close to work in a decent part of the city. Gunnery Sergeant Garrett, the guy I would be working for, told me to take all the time I needed to get settled in (two days). I bought new furniture, had it delivered and in no time my new place looked like home.

My new unit was small (about thirty active duty personnel) but had the distinction of having a light bird (LtCol) full bird (Colonel), a Master Sergeant, Master Gunns and a Sergeant Major. A Navy and Marine Corps Reserve Training Center, Marines on one side sailors on the other. Independent duty requires special training for administrative personnel, three months after checking in, my Admin Chief gave me the good news. I was going back to Parris Island for Reserve Admin Training. Training which was altogether different from the active duty side of the house. I didn't mind the additional training, but Parris Island again? Reserves drilled one weekend a month and attended annual training duty for two weeks during the summer. If they wanted to earn extra points toward retirement, they could come in between drills on Equivalent Instruction or Duty (EIOD). Some could work full time on what was called the Extended Active Duty (EAD) program. Our task was to train these weekend warriors which I later learned would be no easy task.

Heading back to Parris Island, I had none of the fear and apprehension of my last two visits. I was now a Sergeant a few steps higher on the food chain. I arrived and was greeted by the same vintage barracks. Though now as a Sergeant, I would have my own room, or so I thought. Unfortunately, I was assigned to a barracks with (you guessed it) an open squad bay. The newer barracks were reserved for recruits and permanent personnel. My course would only be about six weeks long, no reason to sweat it. Parris Island was never one of my favorite spots, this time it was more bearable. We were told not to screw around with the recruits on the island and not play DI with them. We attended school from about 0800 to 1600, Monday through Friday with scheduled barracks cleanup (field day) on Thursday nights.

The rest of the time was basically ours to do whatever we needed. The class had about forty Marines and one of the first guys I met was a skinny light green Marine named Henry Green, who was immediately tagged "Thin Man" by the students in the class. Thin Man was a re-tread (former Marine) in and out of the corps about three times, a Vietnam vet. He stood 5' 8", weighed 120 pounds and had an affinity for talking shit. He along with two dark green Marines, Davenport and Ronnie Mack were the guys I hung out with throughout the course. Service Schools are no break from military discipline and protocol. PT was scheduled three times a week with a physical fitness test scheduled for the last week. Personnel inspections were scheduled each Friday morning. On one particular Friday morning, Thin Man was standing in the first rank. I was directly behind him in the second rank. We were being inspected by the Regimental Commanding Officer accompanied by the Regimental Sergeant Major. Inspecting the first rank the Colonel stopped, made a left face in front of Thin Man and said, "I see you're wearing a Purple Heart Marine, where did you get it?" There was complete silence for what seemed like five minutes before Thin Man spoke up and said "Vietnam sir." Well hell Marine, I know you didn't get it in Korea, where in Vietnam? Again silence, total silence, can't remember huh? No sir. The Colonel made a right face and moved to the next Marine.

Of course when we got back to the barracks we replayed that scene over and over which irked the hell out of him. He said, you motherfuckers don't know a damn hero when you see one; that's your problem. Some guy named Anderson told him he needed to get his tubes tested because his screen kept blacking out. He got irate and threatened to kick his ass which was highly unlikely since Anderson was about twice his size. I had to admire him though, he had tenacity and a fighting spirit.

I broke up the excitement when I told them "we've got to get to class." Occasionally we did things to break up the monotonous class routine to include the "Thin Man, Ronnie Mack Revue." Before we split on Friday afternoon, we were entertained by their kick off the weekend show. Beer was allowed in the barracks; everyone had one for the show. Our weekly show was headlined by Thin Man and Ronnie Mack with other entertainers joining in from week to week. No matter how the show started out it always closed with Thin Man and Ronnie Mack backed up by three other Marines, treating everyone to a rendition of the O'Jays Living for the Weekend. The starting acts were pretty good, but those guys were definitely the headliners of the show. Ronnie Mack opened the song with the flair of a club DJ pumping up the crowd for the main event, but the guy with the pipes was Thin Man. He finished the song in a way that would have made any professional singer stand up and cheer. Thin

Man was a natural; maybe singing is what he did when he wasn't in the Marine Corps blanking out at inspections. The deck of the barracks was highly polished and buffed. With a swab (mop) and push broom substituting for mikes, this duo put on a hell-of-a-show sliding across the deck as if they were live on stage which, in fact, they were. Damn near everyone in the barracks joined in. Those who couldn't sing hummed and those who couldn't dance moved their feet and bobbed their heads. We were all living for the weekend covering as much territory as we could. One weekend traveling to North Carolina, Georgia the next and then Tennessee.

The weekend we visited Thin Man's parents in Memphis opened my eyes to some things. The lady that opened the door and hugged us, the one he introduced as his mom, was black. He never mentioned it, never thought it was necessary. Now a lot of things fell into place, no wonder this guy was a skilled vocalist, he had perfected his craft in the community of rhythm and blues. He knew as much about black culture as I did. And since he lived the black experience as a white guy, he probably felt the vicious sting of prejudice from both sides of the fence. He never mentioned his mom was black, for the same reason I never mentioned my mom was black. It wasn't because he was ashamed of her; he didn't think it mattered. We carry enough labels; he didn't want to be labeled as "acting black" any more than I wanted to be labeled as "acting white." I never questioned him about it, Thin Man was my "Homey," that's all that mattered.

This was my third visit to the Beaufort area and this time I was determined to get a feel for what the locals had to offer, other than Parris Island. Throughout the week after class, I took the time to explore Beaufort and the surrounding area. Beaufort offered horse drawn carriage rides and tours of antebellum homes that survived the Civil War. A tour of these homes provided you a quick glimpse of Southern History, although I wasn't looking for that kind of history. I had lived that history. I was being selective wanting to see something not readily available in an American History Book. I knew the city had areas with a rich African heritage and culture. I wanted to see those artists', painters, basket makers, sculptors and others honing their craft.

What I was looking for could be found on the Sea Islands a short distance away. There was a nearby town named Frogmore located on one of the local islands (St. Helena). Town may not be an accurate description there was only a post office on one side of the road and a two-story white country store on the other. I met a girl named Mariami Moran picking up her mail at the post office. Mariami was what Beaufort residents called a "Gullah" a native islander. She had a strong accent; it was difficult for her to pronounce certain words.

Thing was pronounced "ting," them was pronounced "dem,"and to came out as "ta." She lived on the island with three generations of her family including her grandfather. A grandfather who in English terms could be described as a storyteller and in African terms could be described as a "Griot." Her people gave me a direct connection to Africa; her culture had retained ethnic traditions from West Africa since the mid 1700's.[34] I loved the exotic sound of her dialect that linked me with far away kinsmen and faraway places. In Mariami's family there seemed to be no gap between generations. Words they used such as "ashish" for ashes, "bettuh" for better, and "chillun" for children, weren't new words to me. They were words used by older generations in my own family. The difference was my generation didn't use them. I asked Mariami about the terms "Geechee" and "Gullah" she told me Gullah and Geechee are not synonymous. Both identify the people of Sea Island cultures. Gullah is the accepted name of the islanders in South Carolina. Geechee is the accepted

---

[34] The New Georgia Encyclopedia (2010), Geechee and Gullah Culture, retrieved

name of islanders living in Georgia. Every time we met she taught me something about the ways of a bygone era. A short distance from Beaufort we visited an actual African Village in America, located near the small town of Sheldon, South Carolina. Named the Kingdom of Oyontunji it had a royal palace with open air shrines including carved Yoruba godheads. There was a courtyard with a bazaar and shops selling African artwork, jewelry, herbs and clothes. Mariami seemed to enjoy the trip, I purchased several souvenirs.

She loved cooking and made me a spicy dish called Frogmore Stew. It was made with sausage, shrimp, crabs and other delicious ingredients served over rice or rice was used as a side dish. Sometimes I invited her over to my barracks for blue crabs boiled in beer. When I learned of her belief in Voodoo and hexes she explained them to me, our relationship didn't change. She confirmed what some guys in class told me about people on the island working roots and collaborating with a witch doctor. One guy told me an island girl had threatened to put a spell on him; I sincerely felt he believed it. He warned me to stay away from the island if I wanted to avoid a hex or being turned into a Zombie. I didn't follow his warning, continued to see Mariami and never kidded her about her religion. I didn't think she would turn me into a frog but why take the chance. She taught me words in Gullah such as "joso" which meant witchcraft and "gafa" which meant evil spirit. She had her faith, and I had mine, we both believed in a greater power that protected us from evil spirits.

There was a holiday coming up giving us a three day weekend. I told Mariami I was visiting my brother Bennie in Augusta, she asked if she could tag along. We had become good friends I said; I'm glad you asked now I won't have to ask you. We took a picturesque route along South Carolina's U.S. Route 125, a rural road with small towns and open farmlands. The hitch to this route was having to cross a government nuclear facility called the Savannah River Plant[35] located about 25 miles from Augusta. Built in the 1950's its purpose was to refine nuclear materials for deployment in nuclear weapons. Once you entered the installation grounds your vehicle was timed until you exited.

Stopping, taking photographs or taking too long to get from the entrance to the exit was cause for a pull over and search of your vehicle and person. I noticed the odd features of some trees we passed, malformed in some manner. Who knows what other unnatural effects the radiation was having on the environment? Or what kind of radiation treatment we were getting as we traveled through.

When we got to Bennie's the grill was fired up and the cooler full. He was completely enamored with Mariami and wanted to know everything about her and her family. He treated her like royalty the entire weekend; she loved him for it. Bennie could be a great guy when he wanted to, unfortunately, he preferred being obstinate and sometimes intolerant. On our way back to Beaufort, Mariami could not express her gratitude for Bennie's gracious welcome. I told her don't think he's always like that, he was trying to impress you. He did impress me she said and so did you, both of you treated me like family. She leaned over and kissed me on the cheek, my first kiss from her. For some unknown reason, I had envisioned our relationship as strictly platonic, now my spidey senses were telling me something else. Mariami told me stories very similar to the ones I heard from my own family. Stories of hags and haunts (spirits) visiting and sometimes terrifying the living. We were a short

---

[35] Wikipedia (2010) Savannah river site, Retrieved December 8, 2010, http://enwikipedia.org/wiki/Savannah_River_Site

distance from Beaufort approaching Yemassee when out of nowhere I saw a vision of a pond. It appeared as if it were a billboard alongside the road. The second time I saw it, I turned into a gravel lane that led to a farmhouse. I stopped halfway down the lane and got out; the pond couldn't be seen, but I knew it was nearby. Looking around I saw a woman standing on a hill, I could faintly hear her voice, but could see her hands feverously waving at us. I started running towards her so did Mariami. As we approached, we could see the pond on the other side of the hill she was standing on. On the far side of the pond was an overturned tractor with someone pinned underneath.

It was a fourteen-year-old boy, and his mother had been screaming for help. I used a short log as a brace, a longer one for leverage and lifted the tractor enough for Mariami and the boy's mother to get him out. He was badly bruised possibly had broken bones but was alive and breathing normally. I didn't want to move him though the mother insisted I put him into her car. We followed her to the hospital in Beaufort. Mariami ran inside and came out with two attendants pushing a stretcher. I can't remember how many times the mother thanked us. A short time later when the father arrived he picked up where she left off. The kid was going to be fine and when we got that word we decided to leave. The mother would not let us leave without a hug and a kiss. There truly is nothing in this world like a mother's love.

How did you know asked Mariami? I don't know I saw an image of the pond and something told me to stop. Are you a Baptis' (Baptist)? No, my mom worships with the Church of Christ. But what church do you belong to? I don't attend church. I think maybe you should, Gawd (God) gave you a vision that saved one life maybe someday you'll save others.

Normally I never took the time to say goodbye to any of the ladies I met. Mariami was different she was a good friend. At the end of my class, I stopped by her home to let her know I was leaving. She gave me a kiss and said goodbye Bobby Wade and whenever you return "Kumbayah," which meant come by here. I hoped I would see her again, but only God knew if I ever would.

I loved everything about Atlanta. From the beautiful women in my apartment complex to the underground clubs. The Varsity hot dog and hamburger joint and my duty station on Georgia Tech campus. I was the lucky son-of- a gun that would spend the next three years there training reserves. About two months after my return from Parris Island, I was scheduled to participate in my first color guard detail.

Atlanta has several professional teams; our unit provided them with color guard details from time-to-time. To ensure everything went off without a hitch, we practiced before the actual detail. This particular game was being broadcast on national television and as usual there could be no mistakes. We were scheduled to meet at the reserve center at 1100 on Sunday, have a practice run and head out for the real thing. The Color Guard Detail included me, Sergeant Summerville, Sergeant Sanders and Staff Sergeant Payuma the senior man on the detail. Staff Sergeant Payuma showed up thirty minutes late barely able to stand up. He looked like shit and his breath smelled like cheap whiskey. There was no time to get a replacement. We got him cleaned up, had him wash out his mouth with aftershave and headed out. Luckily as the senior man he was designated to carry the American flag and didn't execute any movements. We formed up and squeezed his ass in so tight he could not possibly fall down. He was in no condition to give commands, Sergeant Summerville took over his duties. The color guard went smoothly, usually after the detail each member was given a free seat to the game. This time was different. We couldn't take the chance of someone smelling alcohol on Payuma's breath, which anyone coming within ten feet of him was sure to do. That aftershave wouldn't last much longer. We got back to the Reserve Center and gave Payuma plenty of shit. He stayed at the center to get some sleep before driving home. The last thing we heard from him before we left was, "I owe you motherfuckers one." I knew this was going to be a great duty station and the guys here already felt like my extended family.

We had drill weekend once a month and usually got a three day weekend the next week. As an added bonus at noon on Wednesdays after a ferocious game of volleyball, played according to "jungle rules"[36] we got the afternoon off. Training reserves was a good though sometimes frustrating experience. What they learned this month they all but forgot the next month. But, it was okay because these guys and gals were primarily civilians in military uniforms. It was a constant cycle of training and re-training. Some of these civilian warriors had the hook up in the real world.

Knowing the right ones could get your electricity, and other utilities hooked up without a deposit, or a great meal at a fancy restaurant. "Quid pro quo" was all right with me as long as the shit didn't get out of hand. Go overboard with it, and you'd find yourself standing on the carpet in front of the old man answering for your transgressions. We were a few Marines representing the entire Marine Corps; everything we did had to be above board. It didn't take me long to learn the city and after a few months it felt like home. I frequented many clubs and hot spots and knew all the places I needed to keep my ass away from. One of my favorite restaurants

---

[36] Jungle rules, anything goes short of tearing down the net.

was a small Muslim fish shack, located a short distance from historic Ebenezer Baptist Church on Auburn Avenue. They sold an awesome fish sandwich for seventy-five cents; their bean pies were outstanding. I pulled into their parking lot, went in and placed my order. A few minutes later I was watching a young lady pretending not to be watching me. She had my attention; I didn't take my eyes off her. I had no reason to be pretentious, walked next to her and asked for the time, though she could see I was wearing a watch. Mine doesn't work. Seeing the second hand moving she said it's working now. It was and so was I. Turns out she was a teacher named Penelope. The next day I picked her up after work and we caught a movie. For the next month, she was my constant companion. After a month and no sex, I was starting to worry. She was lively and fun loving but withdrew whenever things got too heated. Named Penelope Crabtree and a school teacher. I was sure her panties were frosted over; I couldn't wait to heat her up.

Maybe I was wrong; maybe she was a fireball in bed. A week later I was on top of her and cursed the fact I was right. I felt like a necrophiliac[37] the corpse was underneath me. She showed no passion, no moans of ecstasy and pleasure. No tearing at the flesh on my back, no heat from within her love canal. My first catch in Atlanta was a dead fish. I called on all my experience giving pleasure and gave it all I had, just could not light her fire.

When it was over she had the balls to ask me "how was it?" I wasn't lying when I said "you took everything out of me." I kissed her goodnight at the door, got into my car and tore her name out of my little black book. Tonight I had been a teacher and Mrs. Crabtree was a lousy student.

---

[37] Someone having a sexual attraction to corpses

Daydreaming at work the next day, I thought about Penelope and wondered if Odysseus[38] had gotten the same kind of lovemaking from his Penelope. Maybe her frigid thighs were the real reason he was always away on some expedition. In the middle of my daydream, I looked on the deck (floor) and saw a lone dime heads up. One thin dime as my dad would say. I remembered an experience at my first duty station in Norfolk. It was payday, and I was headed to work. I lived in Portsmouth a short distance away; my car was in the shop and Gunny Branson was on leave. Getting to work by bus required catching four buses.

Twenty five cents for the Craddock bus, ten cents for the Tunnel bus, thirty five cents for the Naval Base bus and then a free ride on the base shuttle. Just my luck I was a dime short, after searching underneath every seat cushion; checking every coat and pants pocket every possible place a dime could hide. Only someone on the lower rungs of the economic ladder can understand what I'm talking about here. Finally running out of time I decided to catch the bus with sixty cents in my pocket. I caught the first two buses with no problem and was waiting for the Naval Base bus with twenty-five cents in my pocket. I thought about hitching or walking the rest of the way.

I remembered the morning I was walking downtown near the convention center named "Scope." Some clown pulled a knife on me attempting to rob me, so happens I had a bigger knife. Even so I really didn't feel like going through that crap again. There was no option that would get me to work on time. A small black lady was

---

[38] Legendary Greek king of Ithaca and hero of Homer's epic poem the Odyssey

standing next to me, a daily rider. She carried a large bag slung over her shoulder, as clichéd as it sounds she reminded me of my mom. The bus would be coming soon; a decision had to be made. Swallowing my pride, I asked the lady to borrow a dime. She reached into her purse and gave it to me with a smile. I thanked her and quickly put it in my pocket not wanting anyone to see me borrowing a dime. A Marine in uniform borrowing a dime. I felt like a thief stealing candy from a baby. Should have started earlier and walked the first leg of my route. Should have planned better or did something to keep from totally embarrassing myself. Borrowing one thin dime made me feel lower than the snail nuts my DI talked about.

The next day I met her at the bus stop and offered her a quarter, her dime plus a little extra. She smiled and patted my hand, honey I can't take that. I'm on the bus with you every day going to work. You're a nice young man who needed my help. If I let you pay me back that dime, I might lose my blessing. Looking me directly in the eye and still holding my hand she said "don't ever let pride keep you from asking for help, everyone needs a hand every now and then." She told me there are some people who try to live a Christian life, people that are happy to help others. You can repay my charity by extending charity to someone else. What a sweet lady kind and unselfish, she was indeed just like my mother. Why couldn't I meet more people like her instead of the sons-of-bitches I regularly met on every corner? I reached down and picked up the dime, looked at it and shoved it into my pocket, one thin dime.

When we weren't having drill weekends things around the training center were pretty routine. Days were spent working in you MOS, nights, and most weekends were primarily spent doing whatever you wanted. There was no all-night duty. After regular working hours usually around 1630 we closed up and went home. If you were the lucky soul who had the duty for the day, you stayed a couple of hours extra. After ensuring the building was secured, the armory locked and ADT notified, you headed home. Duty on the weekend meant coming in for an hour or so and checking the grounds. Wherever you find Marines, sailors are not far away and for the most part the ones we had were a pretty good bunch. A few of the single ones loved to hang out with Marines improving their image. One of the guys that hung out with us was a First Class[39] by the name of Kevin Butler. A good friend and fun loving guy who, unfortunately, was killed in a motorcycle accident. I had duty on a Saturday about two weeks after Butler's death. Checking out the building and grounds, I thought I saw Butler walking down the hallway. It turned out to be nothing, just my imagination, I chalked it up to being tired. I checked out the Sergeant's Major office and took a time out on his couch first sitting and then stretching out. I fell asleep or thought I did. Butler was in the hallway again and when I looked around I saw myself lying on the couch. Butler was beckoning; I was lying on the couch, yet looking at myself and Butler. Even in this state I didn't think following Butler was a good idea. I decided to get off the couch, and nothing worked.

My arms and legs were frozen in place; my eyes would not open. Determined not to follow Butler, I put all my energy into getting off the couch and suddenly woke up. I got off the couch closed up and left with no idea what happened. It was similar to the eerie light that appeared on my mother's bedroom wall before Pap died. She could see it no one else could. One of those freaky things that happen and defy explanation. Although no explanation was needed, it was the weekend there were other things to wonder about.

---

[39] First Class Petty Officer (E-6)

Most of the Marines and sailors stationed at the center were strictly "top shelf" but no matter where you go there are always the guys who make up the ten percent, the ten percent known as "Shitbirds." On Monday morning around 0500, I received a call from one of those shitbirds called Perkins. As shitbirds go, Perkins was at the top of the list. A big mystery was how he got into the Navy; an even bigger mystery was how he got assigned to independent duty. I knew Navy standards were lower, but not that much lower. He lived a few miles from me and was calling for a ride into work. Ten minutes after I picked his ass up he fired up a joint. Hey, you can't smoke that shit in my car. No one's going to bust you. I don't give a damn; you can't smoke that shit in my car. Ah, come on now you care too much about what people think, fuck them if they can't take a joke.

Look asshole I'm telling you for the last time put the shit out. What are you going to do, put me out? I pulled over and told him to hit the curb or be thrown out. Okay man I'll put the shit out. No, you and your shit get the fuck out of my car, now. He got out and was standing on the curb as I drove off. The dumb bastard liked his weed more than riding. He only had about five miles to go and the walk would do his fat ass some good. I was no puritan; didn't give a shit what he smoked as long as he didn't smoke it in my car. I would not allow him or anyone else to put my career in jeopardy, definitely not for a shitbird. The Navy wasn't the only branch of service with its ten percent shitbirds. We had our reserve ten percent, as well. Reservist who came in wearing a wig[40] and looking like crap or worse the ones who didn't bother to show up for drill. These guys made my day because if they missed a certain amount of

---

[40] During this period Marine Reservist were authorized to wear a wig that conformed to Marine Corps haircut regulations.

drills they could be placed on involuntary active duty for a period of two years. Pete Garrard was one of those guys who loved to miss drills and today we were going to present him with involuntary active duty orders.

Sergeant Summerville and I were headed to a section of Atlanta called East Point driving down Lee Street to deliver the orders. I wonder what Mr. Garrard is going to say when he finds out he's being placed on active duty for two years. You know what said Summerville; I bet he starts crying and moaning. I didn't get anything about missed drills. I've been sick and planned to make up those drills when I got well, can't you give me another chance? Hell, I think they should let us cuff the bitch in front of his momma and drag his ass to the car.

We were laughing about Garrard when Summerville turned on the radio and caught Wild Cherry's "Play That Funky Music" bumping. He was singing and bobbing as we headed for Mr. Garrard's home. Turn it down, that's his house. I've got the orders, let's go see Mr. I can't come to a drill. Garrard had a gated fence around his front yard; we opened the gate and went to the front door. I knocked as Summerville stood behind, after several knocks I figured either he wasn't home or the dip shit wasn't going to answer his door.

We were walking away, heard the door opening and turned around. There staring us in the face was a vicious looking beast of a dog with a hundred teeth in his mouth. He leaped out the door; I almost ran over Summerville trying to get out the gate. Summerville couldn't get his footing; I knew both of us would not make it out the gate before that meat eater had us for lunch. I moved to Summerville's side and decided to jump the fence, when I did the wire running along the top

106

shredded my new dress blue trousers and my leg underneath. I stood on the sidewalk looking at my bloodied leg and cursing. God dammed that asshole if I had a gun they would be burying that son-of-a-bitch and his crappy dog. Wait until I get my hands on that gap-toothed cocksucker. I looked up and saw an old lady staring me in the face. She said, "You have a filthy mouth young man and you should not be using the lord's name in vain." She was wearing a black ankle length dress with a matching black hat festooned with a white bow. She had on bifocals, carried an umbrella and wore black leather shoes with thick granny type heals. Here I was being confronted by an officer of the morality patrol.

Young man did you have a Christian upbringing? Yes ma'am I did. Then somewhere along the line you've forgotten what your parents taught you. Do you go to church? No ma'am. You need to go. Yes ma'am I should go to church. She gave me an "I should slap the tongue out of your mouth look" and walked away. I'm hurting like hell; the old biddy never showed any concern for my injured leg and then the witch tells me I needed to go to church. That took a lot of gaul, to hell with her!

Summerville rubbing his ass said, "that damn dog bit me." Did he bite you on the ass? Not on my ass on my leg. You were rubbing your ass. Fuck you, wait until I see that bastard. I'm going to cut his balls off and feed them to that shit eating dog of his. Hey, I don't know I'm not really into screwing around with some guy's balls. Summerville looked at me and said, eat shit! He walked towards the car thought about the old lady and turned around. Hey, what did that old lady say to you? Oh, man you wouldn't believe what that old horny broad said. What the hell did she say? Here I am standing on the sidewalk bleeding like a stuck pig and all she wanted to

know was how much pipe I was packing. He laughed; you're
a lying ass, let's go. We took our bruised bodies and egos
back to the Reserve Center and reported what happened. The
Inspector Instructor told the Admin Chief to prepare a DD
Form 553[41] and have the dip shit picked up. Sometime later
we received a call from the Fulton County Police Department
informing us of Mr. Garrard's apprehension. Sergeant Major
Pinson was sending me and Summerville to pick him up, but
first he gave us a warning. "When you get back here with that
turd he better look the same way he did when you picked him
up, understand?" Am I making myself clear, Summerville,
yeah, Wade, yeah, all right go get the bastard.

On the way to pick up Mr. Garrard, we worked on ways to even
the score without the Sergeant Major being able to tell we did the
deed. We picked him up and placed the cuffs on him tight enough
to restrict his blood flow. I planned to crack his head a couple of
times getting him into the car. We could get away with a few bruises.
Before I could put my plan into action, the asshole tripped and
cracked his head on the sidewalk. He tripped on something; I have
to be honest I didn't try to catch him before he fell. Of all the rotten
luck, landing full force with his hands behind him had loosened one
of his teeth and chipped another. Blood was coming out of his
mouth and nose, there were some nasty bruises on his face. I didn't
have anything for him to wipe the blood off and wasn't going to look
for anything.

---

[41] Form used to notify civilian authorities of a Deserter/Absentee
wanted by the armed forces.

The bastard got what he deserved. He was looking like shit when we got him back to the center. I was hurrying to get his cuffs off and get his ass into the head when Sergeant Major Pinson walked up. Pinson looked at Garrard with his bloodied face and protruding tooth. He asked him what happened. I tripped on the sidewalk Sergeant Major. Oh, he said, you tripped and damn near knocked your tooth out. Did these two tell you to say that? No sir, they had the cuffs on me I tripped on the sidewalk and fell. Okay, get in the head and get cleaned up. Garrard left for the head Pinson turned to me and Summerville. How many times did you guys rehearse that lie? What did I tell you before you left? I said Sergeant Major what he told you is what happened. I can't tell it any other way; that's how it happened. Yeah, it's what he told me are you going to stick to that story? It's not a story it's what happened. All right you two just volunteered to help Staff Sergeant Akins clean weapons.

Summerville said for what we didn't do anything wrong. Oh, you're not being punished; Akins needed some help. Walking off, he said let me know if you want to volunteer for anything else. Summerville turned to me and said isn't that some shit; that son of a bitch, we do what we're told and still get screwed. Yeah but think about it, I was there, and it's hard for me to believe that story. Garrard got over on us again. Garrard wasn't the victim here we were the victims, victims of circumstance.

Time never stops, and it doesn't slow down when you're having a good time. My time in Atlanta could not have moved any faster. My three years (normal duty assignment) were almost up; I decided to send an Administrative Action (AA) Form to Headquarters Marine Corps (HQMC) requesting a one year extension on station. In true puzzle palace fashion, my AA Form was never answered. Two months later I received orders back to Parris Island directing me to report to the CG, Marine Corps Recruit Depot, Parris, Island, South Carolina for temporary additional duty with Drill Instructor (DI)

School. I wasn't sure DI School was what I wanted; with only a few months left on my contract I could decline the orders. Why are they sending me back to Parris Island I wondered, why don't they just send me straight to hell instead? Before I could make a decision one way or the other I got the word my CO, Colonel Paulson wanted to see me. I knocked on his door; he said come in Sergeant Wade I want to talk to you about something.

Colonel Paulson was a Limited Duty Officer (LDO) one of the few Marine Officers I knew that once held the rank of Private. That fact alone garnered him an immense amount of respect and there was no one in the Marine Corps I respected more. He was sitting at a small round table with photo albums on it, pull up a seat he told me. You're about to take on one of the greatest challenges of your career. I want to let you know what to expect, take a look at this photo. I took the photo; it was a picture of him as a young Marine Corporal with one hash mark. He was wearing a campaign cover and DI belt. I had made Sergeant in two years and forgot at one time promotions were so slow, four year Corporals were the norm.

He started to tell me all about DI School and the challenges I would face. He spoke of the pride I would feel turning raw recruits into Marines and the impact it would have on the future of the Corps. After forty-five minutes with the Colonel, there was no way I could decline the orders. He gave me a fifth of "Old Barton" whiskey. He told me after I finished a successful tour as a Drill Instructor to pop the top and have one on him. He added if I didn't have a successful tour not to bother taking a drink, just break the bottle.

During the entire time I spent with the Colonel, not once did he ask if being a DI was something I wanted? He never gave me the option of saying no. I left his office, bitched and swore, then decided it was time to head back to Parris Island, and it wasn't because I wanted a taste of "Old Barton."

DI School was boot camp all over again only worse. Worse because, as a student, you were a noncom[42] or staff noncom going through the same shit recruits went through. Worse because every aspect of training was more challenging and demanding. Once assigned to a barracks (open squad bay again) we wasted no time starting training. We were broken down into eight to ten man squads and assigned a squad instructor from the school staff. Our first day of PT (physical training) consisted of the standard physical fitness test pull-ups, sit-ups and a three mile run. From there it expanded at every session to include the circuit course, confidence course, obstacle course plus a five or six mile run.

Instructions were provided in first aid, Marine Corps history customs and courtesy, weapons training, and what Marines are famous for drill, drill, and more drill. It's a school that truly separates the water-walkers from the rest of the pack. Becoming a Drill Instructor is an ambitious endeavor, being given an opportunity to shape the future of the Marine Corps. Not to mention getting a chance to exact payback for the shit you took as a recruit. As I mentioned earlier, the training is grueling mentally and physically. PT is rigorous; academics is challenging, and personnel inspections are demanding.

Inspections started from the top of your head. Was your cover (hat) clean, did it fit properly? Was it properly marked with your name, and was there any hanging Iris Pendants (strings)? Was the Marine Corps emblem properly placed, was there any unpainted brass

---

[42] Non-Commissioned Officer

that showed through? Did you have a regulation haircut? Did you have a proper shave and was your mustache properly trimmed? Were there any zits or blackheads on your face or blood stains from an improper shave? Moving down did your shirt have collar stays, was it clean and pressed? Was your tie correctly tied, was the tie clip placed between the fourth and fifth button, and was the tie clip polished or tarnished? Was your blouse (coat) properly tailored, was it clean, were stripes and hash marks properly centered? Were ribbons clean and properly centered and in the right order of seniority? Was the belt to your blouse the proper length, was it clean, was it marked? Was the buckle clean and polished? Were there any Irish pendants hanging from your belt loop, were there any Irish pendants inside your pockets? Were your emblems correctly placed and serviceable any missing or cracked buttons? Did your trousers hang properly in front and back? Were they clean with no double press marks? Did they match the blouse in color and texture?

Was your web belt clean, was there no more than two to four inches from the belt buckle to the belt tip? Were both highly polished, was there any cleaning residue left on the web belt, buckle, or belt tip? Were your shoes highly polished with edge dressing placed around the soles and heels? Were shoe laces inserted left over right? Did shoe heels have excessive wear? Everything was checked for fit and functional service, in other words did you look like a Marine Drill Instructor? In addition, every question asked by the inspecting officer required the right answer. Questions ranged from current events to military subjects to personal; nothing was out of bounds. If you possessed any dark secrets, those were usually exposed during one of your required visits to the shrink.

Another challenge was the method of teaching drill movements to your fellow squad members. Your squad instructor held a handful of drill cards; you pulled one from him. You were given five minutes to go over the movement and then present it. Of course, you had to memorize all the movements beforehand. To present your movement, you stood before your squad and moved to a modified position of parade rest with one hand behind your back. You introduced the movement by saying "the next movement I will explain and demonstrate is "Parade Rest" or the position of attention etc. Following the drill card verbatim you explained the movement and after explaining it you demonstrated it by giving yourself both the preparatory command and the command of execution.

Staff Sergeant Amos, one of the students in the class, would start to present his movement by saying the next movement I will explain and demonstrate is (insert movement here). He could never get beyond this point, even after backing up several times. I don't know if the Squad Instructors thought he was for real or faking it. Not everyone wanted to be a DI. They kept him in class until the last week before dropping him. This was too bad. No one working on the street taught recruits that way they were taught by the numbers. It's the easiest way the little shits can learn drill movements. Finally after eight grueling weeks forty-three Marines from a class of sixty-two graduated and were given the Leatherneck Magazine certificate of achievement.

The graduating class was split up with some being assigned to each of the four recruit training battalions. I wanted third battalion, my old alma mater so naturally they sent me to second battalion. The barracks housing DI's were not open squad bays but very close to it. The same old world war two leftovers with individual rooms. Rooms were equipped with a closet and sink, communal shitters and showers were clustered at one end of the building. If you hate working a forty-hour week don't think about becoming a Drill Instructor. For a DI, the day started around 0330 when you got up showered, shaved, got dressed and looked over the training schedule

for the day. DI's were expected to be at the recruit barracks by
0430, a half hour before reveille. The work day went to 2100 if you
were lucky. If you were unlucky enough to catch duty that day, you
spent the night in the barracks with the recruits. By the way having
only three DI's meant duty every third day. Otherwise, you went to
your barracks and checked your schedule for the next day. If there
were a class, you were teaching, lesson plans had to be pulled and
reviewed along with any special uniform requirements. The next
day it started all over.

After forming week, the twelve week boot camp training
schedule was broken down into three phases and for the first two
phases it was usually an all hat (DI) requirement. When recruits
reached the third phase of training, they had received sufficient
training and discipline to perform some functions on their own
"automatic pilot." During this phase, only one DI was needed per
platoon/series. Suffice it to say the hours of a Drill Instructor are
grueling. Because of long hours with little sleep, your body is in a
constant state of tetchiness.

On a blistering July day, I had my platoon on the parade grinder
going through drill movements. A day I thought should have been a
black flag day.[43] One recruit was having problems properly executing
his rifle movements. I called him out of the platoon and had him
standing directly in front of me. Giving him one-on-one
instructions he was still screwing up. Frustrated I reached out and
snatched the weapon from him and he flinched. Screwing up the
movements, then flinching was enough to push me over the edge. I
used his weapon to give him a vertical butt stroke which knocked

---

[43] Black Flag (WBGTI of 90 and above degrees F): All nonessential
physical activity will be halted.

him down, down and out. I stepped over him and asked if he were dead, to my amazement his eyeballs fluttered and he said, no sir. Good I said, get on your feet you're holding up the rest of these recruits who want to drill. I discreetly looked around for a Depot Inspector. These were former DI's now working as Depot Spies watching for recruit training violations. Had one of them seen me and reported my actions the outcome could have been voidance of my secondary MOS as a DI (8511). As a result of that action, I would have been sent back to the Fleet Marine Force with my career in jeopardy. Later I thought about this incident and realized maybe it could have been handled differently.

I owed that recruit an apology, but one would not be forthcoming. I made him better at drill and he should have been thanking me, besides apologies could easily be misinterpreted as a sign of weakness. My old DI Sergeant Jones told me DI's had the power of life and death. I remembered the "Ribbon Creek Saga" and how he loved telling how six recruits were marched into a swamp and died. Turns out it was a true story, however, Sergeant Jones never told the rest of the story as [44]Paul Harvey[45] would say.

Staff Sergeant McKeon the DI in Sgt Jones' saga marched six recruits to their death.[46] McKeon was brought to a court of inquiry on the next day. At first, he was classified mentally and "emotionally stable" and "a mature, stable appearing career Marine." Later, the court recognized the detailed directives regarding and prohibiting certain Marine training methods were "correct and adequate." McKeon had launched an unnecessary and unauthorized disciplinary action. It was also found he was drunk; McKeon was

---

[44] A popular radio announcer

[46] http://www.en.wikipedia.org/wikiBGTI of 90 and above degrees F): All nonessential physical activity will be halted.

recommended for court martial. McKeon himself claimed he held a minor degree of guilt, and suggested only being "part of the system" and that the supervision regarding basic training should be restructured. In the end, McKeon was acquitted of manslaughter and oppression of troops. He was found guilty of negligent homicide and drinking on duty. The sentence was a $270 fine, nine months of confinement at hard labor; rank reduced to private and a Bad Conduct Discharge.

The Secretary of the Navy later reduced the sentence to three months in the brig, reduction to Private with no discharge and no fine. McKeon went back on active duty. He was never able to regain his former rank and was medically retired from the Marine Corps in 1959. He did it under the influence of alcohol a mistake he later admitted gave him a lifelong burden of guilt. Sergeant Jones never mentioned how McKeon prayed to God every day for forgiveness and the safekeeping of those recruits.

I hated what happened to those recruits and deeply regretted what happened to McKeon. I realized I crossed the line and decided to keep myself in closer check. As a DI, I took a pledge that stated: "These are my recruits; I will train them to the best of my ability. I will develop them into smartly disciplined, physically fit, basically trained Marines, thoroughly indoctrinated in love of Corps and country. I will demand of them, and demonstrate by my own example, the highest standards of personal conduct, morality, and professional skill." My job was to train recruits. Killing one was not part of my pledge. Being a DI carries an awesome responsibility. Not only to the recruits but to the parents who entrusted us with the care and training of their children. There is a thin line between pushing a recruit to his limit and abusing him. No manual can tell you how close you will come to that limit on any given day.

You have to trust your judgment, control your temper, and above all use common sense. I said earlier that there are few jobs I know of that are more stressful than being a DI. Some could handle the stress of a 100 hour plus work week and some could not. After months of that pressure, fissures had begun to appear in some and others had ruptured. Two of the guys who graduated DI School with me had exploded. One committed suicide in front of the recruits; the other one shot a recruit on the rifle range. These were the ones that got the attention. Others that went undetected were the wife beaters, child, alcoholic and drug abusers. They were all there; I knew them by name.

Marines are after all still human and make human mistakes. I trained recruits mostly within standard operating procedures outlined in the recruit training (SOP) and kept my nose clean most of the time. I received excellent fitness reports and managed not to kill any recruits. After two years my tour was finally up, I received a west coast assignment. Colonel Paulson was right. There is no greater feeling of pride than turning raw recruits into Marines. Training recruits was my greatest challenge and had given me my greatest reward. I could now open the bottle of "Old Barton" Colonel Paulson gave me and have a drink. I chose not to, having earned the right to have a drink was enough. I would save the bottle as a reminder of Colonel Paulson.

After a successful tour, I was given a choice of duty station, I chose California. I was headed for the 1st Marine Division at Camp Pendleton, California. I had never set foot in California and was looking forward to the transfer. The Transportation Management Office on base made arrangements to have the majority of my gear picked up and transported to my new duty station. I could carry the rest on the plane though taking a flight to California wasn't my best option. I couldn't do any sightseeing that way. I was now a Staff Sergeant and decided I needed a car. My old Beetle was given to

Jason, who had a family and needed transportation for work. It was 1979; I wanted a new Volkswagen Scirocco. Danny, a fellow DI, dropped me off at a local Volkswagen dealer to check out the car I wanted. I bought used cars all my life, and now it was time for a new one. I didn't know the Scirocco I wanted was out of my price range. My entire paycheck wasn't going into a car payment. I walked out of the dealership thinking this was another busted pipe dream. I started walking and wound up in front of a Toyota dealer. I didn't know a thing about Toyota's. There was a red Celica coupe parked on the front row; I was locked onto it. It was a sporty five speed with custom wheels and a sunroof. As I was about to pull myself away, a saleslady came up and said get in. She drove a few blocks got out and told me to drive. It was, as they say, better than expected, much better.

It drove like a precision machine in-tune with my every movement and best of all it was $2,000 less than the Scirocco. Arriving back at the dealership, she asked me how much could I pay down and when did I want it? I said $1,200, and give me a couple of weeks. Two weeks, twelve hundred dollars, counting the five dollars in my pocket I only needed another eleven hundred ninety-five. Sometimes the stars align in your favor. With my next paycheck and a loan from the credit union, I bought that new Toyota.

There was a five-hundred mile break-in period; I reached that mark in two days. My Permanent Change of Station Orders directed thirty days leave; four days proceed and seven days travel. Time for some well-deserved R&R (rest and recuperation). Time to unwind, visit the alley, and for the first time in my life go home in a new car of my own.

I checked swoop circle to see if there were Marines going my way that needed a ride. There was a Corporal Gold hitching to Jackson, TN. Jackson was a couple hours off my route, but what the hell I had plenty of time and it was a good deed for a fellow Marine. I packed my gear, picked up my rider and drove out the main gate of Marine Corps Recruit Depot, Parris Island, South Carolina playing McFadden and Whitehead's "Ain't No Stopping Us Now," which somehow felt appropriate. Other than a combat tour I completed possibly the most challenging tour the Corps had to offer and survived. I had seven years under my belt, re-enlisted for six more turning me into a lifer"[47] and I felt damn good about it.

---

[47] An enlisted Marine or Officer who decides to make the Marine Corps a career.

J. Wesley Gold

6 THE ROCK

Turns out Corporal Gold was a WM (Woman Marine) and quite a looker with a body that showed the benefits of exercise, firm but supple. Not one of those hard ass penis envying want to be a man types. Thanks for the ride Staff Sergeant, I was going to ride with three other Marines until I saw the derelict they were driving. I wasn't confident it would make the trip and opted out. I'll split the cost of gas with you Staff Sergeant. Wait a moment, we've got a long way to go, don't be calling me Staff Sergeant all the way, my name is Bobby Wade just call me Bobby. Okay, my name is Zakiyaa, Zakiyaa Gold. Is Zakiyaa an African name? No, my last name is Gold why didn't you ask me if I were a Jew.

Hey, no need to get touchy, I'm just asking, besides there is nothing wrong with having an African name. I know; I'm sorry; it's a Muslim name and no I'm not a Muslim, my dad is. He gave me the name. I asked what it meant. It means pure. And does that make you pure gold? She laughed; my dad thinks it does. Well dads are usually right. Sometimes they are she added. Hey, I'm cool with that. She smiled, slipped off her shoes and tried to get comfortable. Three hours into our trip Zakiyaa was telling me all about herself. Her dad was former military but preferred she chose another occupation. For her, joining the Marines was a pathway to a college degree. She had completed two years of college and needed money to finish. I was surprised to find out she was only a couple of years younger than I was. Now that I knew her age I could pick up a six-pack the next time I stopped for gas. Not that I needed anything to loosen her up; she was a great girl completely at ease with me. I already decided not to try putting another notch in my gun handle. I was happy sharing her company on an otherwise boring trip. We finished a six-pack and I remembered how many hours had passed since I slept, I was dog tired. Can you drive a stick shift I asked? No, but I'm tired too why don't we get a motel room?

Okay by me, I intended to get separate rooms she was the one who told the desk clerk we only needed one room with two beds. She went into the room. I went across the street to a convenience store and picked up a six-pack, something to help us sleep. I got back to the room; she was coming out of the shower. She came out wearing sweat pants and a tee shirt. Its' all yours she said. I brought your PT Bag in, its' on the bed, thanks I said. Sleep not shower was what I wanted but what the hell; maybe she was telling me I needed one. I got into a hot shower and began to wonder what she looked like standing nude in the shower. I felt "Mr. Willie" starting to come alive and immediately thought about something else.

My sweats felt good, and so did my tee shirt. I wiggled my toes into shower shoes. I came out of the head and saw her sitting on the bed with her knees pulled up arms wrapped around them watching TV. What were you doing in there? What do you mean? You were in there a long time. It was only a few minutes, did you miss me? No, I was just wondering what you were doing. I wasn't in there playing with anything if that's what you mean. Playing with what she wanted to know? Never mind, I opened a package of cups and poured a beer for her and one for me. So what would your wife say if she knew you were drinking beer and sleeping in a motel room with another woman? Now why do women do that? If you want to find out if I'm married ask me, no need to be coy. Coy, is that a word you use often? No, I heard it on a TV soap

122

opera. Are you married? Not at the moment no. Would you tell me if you were? Sure I would I don't have any secrets. I was more direct, are you married? No. Someone like you should have guys waiting in line to put a ring on your finger. Why aren't you? I want to finish college and become a professional before I get married. Now what's your reason? Me, I don't want to be married. She wanted to know if that were true. I stretched out on the bed and stared at the ceiling. Yeah, it's true, at one time it seemed like a good idea but it didn't turn out that way. So one girl screwed you over and now you've damned marriage and don't trust any woman is that it? You make a lot of assumptions from a few words I never said that.

She was sweet and likable the more she talked, the closer I was drawn to her. A few beers later I thought it was a good idea to get some sleep. I pulled back my covers and got into bed. I was sleepy and Zakiyaa wanted to talk. I'll answer any questions you have about me. Okay, are you pure? She came over to my bed stretched out on top of me, looked into my face and said "what do you think?" I guess being pure is a state of mind, you are as long as you think you are.

She felt me growing beneath her and gave me a kiss, a delicious taste of sweetness slowly exploring my mouth with her tongue and finally pressing full sensual lips into mine. She eased off me and walked to her bed. Turned back the covers, slowly slipped off her sweats and pulled off her tee shirt letting me get a good look at her body. I didn't think it could get any better before she unhooked her bra, slowly stepped out of her panties and got into bed. In an instant, I had scanned her from top to bottom. A Nubian beauty with silky black hair, beautiful angelic face, lean, athletic body, small, soft supple breasts, gorgeous firm butt with long sculptured legs. I got out of my bed and started towards her; she stopped me; you should take those clothes off you won't need them in my bed. Sex with Zakiyaa could never be described as a casual encounter. It was a fantastic sexual voyage to be savored and forever chronicled in one's consciousness. We pulled into the front yard of her parent's home; she grabbed her bag, glad to be home. She started to walk away quickly turned around and gave me a kiss, thanks. I know we'll probably never keep in touch but here's my parents address, pressing a slip of paper into my hand. You can always contact me through this address. Stay pure, I will she said, smiling as she went through the front door. Zakiyaa, a beautiful name for a beautiful woman, as I drove home the erotic scent of her body lingered inside my car, she was unbelievable. Mom was right. Doing good deeds has its own rewards.

I got home around three in the afternoon and dropped by Mr. C's for a quick trim and the latest neighborhood info. Mr. "C" greeted me and said "how's your brother?" Which one? The one that got shot! Got shot when? You didn't know your brother got shot at the 300 Club last night? I left the shop, got back into my car and drove home. Mom was watching TV when I went inside; I blurted out who got shot?

You can say hi before you start asking questions. It was Tommy; he's all right. Oh, hi mom I said giving her a hug. How did he get shot? You know they don't tell me anything; you'll have to ask your dad or one of your brothers. They hide things from me I'm sure you know that. Sit down and talk to me, if your brother were hurt very bad he would be home and not out there in the streets. How long are you going to be home? I started to tell her I had about thirty days to kill before going to my next duty station. Before I said anything, I thought about the work to be done around the house and told mom I would be home about fifteen days. I didn't mind helping out around the house though I didn't want to get stuck working around the house every day of my leave. Tommy came running through the door, what's up he said slapping my palm. What's up with you, what's that bandage around your neck for? I've got to ride over to Sweet Peas' come ride with me. I'll be back mom; okay, what do you want for supper? Don't fix anything for me, I'll get something later. Tommy had a nice ride, a tricked out Chevy Nova; we jumped in, I said, what the fuck happened to you.

You know the wench that shot me it was Tina Skelton. What, why did she shoot you, catch you with another coochee? No, that's not it I never tried to talk to that scab. I asked if he were trying to take some. Hell no, not from that skank, I and Leroy were kicking the shit out of her boyfriend at the "300." That bitch went ballistic shot Leroy in the chest and shot me in the neck. What did she hit you with? It was a "25" automatic the bitch knew how to use it. The paramedics took me to the emergency room where I was treated. They took X-Rays, said I was okay and sent me home. Leroy needed surgery; a bullet went through his chest, pierced a lung and lodged near his spine, isn't that some shit. So Tommy, who's her boyfriend? Dumb ass Sand Man, he left town and his old lady is in the slammer, what a man, huh.

So besides you getting your ass shot, what else has been going on? You know same old shit, different day. But it's good to see your ass, how long are you going to be home? About thirty days, but don't tell Mom. Yeah, I know she will have your ass in high gear. Tommy you would not believe what happened to me yesterday on my way home. Hey, I saw your new ride did you find a wallet stuffed with cash to go with it? Better than that, I found the woman I'm going to marry. Marry, what the hell are you talking about, I'm not thinking about any marriage until I'm forty. Sure you're right at forty your ass will be too old to get it up. Not me, I'm going to be just like old Smitty still getting it at sixty-five. That's your dream Tommy. Hey Bobby, guess who's been asking about you? Miss Vanessa, the love of your life, that's the girl you should be marrying if you're going to marry anyone. Where did you run into her? Down the way, you know at Big George's place; she still stops in every now and then. She's teaching school. Miss Vanessa is working her way up the ladder. Tommy it's nothing wrong with being ambitious. Yeah, I know I'm proud of her. So what did she say? Say about what? Say about me? You know, how's he doing, when was the last time you saw him, when is he coming home? I think the girl has a Jones for you.

Yeah, I love Vanessa but I'm not ready to do that settling down thing right now. When I'm ready to be faithful to one woman that woman will be Vanessa, I hope she waits for me. So big brother where are you headed when you leave here? I'm headed for California. No shit, hey, I'll be there, that's a place I've always wanted to visit. You say that shit all the time but never go anywhere. Hey, I know I've said that shit a lot, but this time I mean it. I'll be there, maybe bring a babe with me, or maybe not. Don't forget I came to visit you in Atlanta. Yeah, I know, once in three years.

We rode around for a while, when we got back home dad was sitting in a swing on the front porch. He was cleaning underneath his fingernails with his pen knife. I asked him if he carved anything lately? My dad was a skilled artist with a pen knife. For as long as, I could remember he turned peach seeds into unique carvings using only a penknife, a long needle, a small vise and magnifying glass. Wait a minute he said and walked into the house returning with a cigar box. Take a look at these. I opened the box and inside were exquisitely carved peach seed treasures. Some were carved in a natural state; some painted, some sanded smooth with a clear coating, and each one was different. I wondered why I didn't have some kind of talent. Maybe mine couldn't be God given maybe I

126

had to develop it. Three weeks at home I was restless and ready to leave for California. My goal was to drive to the west coast nonstop stopping only for food, gas and head calls. My cooler was packed with sodas; beer and sandwiches mom made for the trip. It would be a long and boring trip with no rider to help me pass the time. After eighteen hours of constant driving, I started to get muscle spasms in my back. I stopped the car got out and stretched for about fifteen minutes and got back in. Thirty minutes later the spasms were back, I decided to hit a rest stop. Before the next rest stop came up I stopped for gas, bought a six pack of beer and a bucket of chicken.

I would have a quick snack before I crashed. It was a mild October day, good weather for a nap. I pulled into a rest stop, had a snack, locked my doors, rolled my windows up, opened the sun roof and reclined my seat all the way back. I was probably out in less than five minutes.

I woke up to the groans of someone straining, reaching their hand into my sun roof and making off with my bucket of chicken. Quickly popping my seat up I retrieved my pistol from underneath and began to chase the chicken thief through the rest stop. He had a few seconds start on me, but I was gaining fast. I yelled for him to stop; he kept running holding onto the chicken bucket. Holding my gun with one hand and grabbing the collar of his shirt with the other, I slammed him to the ground with enough force to send my bucket of chicken rolling across the parking lot. I stuck my gun in his face; he brought his hands up to cover his face and begged me not to shoot him. A small Hispanic girl maybe six or seven with long braided hair, and sparkling eyes was watching me. Holding her mother's hand, she asked me not to shoot him, even though her mother tried to shut her up. Please, please don't shoot him he's just hungry. I couldn't fight someone who made no attempt to fight back, and never had any intention of shooting him. I told the little girl I wasn't going to shoot him, cleared my gun removed the clip and placed it in my pocket. What was I doing running through a public place with a gun in my hand chasing some dumb ass for a bucket of chicken that wasn't even full? I watched him pick up pieces of chicken off the ground, brush the dirt off, and place them back into the bucket. He ran off into the Arizona desert with my chicken bucket.

I wondered how hungry I would have to be to risk my life for a few pieces of chicken. If he were hungry, all he had to do was ask I would have given him the bucket. Everyone gets down sometimes; no one should ever risk losing their life because their pride prevented them from asking for help. I got back to my car where a small crowd had gathered. A burly trucker wearing a hat that read "keep on trucking" asked me if I caught him. I told him I let the guy go. He said you should have shot the bastard. A chubby little woman standing nearby said no honey you did the right thing; you don't want to kill a man over a few pieces of chicken. She was absolutely right; I could see the headlines "Marine shoots man over bucket of chicken," what would my mom think?

I pushed my gun into a sea bag inside my trunk thinking someone may have called the cops. Now I was wide awake, I got into my car and hit the road. I would sleep at another stop. What a crazy, not only did he take a risk of getting shot, the loopy guy didn't take a beer with him to wash down his chicken. I hit the next rest stop locked my doors, cracked my windows and sunroof and crashed. I woke up well rested and decided it was time to continue my journey.

At the entrance to the interstate, a lovely young thing was holding a sign that read California. Why not I said and pulled over to give her a ride. I needed someone to break up a

monotonous trip. A curvaceous honey wearing white
sneakers, cutoff jeans, halter top and some weird kind of hat.
She had a nice body but what struck me the moment she got
in was her body odor. It literally slapped me in the face this
lovely lass had avoided soap and water for way to long. I
attempted to carry on a conversation asking her what part of
California she was traveling to. No matter how I tried to
ignore the smell it was impossible to overcome.

With windows down and sunroof open nothing could
shake her stench, it was overpowering. Twenty miles down the
road I stopped at a service station. She got out to use the head.
I placed her backpack near the pump and left. Marines coming
off a week in the field weren't that foul. Not only was her
body odor atrocious, her breath was just as offensive, her
stench was still on my seat. I pulled over and sprayed it down
with a can of "right guard" and tried to de-funk my seat, it was
the best I could do. Those truckers who passed her up
probably got the word she was toxic. A CB would be a
necessity for my next road trip.

Hours later I turned off interstate 5 and pulled into Oceanside,
California exhausted and looking for the nearest and cheapest
motel. I found one got a room and crashed. Camp Pendleton was
only a few miles away, but I didn't plan to check in right away. I
opted for a good night's sleep. The next day I went onto the base
found my unit and checked in with the duty NCO to stop my leave,
no need to waste leave days. All my time in the Corps had been
spent as an east coast Marine. This would be my first west coast
assignment. It was a lovely day out; I wanted to recon the area.
Any Southern boy would be impressed with Southern California.
Not because of the ocean and beaches or palm trees and sunshine,
what caught my eye was the mix of people. Since joining the
Marines, I no longer lived in an exclusively black environment. I

lived in a mix, that mix was usually exclusively military; civilians were seldom included. This was a civilian world of blacks, whites, browns, yellows and reds all in one homogenous group.

For some unknown reason, I felt like a part of this mix. Eighteen-hundred miles and I entered a new country. Hill Street was the main drag running through Oceanside only blocks from the beach. There were all kinds of people coming out of clothing stores, barber shops, bars, pool rooms and restaurants. I stopped at a taco stand and ate my first taco filled with shredded beef and not ground beef. I ate a Nacho Chili Burrito; it was the hottest thing I ever tasted. I wondered if California was like North Carolina where I could get sex for a bucket of chicken and a Nehi Grape Soda. After eating that burrito, I would have settled for the soda without the sex. I didn't know if Nehi Sodas were sold in California, hopefully they were, Bennie said it was a valuable sex aide.

I joined Headquarters Company, Headquarters Battalion, 1st Marine Division at Camp Pendleton on 22 Oct 1979. Assigned as a team leader with the division Admin Assistance Unit. After the stress of Parris Island, this seemed like a "chill out" tour. Basically, my job was to go from unit to unit throughout the base conducting courtesy inspections. Or being part of the Commanding General or Inspector General's inspection team. It was eight hours a day, a sweet reward for the long hours put in at the island. There were no single Staff NCO quarters available on base; I crashed out in another Marine's room. He had an extra rack; it worked out for a while until I found out his room was party central. After a week, I decided to look for something of my own. Luckily the guy I replaced on the admin assistance team was giving up his apartment. We went to his landlord, and she gave me a deal. Accept the apartment as is and move in with no deposit, a one bedroom apartment in need of a thorough cleaning, I took it. My household goods arrived shortly thereafter and soon I was enjoying Southern home-cooked meals in California. The guy whose room I tagged party central honestly was party central. We hung out there playing spades, drinking beer and shooting the breeze. Women were always around; they were as wild as the guys and drank as much beer and liquor. Sometimes we went there for lunch and never left. We would call the units scheduled for a courtesy inspection, talk to the Admin Chief and let him or her know what was going on, they always covered for us. After all, we were the same guys performing the actual Commanding General's (CG) and Inspector General's (IG) inspection. We spent the rest of the day playing spades, drinking beer and Black Velvet.

One of the greatest things about Camp Pendleton was the Sierra Madre Staff Non-Commissioned Officers (SNCO) Club. Located a couple of miles from the beach and the main gate. This was the pound where most of the dogs I hung out with gathered on the weekend. The drinks were cheap, and the place was always crowded. Whenever there was a familiar dog spotted, there was a bark given out to let them know you were in the house, a barking ceremony that went on throughout the night. Women joined in. They loved the pound as much as we did. I had most weekends off and looked forward to Friday night at the pound.

My routine was to start off at the bar with a couple of beers and move to my favorite drink, a vodka screwdriver in a bucket. From this vantage point, I could separate the couples from the singles and observe where the strays were gathering. To keep an accurate track of the ladies I broke them down into three categories. There were the Friday night "searchers" looking for a husband or boyfriend. The "deployment wives" horny babes looking for some meat and a few extra dollars until their husbands returned. And there were my favorites the "party girls" those looking for nothing more than a memorable one night stand. One honey I was hitting on kept me off balance, she had the looks and the body though her head seemed to be somewhere else. Sometimes she pulled me towards her and sometimes pushed me away. There was something about her I couldn't put a finger on. She was a black Staff Sergeant who hung around with another Staff Sergeant, a white chick, the cowgirl type. They were always together; I wondered if it was "don't ask don't tell."

Or perhaps we were not on the same frequency either way she was good company when there were no other skirts to pursue. I had been scouting her for weeks and still hadn't figured her out. Although it was no big deal, scoring with some "party girls" had prevented me from reaching "horny goat" status. Maybe I would get the cookies; if not, no problem.

This particular night was on the Marine Corps Birthday weekend; everyone was in a festive mood. I put away a couple of screwdrivers and planned to relax at the bar. Someone tapped me on the back; I turned around; it was the Staff Sergeant I dubbed "cowgirl." She pointed to the stool next to me and asked if anyone were sitting there. It's all yours. I noticed she was dressed differently, wearing a nice skirt with low-heeled-pumps and a pretty form-fitting sweater, a very attractive lady. Can I buy you a drink? Yes, thank you a rum and coke.

She took a sip of her drink and said what's wrong you're not out there womanizing tonight? You've mistaken me for someone else, that's not me. Oh yes it is, I'm Dee Dee's friend remember. I've seen you around, and that's what you do. Have you been watching me? Yes, I have. Why? Because you give all your attention to my roommate and every other girl you meet, but never say more than two words to me. Whenever I'm with Dee Dee you have plenty to say to her, but barely say a word to me. She caught me with my pants down I could only stare at her. Surprised? Yeah, I am, why didn't you say something? I was waiting for you to make the first

132

move. I'll be honest; I didn't think I was your type. You thought because I wore jeans, shit kickers and listened to country music; I was another Hilly Billy. I didn't say that. No, but you wanted too. Come on now give me a chance to speak. Why do think you and Dee Dee never got busy? I tried to think of a reason, don't go there. You two never got together because she knew I had a thing for you.

All I wanted was for you to get to know me. What could I say I was dumbfounded? Taking my hand, she led me to the dance floor. Heat Wave's "Always and forever" was playing, she felt the music. Did you really think we were lesbians? No are you reading my mind where in the world did that come from. Was it the way I dressed? No! Then it must have been because I'm white, you wouldn't overlook me because of that would you? That's not it definitely not I didn't go after you because I didn't think I was your type. I would never discriminate against anyone especially you. She leaned in and kissed me. Sometimes we never find out what our type is unless we give everyone a chance. That's exactly how I feel about it.

We walked back to the bar; her sister was there waiting. She introduced us and told me they were leaving. Before she left she wrote her name and number on the back of a card. Janice, I never knew her name. She kissed me again telling me if I ever got rid of my hang ups to give her a call. She made me feel like I saw black women and no others. Black men had been murdered in the South for allegedly whistling at white women. My dad taught me to stay away from them because in his words "they weren't worth the trouble." That was another time and another place, though I may have consciously or subconsciously pushed myself away from any relationship with women outside my race. I thought about what she said. Was I really that perplexed about race or was I taking the safe route. If the answer to either of those questions was yes, then there were some changes to make.

My assignment as a Division Inspector lasted about a year. I was transferred to a Grunt (Infantry) Battalion. Seventh Marines located at San Mateo one of the outlying camps of Pendleton. The thing about being assigned to a Grunt Battalion is no matter what your MOS. You're a grunt. Twenty mile humps and field maneuvers were all part of it, so were deployments. I arrived at 7th Marines just in time for a six month deployment to Okinawa, Japan, commonly referred to as the rock. I got together with my troops and went over the pre-deployment checklist. We kept an extra set of publications and directives for deployment. Those had to be updated and packed securely in mount out boxes along with six months' worth of office supplies. A pre-deployment stand down was conducted where we checked dog tags, medical tags, ID Cards, Servicemen's Group Life Insurance (SGLI) Forms, and Records of Emergency Data (REDS). In addition Officer Qualification Records (OQR's) and Service Record Books (SRB's) were checked from top to bottom.

On May 16th, 1981, I and the rest of my battalion were aboard a Flying Tigers 747 headed for the rock. We arrived there after a seventeen hour flight from San Diego. Landing on the southern end of the island at Kadena Air Force Base after a short layover in Anchorage, Alaska. Our destination was Camp Hansen (Grunt City) located at the northern end of the island. We got there by way of a deuce and a half convoy style. The Staff NCO barracks I was assigned to was a real dump. Rooms were no more than cubicles only large enough for a rack, wall locker and small desk. There was no room door. The door opening was covered with a blanket, shower curtain or whatever you wanted to use.

This place was called the swamp for good reason. The communal showers and shitters were located at one end of the building. Rooms provided no expectation of privacy with concrete floors, and flimsy divider walls between rooms. There was one bright spot in this shithole, room service. All of the barracks had a local domestic worker, (Mama San) assigned to it. For a nominal fee, your skivvies could be laundered; boots shined, and uniforms pressed. For exceptional service, give Mama San a bottle of liquor or a carton of cigarettes from time to time.

Probably the most inconvenient thing about being overseas is that you can't jump into your car and go home. You're basically stuck on a foreign piece of dirt for six months. This was pre-satellite phone days; a free call home required using a radio system called the Military Auxiliary Radio System (MARS). I think the system was managed by civilian ham radio operators. The line carried a strong echo and whenever you finished talking you yelled "over" which let the individual on the other end speak. It was a crude and cumbersome system, but better than nothing; it kept me in touch with everything happening stateside.

Just outside the main gate of Camp Hansen was the town of Kin Village or Kinville. Okinawa had its share of scenic attractions but for Marines the biggest attractions are always bars and houses of ill repute. Kinville had plenty of both. Staff Sergeant (SSgt) Taliaferro a Comm Guy[48] bunked out in a room directly across from my room in the swamp. He loved those bars and houses and after only a few weeks of being deployed, was well on his way to becoming both a degenerate and a certified alcoholic. He was one of those guys with a shitty attitude. The son of a bitch became downright obnoxious with a few drinks under his belt. Personally I didn't give a shit if he had a chip on his shoulder as long as he kept his chip away from me. I didn't care for his attitude and let him know it. After a round of binge drinking, he stumbled into my room around 2330 and stood inside my door looking like a lost alley cat. I placed my hand on the back of his neck and guided him into his room; this was incident

---

[48] Comm. short for communication

number one. I told him about it the next day; he gave me one of those "no big deal" responses. A few nights later I awoke to find him sitting on the end of my rack. Again I escorted him into his room, the second occurrence and the second warning. I told him I was fed up with his ass wandering into my room at night; he became hostile.

I warned him he was treading in dangerous waters and not to make the mistake of setting foot in my room again. The third time, as they say, was the straw that broke the camel's back. I woke up about 0200 to the sound of what I thought was water running. I sat up in my rack and saw someone standing against my bulkhead[49] pissing into my shit can. I got up and saw that it was none other than Taliaferro.

This was it; all warnings were past, and the gloves were off. Whether he was drunk or sober was not a consideration. I waited patiently until the bastard got through pissing and spun the dip shit away from the bulkhead, hitting him hard in the mouth. I knocked him from my room into his room; the fun didn't stop there. Inside his room, I snatched him up and popped him again tearing down the wall between his room and the guy next to him. I wasn't through; he was going to pay for his disrespectful and belligerent attitude even if it meant having my foot surgically removed from his ass. We tore through several rooms, woke up the entire barracks and finally four or five Marines got me off him. I gave him a beat down and felt no pangs of guilt for doing it. I don't know if he ever sobered up, but I knew in the morning he would have more than a hangover. I saw the company 1st Sergeant the next day. He told me about some personal problems Taliaferro was experiencing. Although he

---

[49] Bulkhead nautical term for wall

acknowledged his personal problems were no excuse for his actions, and he questioned mine. I was no longer a Private and made no excuses. Maybe I could have shown more restraint but I was fed up with his ass and tired of his bullshit. He flat out needed his ass kicked. I left the 1st Sergeants office and went to work, when I got back to the Swamp there was no Staff Sergeant Taliaferro. I never had the pleasure of seeing that ass wipe again.

Getting back to those bars and houses of ill repute, I mentioned earlier. They had a certain amount of relaxation within their walls, though both could become addictive. Marines are always in search of new adventures, after three months of the same bars and ladies they become restless and want something new. Something new meant a trip to the Philippines. A trip to the Philippines meant going south on the island to Kadena Air Force Base. From Kadena, we could catch a hop to Clark Air Force Base, Cubi Point or Subic Bay Naval Base. Clark was my favorite because its neighbor was Angeles City a quick trip outside the base gate.

I usually arrived with four or five other Marines, when we walked through the gate there was a line of taxi's waiting. Not taxi's in the conventional sense but modified taxis. Some were World War II jeeps cut in half, extended and painted with decorative colors. Called Jeepney's they had a variety of lights attached with rooftop mounted horns. Others were small motorized bikes with sidecars. After a few trips, the drivers recognized you on site and scurried for your business. Whenever possible I hired the same driver on every trip preferring to have a private bike driver rather than a Jeepney. My driver would be available during my entire stay always on standby. He would automatically take me to the Clark Hotel where there was a restaurant, bar with ladies in waiting, room service, and best of all water supplied by the base. I started out with a good meal and chased it down with a few bottles of San Miguel Beer. After a quick tryst with one of the ladies in the bar, I was ready to explore the city.

For American military personnel, the Philippines was Fantasy Island without the services of Mr. Rourke or Tatoo. My driver took me to my first stop Joe's Bar. Joe Morgan, the owner, was a retired Air Force guy and you could always count on him having the best in food, women, and entertainment.

In some ways, it was better than jukes back home. A twelve-ounce bottle of San Miguel beer could be bought for the equivalent of 12 cents in pesos. If there were one of the ladies you fancied and wanted to spend some time with, the fee for taking her with you (bar fine) was less than the cost of a bucket of chicken. They were unbelievably beautiful women with long black hair, bronzed skin, and attractive figures. Most of them were bilingual speaking English along with Tagalog. If you were too cheap to spend a few bucks, you could wait until midnight and take them with you without paying a bar fine. A fantastic night on the town with several women could be had for twenty bucks.

Another great liberty spot was Olongapo, a town outside the gates of Subic Bay Naval Air Station and home to the notorious "Shit River." The Shit River was basically an open sewer. Some Marines and Sailors got a kick out of throwing pesos into it and watching the Filipino kids dive in to retrieve them. I saw no need to have someone suffer for my entertainment. I gave them the pesos and got more satisfaction than I ever would from throwing coins into the river. I saw no need to give credence to the term "Ugly American." Seven days of wine, women, and song in the Philippines was all one man could handle. We returned to Okinawa broke and exhausted. Between trips to the Philippines and Korea, my six-month deployment was quickly coming to an end. Soon I would be on that freedom bird heading back to California. It was my last week on the rock, and I was unfortunate enough to be assigned Village Patrol or what we called "Ville Patrol." Ville Patrol teams consisted of a Gunny or Staff Sergeant assigned to walk patrol with a Corporal or Sergeant. Basically, our job was to keep Marines and sailors out of trouble and maintain order and discipline. Normally, I would have paid someone to take my detail but I was running low on bucks after my latest Philippine excursion.

No one wanted to stand Ville Patrol on their last week on the Rock. There were about a million things that could happen to place you on legal hold. A legal hold meant your trip back to the land of the big PX could be delayed indefinitely. Other than the possibility of legal hold Ville Patrol wasn't a bad gig. You were in uniform with an armband, so everyone knew exactly who you were including the ladies of the night. Of course they had to badger you, "hey, Staff Sergeant no Boom Boom for you tonight".

I was teamed up with a Corporal Fischer a real hard charger; probably my biggest concern would be keeping him contained. Tonight was a night to overlook small indiscretions to ensure my seat on the freedom bird. We began our four hour patrol at 2000; it didn't take long before things started to happen. Our first meeting was with a Lance Corporal (LCpl) running down the street being chased by two independent contractors. We stopped him, the women told us he was trying to leave without paying for their services. I asked why he didn't pay the ladies; he told me if he paid them he wouldn't have any money left to buy drinks. You should have thought of that earlier I told him before you acquired their services. What kind of dumb ass are you? Pay them! One of the ladies said, "him bad Marine him not like you Staff Sergeant you know I 'boom boom' long time." I glanced at Cpl Fischer; he quickly wiped the smirk off his face. I didn't want my business being a part of this conversation. I took the Lance Corporal's ID card and escorted him back to the Main Gate. I gave the guard his ID card and told him the young Marine was restricted to the barracks for the night. Our next encounter was with a Butter Bar wearing Platoon Commander (2ndLt) who had the brilliant idea to march his platoon from bar to bar in formation.

I told the Lieutenant he would have to break up his formation and allow the troops to go on their way. He looked at my stripes and started to offer some resistance. Part of my patrol gear was a nightstick and handcuffs. I let him know I was authorized to use both of them in the performance of my duties. His Platoon Sergeant came forward and told me there would not be any problems, the formation was breaking up. He was a smart man who displayed both knowledge and experience; he knew I would risk legal hold to put handcuffs on this belligerent Lieutenant. Around 2300 after a busy night I thought there was a good chance of avoiding a legal hold.

Since the incident with the Lieutenant, we had pulled some rowdy Marines out of a bar. Busted a Marine coming out of a Japanese Pharmacy. Busted a sailor wearing a dress (supposedly as a joke) and escorted several drunken Marines back to base, all in all not a bad night. We turned a corner; there were two Marines sitting in an Okinawan's yard obviously drunk on their ass. Some of the shit Okinawan's drink is laced with narcotics, and Marines knew sharing a drink with them was violating regulations. I called them out of the yard and asked for their Identification Cards. One gave me his card and the other reached towards his back pocket and suddenly broke into a run stumbling as he ran. Before I could even spell legal hold, Fischer was on his trail while I cuffed the other one. It took Fischer a short time to chase him down and when I caught up to him the JP's (Japanese Police) were on the scene. Some other islanders were also there. I didn't understand what they were saying, but I got the gist of it. They were telling the JP's when Fischer caught up to our runaway he slammed him into their car and dented it. The JP's asked for our ID Cards; I thought shit this is it no freedom bird for me. The JP's started to get loud with the guys who claimed Fischer dented their car. If you've never dealt with the JP's trust me when I tell you, they are some tough hombres and did not play. They snatched one of the guys up and started yelling into his face. If they were running a scam, they would pay dearly for it. Those guys started to wave their hands as if to say "screw it" and walked away.

Fischer had probably slammed this dip shit into their car; I'm sure he did it with enough force to make a dent. These guys just didn't want to deal with the JP's. The JP's returned our ID Cards; I had Corporal Fischer cuff our fugitive and let him see me withdraw my night stick. If he decided to run again, the next dents would be on his head. We had no more trouble with him as we took him back to base. We got to the main gate where I released the cooperative Marine to his unit; the other shit head I turned over to the MP's and told them he needed to be piss tested. I looked at my watch it was 0010. Thank God my time on Ville Patrol was over.

The night before we were scheduled to leave Okinawa, me and some of the guys in the swamp stayed up until 2400 drinking a variety of beverages. Since reveille was going at 0200, there was no need to hit the rack we could sleep on the plane. At 0230, each Marine had his sea bag and Val pack staged for our transportation pickup to Kadena. We sat in the staging area getting wet from rain that bothered no one. All our thoughts were on that freedom bird and going back to the real world.

J. Wesley Gold

7 MINISTER BUCKWHEAT

Minutes after that Flying Tiger's 747 took off I was out, dreaming I was back in Atlanta on a burial detail at Daddy King's church. Six Marines were on the casket detail with the shorter guys in front. I was one of those shorter guys and when we picked the casket up it naturally threw more weight on the guys in front. We were moving this hefty Marine from the church to the hearse. As we approached the exit door, a mourner attempted to throw herself onto the casket. Her knee struck the back of my knee and caused me to drop the casket. I woke up.

Strange I should dream about something that happened years earlier. In real life, I was able to maintain my composure and not drop the casket. Thankfully someone grabbed the grief stricken lady, and we were able to get the body inside the hearse. What I thought was a few minutes of flying time were actual hours, we were only minutes from Anchorage, Alaska. We landed in Anchorage with a brief layover, a chance to stroll through the airport and pick up some souvenirs and post cards. We spotted a bar and headed for it on the way passing a glass encased polar bear standing 11- feet tall weighing over 1700 pounds with an angry snarl on its face. I wondered what it was like for a native hunter to face him with only primitive weapons.

We found a watering hole and had a few beers; prices were outrageous $3.50 for a twelve ounce can and it wasn't even an import; I could have bought a case of San Miguel for less. A hamburger was almost ten bucks, now I regretted not having eaten the exquisite food served by the airline staff. One of my fondest memories of Okinawa was not the amorous ladies of the notorious red light districts called Whisper Alley and BC Street. Not the thrill of winning a slot machine jackpot at the club. It was my favorite cuisine, a dish of noodles, eggs, cabbage, carrots, onions and beef or pork called "Yaki Soba." I loved the shit and would leave the barracks at two in the morning to find a vendor that sold it. There were Japanese restaurants in Oceanside when I got back I would find out if any of them served it.

I didn't sleep as much on the second leg of the trip as I did on the first. I caught a movie before I took a nap, waking up when the pilot announced our approach to San Diego. Buses were waiting at the airport to transport us back to Pendleton. Lance Corporal White and Private First Class Jackson - two Marines in my unit - were not on the buses. I had not seen them during the entire deployment. My suspicion was these two were guilty of a crime and unknowing to them I protected them.

Prior to deploying I sat in my car watching two men standing in the parking lot of a local club called the Clown House. They were talking to a female wearing a small piece of a dress, probably a prostitute. It was dark; I used night vision goggles for a closer look. I didn't know I had been watching two dumb shits from my unit giving money to a female impersonator. I started to intervene then decided what the hell let them find out on their own. I needed a drink. Two days later there was a picture of the same female impersonator in the local newspaper. A female impersonator found beaten to death and stuffed into a dumpster. I decided to keep quiet about what I saw, maybe they did it or maybe not, I knew the impersonator probably had other paying customers. Once as a child I witnessed my uncles kicking the shit out of a homo. Because of them I had acquired a certain disdain for homosexuals. Although that disdain, never developed into any desire to kick the shit out of one or kill one. Bad deeds sometimes don't go unpunished; justice has a way of catching up with us. These two were now being detained in Okinawa charged with raping a Japanese woman. Persons indicted by the Japanese were rarely acquitted or found innocent. These two would probably spend years in a Japanese prison eating rice and fish heads.

Twenty four months later I was again returning from Okinawa completing my second pump. I requested and received orders to another unit on base. This time I was going to a wing (aviation) unit located at Pendleton, but headquartered out of Marine Corps Air Station, El Toro, California. A dream come true stationed on Pendleton but not under the base command.

The entire base was broken down into areas; my new unit was in area 22. Area 22 gave me greater access to the commissary, hospital, front gate and Oceanside. Before my last deployment, I gave up my apartment and placed all my goods in storage. I found a one bedroom apartment not far from the beach. It was new, and the price was right. For the same amount, I could rent a three bedroom house in Stamps, Arkansas or Big Rock, Tennessee. But this was California home to some of the most gorgeous women in the world, Disneyland, Sea World and San Diego's Blacks' Beach where nudity abounded. In the short span of three years, I had developed a love for tacos, burritos and enchiladas. Spanish food was like soul food spicy and flavorful but loaded with calories. Calories, however, were no concern, I got plenty of exercise and in my late twenties I only weighed a hundred and sixty-five pounds.

Before I closed the deal on my apartment, I ran into an old friend of mine Brenda White. I was at the Sierra Madre Club my favorite watering hole sitting at the bar. Drinking a vodka screwdriver and talking to the bartender. She said there was someone motioning behind me trying to get my attention. I spun around on the stool;

there was Brenda. Walking over to her table, I could see she had changed very little from the last time I saw her. I gave her a big hug, sat down and started to talk about old times. When she got around to asking me where I was staying I told her I just returned from deployment and was going to lease another apartment.

Brenda was living with her boyfriend in a two bedroom house; they were looking for a roommate. I probably would not have taken her up on the offer if she hadn't told me her boyfriend was seldom there. Brenda was what one would call passionate and fun loving. She loved sharing and shared everything she had, everything. I accepted her offer and moved in; it was a great arrangement. Her boyfriend was often on the road and most of the time we had the place to ourselves. I entertained my guests, and she entertained her guests. When there were no guests, we entertained each other.

I came home one night to find some guy in the living room sleeping on the couch. I went into my bedroom; there was a light tap on my door. Brenda stuck her head in and told me some guy who took her out was sleeping on the couch. She said I don't know if he's dumb or stupid. I told him my boyfriend was home, he asked to sleep on the couch. I thought another dumbass taking an unnecessary risk. Her boyfriend in the bedroom and a suitor on the couch, living a little dangerously aren't we. No, he'll be gone before James wakes up Is James asleep? They both are. Well I'm not. Wait a minute she said and zipped into her bedroom. She came back a few minutes later and got into bed with me. She laughed and said now I'm living dangerously. You sure are. She was a risk taker and a bit of a freak, someone who always added excitement to your life. Every night was something different. Living with Brenda was one adventure after another but there can be too much of a good thing. I decided it was time to move on and got that apartment I wanted earlier. One of the advantages of knowing Brenda was no matter where we met, and no matter who we were with, there was a better than average chance of having a casual fling.

My new unit was a Trainee Management Element, part of Marine Aircraft Group 39 (MAG39). There was a staff of 12 enlisted Marines with only one officer. All other personnel were students going through aviation training to be structure or engine mechanics. There was no duty for permanent Staff NCO's and the shop closed every Friday at 1100. What a difference from spending three years with the grunts with two formations a day and humps every week. Here formations were only for students, and special events, my knees and back could take a break for three years. On Independent Duty as the Administrative Chief, I was the Administrative expert. Here I also assumed both the duties of Personnel Officer and Adjutant. I had "By direction" authority from the Officer-In-Charge and signed the majority of all correspondence.

I wasn't with the grunts anymore; though that did not mean I could take off my pack. Marines are still Marines no matter where they are assigned. Physical exercise is always mandatory, this unit gave me the chance to get in some extra work out time every day. I started lifting weights and after a few months with the aid of two of my partners I was beginning to buff up. We worked out for two hours each day and it showed. I prided myself on staying in shape but wanted to gain some weight. It was good for the intimidation factor and good for my image. Marines should look like Marines even the dip shit actors playing Marines. Hollywood has a problem showcasing Marines. Nothing pisses me off more than seeing a Marine portrayed by some pumped up egotist, with hair halfway down his back and barely able to stuff his fat ass into a Marine uniform. Or the worse imitator of all the android/zombie type who can only follow orders incapable of independent thought.

It's not hard to find the proper image to portray; visit any Marine Base. R. Lee Ermey got the role in "Full Metal Jacket" because no actor could play the part of a Marine Drill Instructor the way a former drill instructor could. Louis Gossett Jr. played a great role in an "Officer and A Gentleman" but the intricacy of being a Marine was not there. Ermey was the real thing; you knew it, and every Marine could see it in his walk and hear it in his voice. You can't get that from an acting class. My buddy Bemo was one of those real Marines and sometimes I hated how real Marines were treated. He was a Vietnam veteran who lost a leg at the age of 19, and was rated one hundred percent disabled by the Veterans Administration.

Yet any time he worked and earned over a set limit, money from his pension would be taken away. A one term Senator made more in retirement than he ever would, and his pension was never docked. When the cameras stop rolling America has a strange way of rewarding its heroes. Heroes used as guinea pigs for pharmaceutical companies and pawns for a government in bed with the industrial arms complex. Americas' military personnel were unknowing guinea pig participants in everything from experimental drug test to nuclear and biological tests. Day by day I was becoming more of a cynic, distrusting of the government I worked for. I was becoming too uptight and decided to take a couple of weeks leave and go home for some much needed rest and relaxation.

I caught a 0700 flight from San Diego which would get me home around 1200 and with the time difference it would be a couple hours earlier. For me getting on a plane was the same as taking a sedative, a few minutes off the ground I was in dreamland. I experienced one of my recurring dreams always centered on things that actually happened. This time it was something that happened before I left home.   It was a scorching summer night. I was lying in bed, rolled out onto the floor and stretched out in front of a fan. Before most of us got air conditioning, summer nights in the South were brutal. The humidity was unbearable; sweat oozed from every pore of my body. Lying under a fan gave me some relief even if it were hot air blowing on me at least it was moving.

I heard voices and sat up to hear what the conversation was about. The voice was coming from my mother's room; it sounded as though she were praying and crying. "God, please don't take him, give him back." She cried, prayed and then there was silence. I wanted to go to her and ask her what was wrong. I looked around; everyone in the room was awake. Whatever happened was over, I laid back on the floor closed my eyes, and went to sleep.   When I awoke the next morning mom, Bennie and Tommy were in the kitchen. So mom how did you know he died asked Tommy.   She said when you love God he tells you things. So what happened? Your dad died last night, I asked God to give him back. He blacked out at the factory when they got him to the hospital he was dead.

Who called you? No one called me. So how did you know? God told me. But how did he tell you? Don't ask so many questions just be happy God gave your father back to us. My mom was a wonderful person but sometimes she felt there were things we did not need to know. My dream was interrupted by a flight attendant asking me to move my seat forward. We were only a few minutes away from landing. I arrived home on a beautiful June day and decided to walk around the neighborhood. Some of my old hangouts were familiar others were beyond recognition.   Things had changed considerably since the sixties. Neighborhood shops and restaurants once neighborhood staples were no longer in business. Small black-owned businesses could not compete with larger white-owned ones now getting the majority of black dollars.   Black mortuaries and barber shops were still there, but so much character of the neighborhood had changed. Houses were vacant with unkempt yards. Young men who stayed in the area no longer looked for jobs or opportunity only a corner to sell drugs. Little did they know, under the new war on drugs policy being implemented, the small amount of drugs they were selling would brand them as felons.

Reagan instituted a mindless war on drugs policy that created career criminals, fatherless children, welfare mothers, and crowded prisons. For a seventeen-year-old black man who seldom had the option of being tried as a juvenile, being branded a felon was a life sentence. Branded a felon meant never getting a decent job, being denied the right to vote and destined to live a life of poverty. Discrimination and segregation had been re-branded and re-packaged from "Jim Crow" to the "War on Drugs." Integration provided what we all needed "opportunity," yet at times it had a negative impact on our village.

To make matters worse, we were contributing to our own demise. Gone were kids on the street hustling to sell newspapers or pushing lawnmowers from home to home, trying to make spending money. No kids manning lemonade or shoe shine stands. Pride, ambition and drive seemed to have packed up and left. Thinking the neighborhood was going to hell in a hand basket I looked across the street and saw Vanessa. She was going into Mr. Ipp's grocery. Mr. Ipp's was the last of the neighborhood grocers. He was practically blind and depended on Mrs. Ipp to run the store. Usually he sat on a stool behind the counter humming and talking to everyone that came in. I started to run across the street towards Vanessa then remembered years had gone by since the last time we met. Not a card or call between us in all those years. Would she give me a hug, a cold shoulder or a hard slap? I didn't know how to approach her. Should I formulate a lie or pretend the years had not passed. I was contemplating taking the cowards' way out and walking away when I heard her voice. I looked across the street and saw her running towards me. She hugged and kissed me as if time had stood still. What are you doing here? I'm getting some much deserved rest and relaxation. How long will you be here? It's a short visit just a couple of weeks. And you weren't coming to see me. Sure I was, I just got here a few hours ago.

Let's go over to Miss Pearl's. Were you getting something from the store? That can wait. She wrapped her arm around mine as we walked. So where have you been and why haven't I heard from you? Did I do something wrong? Vanessa, you look amazing and no you haven't done anything wrong. And because I haven't written you doesn't mean I haven't been thinking about you. You're always in my thoughts. Okay, I'm not going to run you off by asking too many questions. It's so good to see you. Miss Pearls was no longer Miss Pearl's the name was the same though it was being run by Short Barbara. Short Barbara and I went a long way back. When I was a young man, she showed me the pleasures of a woman. I thought maybe she would not remember me, but the hug and kisses on the lips told me she did.

When I was fourteen, I had a paper route and delivered the local newspaper to Miss Pearl. When it was time to collect for my route it was Short Barbara who paid me. She was no taller than five feet, shorter than I was, flirtatious as hell with a brick house body. Before she paid me she always asked if I wanted my money or something else. Didn't know what that something else was, so I always asked for my money. Miss Pearl would tell her to stop messing with me and pay me the money. On one of those collection days, it was cold and snowy. Miss Pearl had given me a piece of hot cornbread with a bowl of beef stew to warm me up. She left for home as I went into the restroom to wash my hands. I had no idea a couple of old heads who hung around the place were about to play a joke on me. When I went into the restroom they spiked my drink with liquor. By the time, I finished eating my stew my head was buzzing, I had no idea why. The old heads were having a good laugh at my expense watching me laughing and slurring my words.

When Short Barbara asked me if I wanted my money or something else, one of the old heads said tell her you're a man you want something else. In my present state of mind it sounded like a good idea, so I told her "I'm a man I want something else." They almost fell out when I said it and were still laughing when Short Barbara took me into the back room and showed me the wonders of life. I'm definitely not an advocate of child abuse, but something called child abuse today was ecstasy for me. If not for Miss Pearl I would have never, ever asked for money again.

We found a booth and Vanessa slid close to me. So what has Miss Vanessa been doing over the years? I can't wait to tell you but before I do, what was that all about? What do you mean? Squeezing you and kissing you on the mouth, an old woman like that. Oh, that didn't mean anything we go a long way back you know that. Yeah, I know, I've heard some stories about what she used to do with young boys. I never heard those stories so I wouldn't know. Are you sure? Come on she's like my - don't say mom. No mom kisses her son like that. I was going to say big sister. She's a friend Vanessa that's all. And am I just a friend? I love you Vanessa. The words startled her as much as they did me. You never told me that. I know; I should have a long time ago. She gazed at me for a moment and kissed me on the lips; her kiss was nothing like Short Barbara's. Let me catch you up, I'm a teacher, I was married, now divorced, no kids, no boyfriend and I live in Queensland subdivision. My mom still lives in the alley; you caught me going to the store for her. No kids I said. I had two miscarriages and then surgery. What about you. No kids, no wife. What happened? I never got remarried. Well my husband was someone who thought I should be taking care of him. You wouldn't understand how some men are these days. I would; I've been walking around the hood. Can you believe it, it's nothing like when we were growing up, and everything has changed. Run down houses, overgrown yards, closed shops and young guys trying to sell dope everywhere.

It's not just here, but you hate to see it happening in your backyard. Vanessa folding her napkin said I see your crazy brothers all the time, what have they been telling you about me? Nothing! Don't give me that, you guys have always been thick as thieves. Well I did hear you got married after that I really didn't want to hear anymore. Why, don't you want me to be happy? Yes, but not with someone else. You are full of surprises today. How are your mom and dad? Still being mom and dad. A waitress brought our order; Short Barbara's burgers with all the fixings were as good as Miss Pearls.

You probably want to spend some time with your family so how about getting together tomorrow? How about getting together later today? You mean you would rather spend time with me than your wild brothers? I must be special. You don't know how special you are. Most of my leave time was spent with Vanessa, when I got back on the plane my thoughts were filled with her. She held a special place in my heart no other woman could ever replace. I loved her, why the hell did it take me so long to accept that fact? Walking back into my Oceanside apartment I knew as much as I loved California, I loved Vanessa more. The bond that held us so close would never be broken. I made up my mind to keep in touch with her; she would be a part of my life every day no more years of separation. It had been an incredible two weeks, tomorrow I would get back to dealing with the same knuckleheads I dealt with every week. After two weeks with Vanessa, dealing with knuckleheads was a breeze. My first day back at work went smoothly and after work I dropped by the bowling alley on base for a burger and beer. The first person I ran into was Sergeant Harris a WM of the Caucasian persuasion. Sergeant Harris was very attractive and a real trip. She did not hesitate to say what was on her mind and could talk shit with the best of them. She didn't pull any punches which is why I liked her. She invited me over to her table and directly across from her at the adjoining table sat three light green Marines who loved to irritate her. Sergeant Harris was dating a dark green Marine they all knew. One of them asked her, is Jackson still feeding you that dark meat?

To Sergeant Harris this was like being on stage and hit with a spotlight. In a loud stage voice, she described one of her sexcapades with her boyfriend. Those guys sat there like the three stooges dumbfounded, she laughed it off. They set out to embarrass her, and she had effectively turned the table with a real gotcha! There they sat with shit all over their faces. She looked at me, did I get those motherfuckers or what? Now I should yell out "attention" and make those dumb fucks stand up. Hell, don't do that I'll have to stand up to. Sergeant Harris, a wonderful girl from Don't Give a Shit, Nebraska. She told me I would never find it on a map, I told her I would never look for it. Sex with her would probably be great, but I knew there would be a battle for the top position.

The years were passing quickly; I was a Gunnery Sergeant, the year was nineteen eighty-four. Today I was scheduled to sit on a Meritorious Promotion Board for Lance Corporal (E-3) to Corporal (E-4). The promotion board consisted of five members - all Staff Noncommissioned Officers, two E-7's two E-8's and an E-9, Sergeant Major as the senior member. All of us were briefed as to the procedures we would follow and the questions we could ask. None of the records of Marines coming before us would be briefed. Our selection would be based on the Marine's appearance, knowledge and confidence. Sergeant Major Redding told us the procedures we would follow and the questions we could ask. Each member of the board would ask candidates three questions either from military subjects or current events. Every Marine came from a different section and naturally each member of the board leaned towards a particular candidate they were familiar with.

There was a Master Sergeant Broady on the board. I bumped heads with him before and had invited him to take off our stripes and settle our differences like Marines; he declined my invitation. His candidate was the first one to come before the board and this dumb ass starts telling us this was a Marines' Marine. He said the reason he looks older than the average Lance Corporal is because he graduated from college before he came into the Corps.

I quickly turned to the Sergeant Major and reminded him individual Service Record Books were not to be briefed and what the fuck is a Marines' Marine? Every candidate we're going to see is a Marine. The Sergeant Major agreed with my assessment. This is when Broady stood up and told me he didn't like my shitty attitude; I promptly told him I didn't give a damn about what he liked. This bastard caused me to do something I ordinarily would not have done. Three of the five members of the board were minorities which meant if we voted for the same candidate our choice was a lock in. On every previous board, I had been a member of, I had prided myself on always voting for the candidate I considered most qualified. However, during a break I was approached by a 1stSgt Fuentes, who suggested we vote as a block and get a minority Marine promoted. Think about all the times we've been screwed over. I couldn't argue with his logic because I knew he spoke the truth. A good argument but it wasn't what convinced me. That job had been done by Broady whom I had nothing but contempt for.

We got our guy in; Broady was infuriated accusing us of forming a coalition. I called him a liar; he stood up and came towards me, as if he were actually going to do something. Other board members kept us apart. We both received a verbal reprimand from the Sergeant Major. I didn't like the bastard and would have been glad to hurt him. Some assholes just rub me the wrong way; he was that asshole. Other than some play on words what the hell was a Marines' Marine? In his case, I thought it could possibly have homosexual overtones. On second thought maybe he did know what he was talking about. Did I make the wrong decision, possibly but I felt justified in making it. Anger caused me to do something I ordinarily would not have done, and I can't say I was proud of it. I had known discrimination; it didn't cause me to seek revenge or payback rather it caused me to strive for justice and fair play.

I always said I was in the business of crisis management, and shortly after arriving at work the next day Corporal Patterson gave me my first crisis of the day. Patterson was my pay clerk and received an advance pay roster from Disbursing[50] about five days before payday. This gave us enough time to handle any discrepancies. Here it was payday, and he was telling me there was one person on the pay roster projected to receive an NPD (no pay due). Why in hell didn't you tell me this earlier? I thought it was worked out with our pay clerk to get him paid. So what happened? When I called Disbursing this morning, Sergeant Green told me they could not pay him. What's this shit head's name? Lance Corporal Whitehead; he's getting an NPD because of an overpayment he received last month, before he got to this unit. Get him in here Patterson, I need to speak to him. Whitehead came in, I told him

---

[50] Provided military pay, travel, and other pay transactions in support of Marines

to take a seat next to my desk. You're getting an NPD any idea why? No, I don't have any idea why I'm not getting paid. I reminded him of the overpayment he received the past month, he told me he thought that was for back pay. Back pay for what? Back pay for something, you know. No, I don't know, and I don't think you do either. Did you save any of the money? No Gunny I didn't. Well let me ask you this can you afford to go NPD this payday. No, I can't. Are you married or single? I'm married. You're married; you took an overpayment you knew you didn't rate, and you spent it, is that it? Well I thought that was back pay for something. Don't give me that bullshit, you knew damn well you didn't rate any fucking back pay. So what do you think your wife is going to say when you don't bring home a paycheck? She won't like it. No, she won't like it, and it was all because of your being a dumbass.

I'm not going to promise you anything, but I'm going to try and get you set up on a six month liquidation and get you a paycheck. I'm not doing it for your dumb ass I'm doing it because I don't want your old lady coming in here dragging some snotty-nosed kid behind her asking me why her dumb ass husband didn't get a paycheck. Understand? Yes, Gunny I got it. I want you to take your ass over to the education NCO (Non-Commissioned Officer) and enroll in an MCI course. It's called "Personal Finance" and when you enroll I want you to bring me back the enrollment card is that understood. Okay, Gunny I'll get it back to you. And next time use a little more common sense.

Whitehead did what ninety-eight percent of overpaid Lance Corporals would do, but I couldn't make it easy for him. He had to be paid; I decided to head to Disbursing and handle it personally. I got to Disbursing and Sergeant Green my pay clerk was out of the office, a Corporal Pacheco asked if he could help me. Yeah, I said I've got a Marine who's NPD, and I need to get him set up on a liquidation and get him paid. He pulled Whitehead's pay folder and brought it to me at the front counter. Gunny he said, there is a note in here from Sergeant Green, and it says this Marine is not to be paid. Where did that come from? That came from me! I looked around and saw Kaye Byrum, a civilian pay clerk who thought she ran things. Why can't he be set up on a liquidation? Yeah, I know he's overpaid but are you going to buy food for his family? No, I'm not he knew he was overpaid and should have been more responsible. And how many Lance Corporals do you know are that responsible Kaye? Look Kaye you're making a mountain out of a molehill. There are Marines who get overpaid all the time and some of them need a liquidation.

Well that's not my problem she hissed. I know it's my problem! You need to take a step back and start thinking about the people you're being paid to support; it's not about you. Gunnery Sergeant the bottom line is he's not getting paid. Well I'm not taking your word for it I need to speak to the person in charge. The Disbursing Officer has already decided not to pay him. Kaye, if you used your time a little wiser and took time to look into that JFPM (Pay Manual) on your desk you would know this. The Disbursing Officer does not make that call. It's the CO's (Commanding Officer) call and my CO wants him paid. I turned to Corporal Pacheco and said get him paid. Kaye flared up; he does not work for you. Listen as long as he's in the Marine Corps and wearing one stripe less than I am, he works for me, and so do you. This last remark hit her button, she stood up from behind her desk her face flushed, and said I do not work for you Gunnery Sergeant. Normally I ease off on civilians, but I was willing to give this bitch some explicit directions to a road that would take her straight to hell.

Warrant Officer Barrett the Disbursing Officer came out and said Gunnery Sergeant I need you to leave. I loved the way everyone dropped the informal Gunny for the formal Gunnery

Sergeant whenever they were pissed at you. Sir, I'm here to get one of my Marines paid. I understand why you're here, but I need you to leave. I told him I would be back and walked out the door. Whether he knew it or not Lance Corporal Whitehead was getting paid. I was headed back to my shop to type up a DD form 114[51] (Military Pay Order) which would override any decision he had made. Twenty minutes later walking back into my office I heard the phone ringing, one of my clerks told me Disbursing was on the line for me. It was the Warrant Officer who earlier asked me to leave. He told me to send Whitehouse over to get paid. He made it clear there was no reason for me to come back. That didn't bother me my job was to get Marines paid. I eased back into my chair and waited for the next crisis.

The rest of my day went smoothly and by 1700 I was on the way home driving down Vandergrift Boulevard listening to my radio. I heard a commercial by someone claiming to be psychic promising phenomenal readings. Some psychic I thought nothing more than another con artist. Just like the one who visited Mount Nebo the last time I attended a sermon. The world is full of insidious people who have developed ingenious schemes to separate you from your hard earned dollar.

As I drove home, I remembered the con man that showed up at Mount Nebo. The buzz around Mount Nebo and the community of East End was all about a visiting preacher coming to spread the gospel. William "Buckwheat" Thomas of the "Little Rascals" fame left the cinema after becoming an adult and became a man of God. The congregation was usually excited when a well-known minister came to town, but no one of Buckwheat's stature had ever graced the pulpit of Mount Nebo. Also coming was the legendary Ida B. Good a traveling evangelist from Faith Temple Church of God in

---

[51] A military pay order directing action for the Disbursing Officer

Baltimore, Maryland. Ida was a fiery speaker whom some would call a heavyweight for Christ. I wouldn't describe her as overweight, just a little corpulent. She was light-complexioned with long salt and pepper hair and a high pitched voice.

The day of Buckwheat's arrival as expected drew a very large audience and the church was packed. Ushers stood by to pass out hand fans and escort little kids to the rest rooms. Ladies were busy in the kitchen; aromatic smells permeated the air. There were attractive women in new dresses with flamingo colored hats and ribbon covered shoes. Men impeccably dressed with double breasted suits, silk ties and wingtip shoes. Children decked out in their Sunday finest. This would be a day of celebrating God's word, and the people were ready. Reverend Winters stood, walked to the microphone and said "let the church say amen." Wearing his customary red suspenders Reverend Winters introduced the guest speaker as a man who traveled from Hollywood to God, the congregation was electrified. Next he introduced Ida and everyone shouted "Amen" giving reverence to a powerful messenger of God.

Reverend Winters said God is in the house today; he's here to give you his word. He quoted Jeremiah 1:9: Then the Lord put forth his hand and touched my mouth, and the Lord said to me: "Behold, I have put my words in your mouth." And today people God is going to put his words into your mouth. Ida spoke first; there could not have been a better opening act. She had perfected her craft and was indeed a powerful advocate for Christ. Musicians were playing; choir members were singing; church members were dancing in the aisles and speaking in tongues. Minister Thomas was up next; the crowd was filled with anticipation. He began speaking and quickly the feverish tempo set by sister Ida began to subside. Not only was he less than a dynamic preacher he seemed nervous and sweaty, a man lost in the pulpit. For the remainder of his sermon, he never got better, the tempo never increased. By altar call, the fire was diminished and in danger of being extinguished. A young man of about nineteen stepped out from his pew and moved towards the altar. He told Minister Thomas and Sister Ida he was a man possessed with evil thoughts. Sister Ida asked him his name, he told her Isaac. Do you trust God Isaac? Yes ma'am I do. Then give me and Minister Thomas your hands. They held his hands, and Sister Ida began to pray; the young man bowed his head.

Without warning his head popped up. His eyes rolled back into his head; he started flailing and jerking violently as if suffering from a seizure. Hold his hand she told Minister Thomas, who seemed on the verge of letting go. Along with the jerking motions, Isaac started to froth at the mouth as if he were rabid; Sister Ida held fast and continued to pray. As fast as the seizure like movements began they stopped, Isaac was calm. Sister Ida gave him a napkin, told him to wipe his mouth and breathe into it. He did as she asked and placed the napkin in an offering tray. She struck a match touched the napkin and watched it burn turning into wriggling black worms that morphed into a vapor. The congregation watched in awe as an evil mist drifted out of the church. Sister Ida said God has healed you today Isaac go and be a witness for Christ. He walked towards his seat with a look of deliverance. The congregation began rejoicing the fire was relit, the flames burned.

It puzzled me why Minister Thomas was lost and afraid; surely a man of God would have more faith. I didn't find out until years later William "Buckwheat" Thomas was never a minister. It was all a hoax I believe perpetrated by a man named Billie English who made a career as a Buckwheat impersonator.[52] Sister Ida never exposed him. I'm sure she sensed he was a fraud. She probably thought the

---

[52] People Magazine, A buckwheat wannabe lands 20/20 on the griddle, Retrieved

experience of seeing the evils of Satan and the power of God was enough to convert him or at least stop him from pretending to be a man of the cloth. Whoever the imposter was he left Mount Nebo frightened and humbled by his experience. For Sister Ida a true believer and woman of faith, it was all in a day's work.

Southern California presented you with a variety of weekend opportunities from visiting Disneyland, exploring desert sand dunes to lounging around on the beach. Occasionally when no one was around I liked to cook a good meal, sit on my balcony, relax to the sound of a jazz record, and listen to the ocean waters. One of my regular visitors was Valerie Carnell, a beautiful girl originally from Baton Rouge, Louisiana with a short afro, beautiful brown skin and a butterfly tattoo. When she came over if I had no other guests, she spent the night.

As far as I knew she was a call girl by profession which is why I was never intimate with her. My friends had sampled her wares and gave her high praise, but this was the eighties. Now things acquired from working girls couldn't be cured with a shot of penicillin. Working girl or not she was good company, I was always glad to see her. I never asked why she chose that profession; she could have told me if she wanted, she never did. Besides I wasn't a priest or a psychiatrist. Whenever she came over we usually had a few drinks. Listened to records and wound up intoxicated, with me sleeping on my couch and her sleeping in my bed. It was an established order, we both accepted it as the norm which was hard for me because she was such a beautiful girl. Southerners can only go the fast food route for a limited amount of time. Their bodies start to crave that Southern home cooking. I was cooking a beef roast, mashed potatoes and oven-baked mac and cheese. For dessert, I made a banana pudding using my mom's recipe. I had finished my pudding placing it in the fridge to chill when I heard a rap on the door. It was

Valerie who came in and kissed me on the cheek. I didn't go for the kiss on the lips, not paranoid just cautious. She was holding three new albums; I knew she brought them over for us to rate. It was what we did, listen to new albums and rated them from 1 to 10. Sometimes we ran across a real dud and gave it a zero. She smelled the aroma of food and checked my pots to see what was cooking. Oh, great she said in her Cajun accent when do we eat? Soon I said my rolls are almost done.

We ate, washed dishes and settled down with a drink to rate our records. We listened to the first one it wasn't very good. Valerie gave it a 3; I gave it a 2. The second one was much better so good, in fact; I asked Valerie for a dance. It was smooth and soft; Valerie felt good her body pressed next to me. I visualized what sex would be like with her. It was the first time I was willing to forego my fears and have sex; I knew she was willing she had suggested it before. I fell weak for a moment then thought about the risk, more importantly I thought about Vanessa. We settled for a quiet evening on the couch listening to music and getting tipsy. We went to bed alone in our usual places. There was an open door policy for her that we both enjoyed. We both enjoyed it until I walked into the bathroom the next morning and saw her sitting on the toilet with a needle in her arm. She came out and began to apologize. I said just get your shit and leave; you're too pretty and too smart to be doing something that stupid. She started to say something else; I stopped her. Just get your shit and leave don't bother coming back, there is no room in my life for junkies. I may have been insensitive and intolerant, but I intentionally avoided trouble whenever possible, someone shooting up in your house was trouble. I felt sorry for her but knew any intervention on my part would have been fruitless. She accepted her fate and so did I. I could not help anyone not even the ones I loved unless they first wanted to help themselves. I hated the choice she made, but it was her decision.

In August of 1985 Headquarters transferred me back to the South assigned to a Marine Corps Recruiting Station, as the Administrative Chief. Transferred to a unit where the CO and XO (Executive Officer) were drunks, the S-3 (Operations Officer) a wannabe country western singer and the Sergeant Major a racist redneck. How much better could it get? The only cohesion in the place came from a Master Gunnery Sergeant, who served as the Operations Chief. My second day on the job Sergeant Major Nathan Bedford Forrest informed me he ran everything. I told him he didn't run Admin, and if that's what he wanted he should get my orders modified and send me somewhere else. He said he was only joking, but I knew the bastard was serious.

We bumped heads from the jump and things did not change for three years. Because of him I came within three hairs of a court martial. I had a light green Woman Marine (WM) who worked for me and every time I gave her an assignment she didn't approve of she ran to the Sergeant Major. Eventually the shit had to hit the fan; we were in his office having a heated discussion. I could show patience with drunks and shit kickers but had no room for bigots and racists. I called him a fucking racist and challenged him to meet me Marine to Marine and not hide behind his stripes; the dumb ass accepted my challenge. I told him if he said one more word I would break his scraggly neck and he knew I would follow through on my promise. If I were going to lose my stripes, they were going for a good cause. The XO's office was next door, even though he was an alcoholic he wasn't deaf. He came in separated us and sent me home with five dollars to purchase a six pack and cool down. Needless to say, this was my longest three years in the Corps and each day was a definite challenge to maintain sanity and keep my stripes. I was working in a real shit hole, but there were times when I loved my job.

There was an occasion when I came back from lunch, and Sergeant Dover told me an older guy came by looking for me. He dropped off a package on my desk. I opened the package and found a 1925 Liberty Head Silver Dollar in pristine condition. There was a note that told me the coin was given to him by one of the first officers he put through Officer Candidate School in exchange for a first salute." He had gotten his medals and wanted to give me something to show his appreciation.

He came into my office months earlier with a faded copy of a DD Form 214[53] and asked if I could help him get his medals replaced. Using his DD Form 214, and the Awards Manual (Secretary of Navy Instruction 1650.1) along with his help I was able to ascertain which medals and ribbons he rated. I submitted the paperwork requesting replacement of his medals and forgot about it. I remembered him as an older gentleman of about sixty-five. He had tried several times to have his medals replaced with no success; some recruiter in the field gave him my name. He was pretty spry for his age; I remembered some of the war stories he told me, a great guy who I was glad to help. Since I had been a Drill Instructor at Parris Island training recruits and not at Quantico training future officers, I didn't know about the Silver Dollar coin or the officer's first salute. It was a custom authorized by Congress on April 2, 1792,[54] the silver dollar tradition is the only coin a newly minted officer gives in exchange for the first salute. It signifies a deep sense of gratitude for the knowledge and training enlisted personnel

[53] DD Form 214 Certificate of Release or Discharge from Active Duty
[57] Something About Everything Military, Retrieved December 24, 2010, http://www.jcs-group.com/military/rank/salute.html

[54] Something About Everything Military, Retrieved December 24, 2010, http://jcs-group.com/military/rank/salute.html

provided in achieving his commission. I didn't expect a reward for getting his medals replaced. As a former Drill Instructor, the coin meant much more than monetary value. A fellow Marine made me a part of his Marine Corps experience; you can't put a price tag on that. I finished my tour and received orders directing me back to independent duty this time in California. I was working with and training reserves again, a job I truly enjoyed. It was here during the first Gulf War my unit was activated and sent to Iraq. However only the Reserves from the Command were deployed. Inspector-Instructor (I-I) Staff personnel were placed on standby and directed to remain in place.

The Reserve CO requested I deploy with the unit and my Inspector-Instructor told me I would deploy when he did. Personally I would rather have gone to Iraq than stay behind having to deal with the spouses who wanted everything, and they wanted it now. Dodging bullets would have been easier; fortunately it was a short operation and short deployment. This was my second tour of I-I duty; I have to admit I did not enjoy it as much as my first tour. I was getting close to retirement and developing an itch. I did three years there and was soon headed to Little Creek, Virginia for my next duty assignment. I was assigned as the G-1 Chief for a Marine Expeditionary Brigade. The Brigade was scheduled for deployment and shortly after I arrived I was on the ship headed for Norway. We floated on the water for about thirty days while the navy conducted their part of the operations. For a Marine that's not a part of the ship's detachment, life aboard ship can be pretty boring. For younger troops, there was cleaning weapons, PT and brushing up on your essential subjects such as first aid and Marine Corps History.

By this time in my career, I had enough stripes to do just about what I wanted with more than enough free time. When our ship got to the coast of Iceland I went topside to take a look; it was beautiful.

Beautiful but extremely cold I went back to the warmth of the lower decks and took the ladder wells down to the ship's library. After browsing through shelves of books, I selected a musty old book with yellowed pages. The title was "The Occult and Occult Practices." I took a seat at an empty table and flipped it opened. Turning the first three pages sent a chill through my body. I continued to read and felt one of the strangest sensations I've ever experienced, forcing me to put the book back on the shelf. Two days later I picked up the same book to see what if any reaction I would get. I got the same peculiar feeling, a second warning; there would not be a third.

Picking up the book, I went directly to the office of the ships' Chaplin. Chaplin Sanderson was in his office and offered me a seat. What can I do for you "Top?" It's this book; there is something wicked about it; I think it should be pulled from the ship's library. He took the book looked at the title, never opened it and said, "I think you're right." I'll make sure it's pulled and disposed of, what else can I do for you. That's it sir. I left wondering why he never questioned me about the book, why I wanted it pulled. Was he going to have the book pulled or was he feeding me a line? This guy was a Chaplain, and I didn't trust him.

Years' earlier mom warned me about the occult and occult practices, satanic practices that opened the door to demonic possession. I had forgotten her warning as I remembered her quoting scriptures from Ephesians, Deuteronomy, Acts and others. I felt God was protecting me through her prayers. More than once she had reminded me there is nothing like a praying mother…..she was right.

After sixty days aboard ship, I was starting to get cabin fever, couldn't wait to get off. Or at least I thought I couldn't wait. We were on an amphibious assault ship (LHA). We began our landing operation coming out the back of the ship riding in an amphibious landing craft, cold air coming across the water penetrated all the way to the bone. I was wearing Gor-Tex extreme cold weather clothing; it felt as though I was wearing pajamas. I could honestly say I had never been that cold in my life. We hit land and set up a base camp and started our exercise. There were "GP" tents set up for each "G" section and temporary heads (buckets with a seat) set up some distance from the main area. The mess tent was operational with plenty of hot wets[55] which probably saved my life. I say saved my life because cold weather MRE's[56] suck. The damn things never completely thaw out until they've been in your stomach for hours.

After being in base camp for a couple of days, the word came down we were going on bivouacs. We broke out the Ahkio[57] sleds and packed in ten-man tents, stoves, fuel, and the other needed equipment. Pulling a sled while wearing full cold weather gear and snow shoes gets your temperature up in a hurry. The Gor-Tex gear we were wearing had zippered slots for cooling and when all Marines on the sled vented it looked like a steam engine running down the tracks. It was an experience I wouldn't soon forget. All under the guise of enhancing our overall combat capability and increasing our snow mobility procedures. By this time, I was approaching forty-years old, when we got to the campsite my ass was worn out. My snow mobility procedures did not need enhancing. We unloaded the tent set up our stove and got a fire going. It was around 0100; I was exhausted. Those MRE's waited until I got warm and comfortable before the damn things demanded out. I couldn't keep them in. Left

---

[55] Hot soups, broths and drinks

[56] Meals ready to eat

[57] Ahkio sleds used to carry equipment can carry a load of up to 200 pounds

with no options, I crawled out of my sleeping bag stepped on two or three people and walked outside the tent. I headed for a wooded area to take care of business. I forgot in the snow your depth perception is nonexistent. I walked out about fifty yards and fell off a steep drop. I hit the ground and never knew snow could be so hard. I got up and with the help of a stick got to my destination. On the way back, I ran into two Captains. Why they were outside I don't know but had my suspicions. One of them said, "Top can you bunny hop down this path back to the tent?" Whether he was bullshitting or not I was in a no bullshitting mood. I looked at him and said are you drunk? You must be to ask me something that stupid. I don't think they wanted me to confirm my suspicions, so the other one said "aw top we're just fucking with you it's just a joke." I turned around and headed back to my tent my ass was freezing, I was in no mood for bunny hopping.

After Norway, I spent the next two years on deployments to England, Germany and Turkey. I tried to remember the number of deployments I had participated in over the years and couldn't recall all of them. I didn't know how many I had participated in but knew I would not participate in any more. I got up one rainy morning in May went into my head and looked into the mirror. I made an on the spot decision to seek employment outside the Corps. My request for retirement was completed and submitted to Headquarters Marine Corps the same day. On 14 Aug 1993 after twenty-three years in the Corps, I stood in my office looking out the window at my unit starting to move into formation. After years of watching others retire from the Corps today, it was my turn. My two-year stint had turned into a long career, and today was my last day in the Corps. I knew the Marine Corps would always be a part of me, and I would always be a part of it. I needed a second career and knew the sooner I started it, the better. I entered the Corps with no intention of becoming a lifer or making it a career. Over the years, I learned to respect the honor and integrity of the Corps.

Besides my parents, Marines in the Corps were my greatest teachers. It gave me an experience few people will ever know. Walking away from an elite organization and leaving my family of Marines would not be easy. I thought about the guys I went through Boot Camp with, my Drill Instructors, about good Marines killed on active duty. About inspections, rifle range details, deployments, PT formations, PCS moves, beach parties and change of command ceremonies. About the jeep, the deuce and a half, the mule and the dragon wagon. About fox holes, leaking tents, sore knees, aching backs and swollen feet. About Mess Halls, C-Rats and MRE's, about Marines I trained and others who trained me. About Color Guard Details, Honor Guard Details and Burial Details.

About all the Marines who had earned my respect and others who never would. Young Marines who were lost and scared and old salts who knew the ropes. About people, I met in foreign countries and above all the camaraderie I enjoyed over the years being a Marine. Something else played into my decision to leave the Corps, I was getting married. I wanted a wife knowing it was too late in my life for kids, besides there were plenty of nieces and nephews to help nurture. Since I left California, I had constant contact with Vanessa. I had committed myself to her and talked to her often. Whenever I went home I always stayed with her, whenever she came to Virginia, she stayed with me. We were already husband and wife. We only needed the ceremony. She had waited long enough, if she would have me I was going to make her my wife. Master Gunnery Sergeant Chalmers had given me a set of Master Gun Chevrons over twenty years earlier, when I was a young Corporal. Given to me upon his retirement I had kept them over the years. I held in my hand my chevrons to pass on to another young Marine deemed worthy. Earlier that morning I gave myself an inspection to ensure my haircut was fresh, and my shave close. I was wearing a white tee shirt, dress blue trousers and spit-shined shoes. My web belt was clean the metal buckle and tip highly polished. My blouse was on a clothes hanger, my cover and gloves on my desk. Lance Corporal Hughes stuck his head in my door and asked if I were ready. All the years of dedication and sacrifice were over for me. It all came down to this day; today was the end of my watch. I put on my blouse with its Master Gunnery Sergeant chevrons, rows of colorful ribbons, pistol and rifle expert marksmanship badges and five four year hash marks.

I pulled on my gloves and adjusted my cover then looked into the mirror to ensure everything was squared away. The image in the mirror was no longer a young and ambitious Marine. Now the reflection showed a seasoned veteran who served his country for many years. One who was ready for the next chapter in his life. I stepped out of the building and headed for the formation and the ceremony that would end my career. I received my retirement orders and end of service award. Later I was taken to lunch and presented a plaque.

An afternoon of bowling was next up on the agenda, and the day ended with a hail and farewell at the club. The club was where I got my biggest surprise. Waiting in ambush was Bennie, Thin Man, Jason, Chris, Bumpy, Tommy, Ronnie Mack, and several Marines I served with over the years. I was toasted, got toasted and chauffeured home. This type of camaraderie is hard to fine these guys and gals would be missed.

8 MOM KNEW

After spending years in the military, it's not easy to wake up and have no job to go to, no uniform to wear. That chapter in my life ended; I needed to turn the page. Not one for looking back I prepared for my journey home, having my household goods packed and shipped for the last time. I spent a couple of days doing nothing saying my goodbyes and sleeping late for a change. Bennie retired a few months earlier, now it was time to move on with my life go home and find a job. I hit the road and remembered a tape someone gave me at my hail and farewell, labeled when you get lonely some oldie but goodies. I popped it into my player. I got home on terminal leave drawing active duty pay. It would be a couple of months before my leave ran out, and I would start drawing a smaller retirement check. Jason found me an apartment to rent until I found a house to buy. I filled out job applications at various places including the Post Office, and VA sending them copies of my disability rating.

Bennie was working at a nearby Army Base and told me I could always get a job there. If I didn't find a job, I could work with Chris and Tommy until I found employment. So there was no rush to get back into the daily grind. My parents had enough work to keep me busy for a while; it was good to be home. I decided to relax and take some time off before I looked for a job. For me, vacations had been few and far between. After being in my apartment for two weeks, I had settled in and got organized enough to invite Vanessa over for dinner. I wanted her to relax, she wanted to help me cook dinner. We had been a divided couple for years. Now it all seemed natural for us to be having dinner together. We talked about things that happened in our lives as though we had always been together. I asked her why she wasn't married and without hesitation she told me she was waiting for me to ask her. I kissed her and changed the subject. I was going to propose but not then. I put on Freddie Jackson's "All I'll Ever Ask" and asked her for a dance, she held me so tightly I thought she would never let go. Listening to that song almost made me propose then and there, but I held off. I wanted my proposal to be something unique. The next day I got up, put on a nice pair of slacks, and sweater went out bought a dozen roses and a ring. I went to Vanessa's classroom with John Hall the school's principal, (my high school classmate) a dozen other teachers and school staff following me.

John stuck his head in her classroom door and said Mrs. Young there is someone here to see you. Before she could move I walked up to her desk gave her a hug and handed her the roses. I got on my knees and asked Miss Vanessa Young if she would become Mrs. Bobby Wade? She said yes after all the students in her class said yes. I placed an engagement ring on her finger, kissed her and walked out with the little girls jumping up and down, the boys whooping and Vanessa crying. I'm no romantic and definitely not a drama queen, but I loved it. This was something to be remembered.

Bennie knew Marines at the local Reserve Center and insisted on giving us a military wedding, complete with flags and an arch of swords. Technically I was still in the Marine Corps, a wedding gave Bennie the opportunity to put on the uniform he loved so much. He loved wearing those Sergeant Major stripes. Bennie planned a wedding that Vanessa called "fairy tale perfect." When it was time to cut the cake, I presented Vanessa my sword placing it over my left forehand with the cutting edge away from my body and the hilt towards her.[58] She took the sword and cut the cake with my right hand resting over hers and my left hand around her waist. She turned towards me, kissed me, and told me this was the day she dreamed of. The day could not have been scripted better thanks to Vanessa, my family and friends. Bennie supervised every aspect of the wedding, from rehearsals and uniforms to decorations, no minute detail was overlooked. As Vanessa and I passed through an arch of swords, I was surprised at what a meticulous job he did. He hired the DJ and selected the first song for Mr. and Mrs. Bobby Wade.

I didn't know what it was, but when he called us out for our first dance and Teddy Pendergrass started to sing "You're my Latest Greatest Inspiration" I knew he picked a winner. Several Marines we knew came for the wedding; some wore Dress Whites and others wore Dress Blues. The sight of beautiful women in sparkling dresses accompanied by uniformed Marines gave us a Kodak moment. A beautiful and colorful wedding filled with pomp, pageantry and military precision, what more could I have asked for?

Dad waited until we opened all our presents before he gave Vanessa a tiny box. This is just for you; it's one of my most prized possessions he told her. She opened it; there was a lovely little swan carved out of a peach seed painted white with black trim. It was dad's favorite gift; he only gave them to family members on special occasions. Vanessa loved it, she told me it made her feel like someone special. I couldn't take my eyes off Vanessa she was such a beautiful woman. She held my hand and made me promise I would never leave her. Why do you think I would ever leave you? I don't think you would. I just want you to promise me you won't that you'll never stop loving me and that you will always belong to me. I

[58] MCO P5060.20 Marine Corps Drill and Ceremonies Manual

promise I will never leave you and that I will always belong to you. As for loving you, I've loved you for such a long time I could never stop. She gave me a kiss. Teddy Pendergrass was right it's so good loving somebody when somebody loves you back. Vanessa owned a heart-shaped jewelry box. She placed the eagle and the swan, our two peach seeds, in the box and told me she was going to keep them forever. After years of being separated my wife was with me, I finally had a love of my own. Someone whom I wasn't afraid to make plans with and making plans for us was a lot easier than planning for war.

I got a job as a VA counselor and built a new home. I was glad to come home to Vanessa each day and be able to visit my family members whenever I wanted. I reconnected with all my brothers and sometimes we met after work or on weekends for a cold brew. All of them were now grown men with wives, girlfriends and kids of their own. Things changed while I was gone. Things had changed, though; it didn't take me very long to get back to enjoying being a civilian again.

I was out of the Corps a year when my mailman delivered a certified letter from Headquarters Marine Corps (HQMC). I opened the letter and discovered I was being recalled to Temporary Active Duty (TAD). Ordered to report to the Commanding General of Marine Corps Base, Camp Lejeune, North Carolina. I retired with a permanent disability; surely they knew I was not physically qualified for recall. They had to know it, they were the official puzzle palace. Headquarters Marine Corps they knew everything or at least thought they did. Placed on active duty this date, report to CG, MCB, Camp Lejeune, North Carolina no uniform required. Point of contact is Lieutenant Colonel Peterson. What in the world could this be about? I called Bennie and said you will never guess what happened. He said you got orders from HQMC ordering you to TAD. How the hell do you know that? Because I got the same orders, I was about to call you. What's happening Bennie is this for something that happened years ago? Nope, I can't think of anything important enough to recall us. I told Bennie about my call to Lieutenant Colonel (LtCol) Peterson, who told me the matter was confidential and could not be discussed over the phone. Did we kill someone and not know it? Some rat probably got into some shit and decided to drop our names in the hat. Bennie said they better have a damn good reason if they plan on taking any of my stripes.

What happens if we don't show I asked? Bennie said they'll probably send some storm troopers to drag our ass back we might as well start planning for the trip. Who knows maybe they want to decorate us for something, everyone loves heroes. Yeah, right I said. Did you ever work with Oliver North?[59]

We wore suits for the occasion thinking we might run into some jarheads we knew, wanting to show them how well we were doing. We also wanted to let the light bird designated our point of contact know we were not intimidated by his ass. Lieutenant Colonel Peterson introduced himself to us and addressed us with sir and no sir. I liked this guy. Gentlemen I don't know where to begin. Sir I said, surprising myself addressing him as sir, old habits are hard to break, let's just start at the beginning. He said okay, "Top" breaking out a manila folder. Take a look at these pictures gentlemen. Bennie asked is this someone we know. It is someone you know; it's your brother. I know this comes as a shock; regulations require the primary next of kin be notified, and that's why you were contacted. I was relieved to find out he had brothers who were retired Marines. I made the decision to contact you rather than your parents.

---

[59] Marine LtCol involved in Iran Contra scandal

Bennie said, "Our brother is dead!" No sir said Peterson; that's your brother and he's not dead. Not dead said Bennie, what do you mean not dead. We buried him over twenty years ago. You buried someone, but not your brother. How can anyone killed in action return from the grave? Where has he been? Peterson squinted and said we're going to cover that later. Where is he asked Bennie? He's in the hospital. When can we see him? You can see him tomorrow. In the meantime, we've got you a room at the Hostess House. Gunny Reyes will get you over to Disbursing to take care of your advance per diem. Gunny Reyes has been assigned as your official escort if there is anything you need let him know and he'll take care of it. I've got to meet some other people, but I'll stay in touch with you two, with that he left.

What's the story, I said could EJ be alive after all these years? You know mom said it wasn't him, remember that? Yeah, but can you believe it? What happened to him and where has he been all these years? The war has been over for years and why did everyone think he was dead? We had a lot of questions; questions only EJ could answer, if it really were EJ. We unpacked our clothes and decided to check out the SNCO Club at Camp Johnson. Things hadn't changed; the beer was still cold; there was one noticeable difference, the Marines looked younger. The military was always a young man's game; I was glad we retired. We had a few beers and listened to some war stories. It always felt good to connect with Marines no matter where you find them.

The next day Gunny Reyes picked us up and took us to the hospital where we met LtCol Peterson. How long has my brother been here Bennie asked? He's been here about a month. A month! A month and you're just now contacting us. Yes, sir, there were some things we had to clarify. So what's his status I asked? It hasn't been determined yet? What do you mean? Well technically your brother is classified as Killed in Action (KIA). Yeah, I know, but he's not dead so what now? How can someone listed as KIA come back from the dead? That's something that will take some time to figure out. Right now he's returned to military control, and we just want to get him healthy. Remember you haven't seen him in a long time, he's not going to look like anyone you remember.

I asked him how he knew this was Edward Wade. We've identified him through his medical records and by his name. You identified him by his name, was he still wearing dog tags? No, his name was cut into his arm. How did he get here? Did you find him or did he find you? I know you have a million questions; I can't answer them now said Peterson. Doctor Cooper is coming in to explain some things to you. Doctor Cooper reminded me of the fictitious Doctor Welby on TV with white hair and personable nature. He shook our hands and introduced himself. I'll start out by telling you something about your brother's condition. From what I gather he's been subjected to extraordinary emotional and psychological trauma. This was created by stressful events that shattered his sense of security, making him feel helpless.

Edward has frightening memories and experiences a sense of constant danger. He's disconnected and distrust other people. When someone experiences the trauma he's been through it takes them an inordinate amount of time to get over the pain and feel safe. Unfortunately for some they never recover. I will tell you with treatment and support from his friends and family one day he may be able to overcome his emotional and psychological trauma. He's suffering from severe memory loss and it overwhelms him. There may be something that triggers his memory and brings him back though that's half of his problems. He has enormous physical difficulties. I'll take you in to see him, he may not know you; you probably won't recognize him. Doctor Cooper was right when I saw EJ he looked nothing like the brother I had known. He was a

stranger in every sense of the word, shorter, stooped and wrinkled with graying hair and rotting teeth. His hands, arms and legs, were deformed as if suffering from a severe case of arthritis. His face was gaunt with hollowed eyes and a look of desperation. I wanted to hug him but was afraid it would be too painful. I reached for his hand; he withdrew, called his name and he said nothing.
Remember me EJ I'm your brother Bobby. His eyes were the only thing I recognized; they told me it was EJ. The rest of his crippled and mangled body was beyond recognition. Bennie called his name and he didn't flinch, he didn't know his name. Only after moving towards him did he look in his direction. Two things were clear, not only did he not recognize us; he was afraid of us. We wanted to touch him to let him know his family was with him and never forgot him. He kept looking around the room as if he were an animal ensnared in a trap searching for a way out. Doctor Cooper said let's leave him alone for a while; he needs rest.

Back at our room I told Bennie; I don't know if mom can handle seeing him like that. Mom's a strong person he said, that's her son for better or worse she will be okay. Bennie, can you believe it, did you see the way he looked? His head and face looked like some guy went crazy on him with a Billy club, and those hands are so crippled I doubt if he can write his name. I've got to find out what happened, and I'm not sure he will be able to tell me. No matter what happens we have to let him know we're still family

Later that day we ate chow with Gunny Reyes. Bennie turned to him and said Gunny, what in the world is going on? What's the story here? Sergeant Major you know I can't say a lot because everything has to be kept under wraps. Another reason is because I know so little about what the story is. What I tell you has to be kept between us, it's not much but it's all I know. Your brother was turned over to the American Embassy by some Vietnamese. From what I understand he was once married to a Vietnamese woman and had been living in the country with her until she died. I don't like that said Bennie those bastards are going to say he was a collaborator, a coward, a deserter who fraternized with the enemy and should face a court martial. Giving EJ a court martial after all those years of suffering would be the ultimate injustice. How could they even mention those words? Bennie I said, they haven't mentioned them yet. I wondered if it were more convenient to declare him dead than expend time and money looking for him. My worst thought was how fellow Marines could have left him behind.

Around 0800 the next day Peterson came to our room. Marines I don't know what to tell you, this is one of the strangest cases I've ever been associated with. I know you have a ton of questions, and I don't have answers for you. We all need answers; we sent for you guys because we wanted your family to know your brother was still alive. No matter what anybody may think, we still see him as part of our Marine family. Are you contemplating a courts martial asked Bennie? Because if you are I'm afraid, you're in for a fight.

Gunny told me you had some concerns about a courts martial. At this point, that's not a consideration. We want to know what happened and to do that we have to convene a Board of Inquiry. It's the only means we have to find out what happened. We're going to beat the bushes until we find some answers. Along the way, we'll conduct extensive medical and psychological tests to determine your brother's mental and physical state and degree of competency. I would like for you guys to keep a lid on this for the time being. Remember our primary concern is for the well-being of a fellow Marine. We're going to send you back home; I promise you I'll keep you up to speed on what's happening.

I asked what about that Board of Inquiry are we going to be involved with that? You bet you are I can't think of two better character witnesses. Sergeant Major, Top, I promise you the Marine Corps is going to do the right thing. Gunny Reyes dropped us off at the Jacksonville Airport and wished us a safe trip home. Our flight was leaving in an hour which gave us some time to kill at the closest bar. I ordered a vodka screwdriver and Bennie got a whiskey. Bennie looked at me, "what the fuck just happened?" Can you believe this shit? Our brother is alive, we should be celebrating instead I don't even know what I'm feeling. Bennie he's alive be thankful for that. He's alive, but I'm not sure he'll ever be the EJ we knew.

Bennie said maybe not the one we knew, but he's still EJ. God it would have been better if – don't say that. We've got a brother and son back from the dead. Thank God, pray for the best and prepare for the worst. Don't believe that bullshit about no courts martial. The Marine Corps can't afford to get a black eye from this. We got back to Ceeville and went directly to my house. So what do we do Bennie? Man I don't know. Do we tell anybody? I don't think we should definitely not mom and dad.

Do you think mom knows? If she does, we should wait for her to tell us. I don't know if I can keep this from Vanessa she'll know something is wrong. Go ahead and tell her; otherwise, she will think you are freaking out. Yeah, you're right I've got to tell her. I had four screwdrivers, when Vanessa got home I was knocked out stretched out in a recliner. She didn't wake me just gave me a kiss. When I woke she was in bed fast asleep, I slipped in next to her and went to sleep. Whatever my problems were they could wait until morning. As the sun came up the next morning, I looked out the window with a slight hangover. Vanessa was already up preparing breakfast. I rolled out of bed and hit the shower. Before I could get dressed, she was in the bedroom. So how was your mystery trip? Was it some secret mission they wanted to question you about?   Sit here on the bed Vanessa I've got something to tell you that's hard to understand. Are you going back into the Marine Corps? No, nothing like that, EJ is alive. What! Yep, EJ is alive. Where is he? He's in a hospital; he's going to be there for a while. Where has he been, is he all right? I don't know where he's been and no he's not all right. What's wrong? I don't know where to start the whole story just sounds so incredible.

It's like a dream or a nightmare we saw him, and he didn't know who we were, he was afraid of us. Are you going to tell your parents? No! What about your brothers are you going to tell them? No! We're not going to tell anyone. The only reason I'm telling you is because Bennie said if I didn't tell you, you would think I was freaking out. Please don't tell anybody not until we figure this out. She sighed and asked is he well? No, he's sick real sick both physically and mentally. I can't tell you anything else because I don't know anything, nobody does.

They sent for us because they wanted his family to know EJ was alive. He was there a month before they contacted us. No one has any answers only speculations everything is in a flux. A Board of Inquiry is being convened and hopefully we'll figure out what happened. My God she said what will your mother think? I don't know, but something tells me she knows already. Dad will handle it okay, but mom will want to see EJ like yesterday and my other brothers will just spaz. Can you blame them? No, it's like something out of a movie I don't know how to describe it. I thought about the last conversation I had with EJ before he left for Vietnam. I hated the idea of somehow contributing to his fate. I didn't want him to leave, but Jesus, I had no idea something like this was waiting for him. Mom always said he wasn't dead and after seeing him I wasn't sure he was alive.

We got home on a Friday. I had such a sense of uneasiness I didn't go to work on Monday, and neither did Bennie. I was lying on the couch watching television when I fell into a deep sleep and began to dream. I was lying in bed and felt an evil presence. It surrounded me and held me down. My body felt as though it was caught in a vice being squeezed tighter and tighter. I could not move and though I wanted to cry out could barely speak, with all my strength I whispered several times "in God's name, I rebuke you Satan."

From nowhere Chris appeared in the dream and came towards me. He drew a cross on my chest, as he did all the pressure on my body was released. I felt the glory of God and all his power, an indescribable, omnipotent power of love and good. I cried out his name and was not ashamed to praise him. I thanked God and rejoiced in being one with him. My body shook; never had I felt such a presence. I awoke and knew it was more than a dream. I still felt the presence, still felt the power and love and the need to thank God for being my God. For the first time in my life, I knew what my mom understood about God and his love. For the rest of my life, no matter the obstacles to be faced in my heart I would know there is a true and living God.

I didn't know how my role in this scenario would play out. Mom said he wasn't dead and after seeing him I almost wished he were. EJ was going to need every ounce of strength we could muster and then some. I was truly my brother's keeper, whatever was needed I was willing to give. No sacrifice I could make would ever come close to the sacrifices he made. When Pap's farm was stolen there was not one person who could make a difference willing to fight for him. Not one person in a position of authority wanted to see justice served. I would fight for EJ with everything I had. I had plenty of experiences with the Uniform Code of Military Justice

184

(UCMJ). Some of those experiences were favorable, some were not so favorable. Courts of Inquiry were covered under Article 135 of the UCMJ; I found a copy to refresh my memory:

(a)   Courts of inquiry to investigate any matter may be convened by any person authorized to convene a general courts martial or by any other person designated by the Secretary concerned for that purpose, whether or not the persons involved have requested such an inquiry.

(b)   A court of inquiry consists of three or more commissioned officers. For each court of inquiry, the convening authority shall appoint counsel for the court.

(c)   Any person subject to this chapter whose conduct is subject to inquiry shall be designated as a party. Any person subject to this chapter or employed by the Department of Defense who has a direct interest in the subject inquiry has the right to be designated as a party upon request to the court.

(d)   Any person designated as a party shall be given due notice and has the right to be present, to be represented by counsel, to cross-examine witnesses, and to introduce evidence.

(e)   Members of a court of inquiry may be challenged by a party, but only for cause stated to the court.

(f)   The members, counsel, the reporter, and interpreters of courts of inquiry shall take an oath to faithfully perform their duties.

(g)   Witnesses may be summoned to appear and testify and be examined before courts of inquiry, as provided for courts-martial.

(h)   Courts of inquiry shall make findings of fact but may not express opinions or make recommendations unless required to do so by the convening authority.

(i)   Each court of inquiry shall keep a record of its proceedings, which shall be authenticated by the signatures of the president and counsel for the court and forwarded to the convening authority. If the record cannot be authenticated by the counsel for the court, it shall be signed by a member in lieu of the counsel.

My dilemma now was how and what kind of role could I play in this inquiry. What rocks would be overturned and what dirt would be dug up. I don't know what the events were that led to EJ's present situation, but I was sure of one thing. Bennie was right if there were any mention of a courts martial there would be a battle. I loved the Marine Corps and hated being involved in a battle against it, but if there were a choice of loyalties it was no question. EJ was always a fighter now Bennie, and I would fight for him. My training taught me not to make any snap judgments. But, I knew I should be prepared for anything. I didn't know if EJ had a crisis of conscience or whether things occurred that were beyond his control.

At times, I questioned my country and the treatment I received in the Corps. Having seen and read plenty of racial incident reports I knew how ugly things could get. Someone as pragmatic as I was couldn't see the world through rose-colored glasses. Black Marines who served in Vietnam told me things very similar to the incidents EJ described in his letters. Different punishment administered for the same crimes. Offensive and demeaning language directed towards blacks, no products for blacks at the PX. Harassment by MP's ordered to break up groups of five or more blacks, a war within a war.   EJ's letters belonged to me; I hoped letters that would not have to be used in his defense. To pretend that life in the military during the sixties or any other time for that matter was one continuous, cohesive unit would only be a lie. There were always racial tensions floating just beneath the surface. The military in my opinion did its best to neutralize prejudices and had made far greater strides in race relations than the general public, though in some areas it still fell short. I could not speak for the Corps of yesterday, but I thought I knew the Corps of today. LtCol Peterson told me the Marine Corps would do the right thing, and I believed it would. That being said I knew there were many factors to consider; I knew the biggest factor was EJ. Had he remembered what I said when I told him Vietnam was not his fight, that he had a cultural war at home to win. I would have given anything to have him speak to me to tell me what happened. How could anyone return from the dead without someone knowing you were alive?

For several years, I had been bitter about losing EJ. Twenty years after his death I expressed my thoughts about Vietnam and the loss of EJ in a Veterans Day Guest Column for my local newspaper. I pulled out the article and began to read what I wrote: "Veterans Day is dedicated to honoring and remembering our men and women who have served in the military. For some, it's a day to watch parades and ceremonies for others it's a day for somber reflections and appreciation.

On a rainy summer day in 1968, I was riding down College Street talking to my brother who would shortly be leaving for Vietnam. EJ had recently graduated from Robin High School, and we were talking about possible career choices when he told me he was joining the Marines. I thought joining the military was the worst decision he could make. For some of you too young to remember the sixties, it was a period of turbulence and turmoil. Much like today we were involved in an unpopular war and many of our citizens wanted to bring the troops home. A revolution was taking place in America with a clash of cultures and ideals. Citizens' black and white disenchanted and dissatisfied with the status quo were being murdered and spied upon by the FBI. Some were beaten by policemen with Billy clubs, doused with fire hoses and bitten by police dogs.

The quest for civil rights had caused a revolution in America in the South as well as the North. Blacks were no longer content being second class citizens. Martin Luther King Jr., Malcolm X, John and Robert Kennedy were all assassinated. America's cities were burning, and its citizens were rioting. Change in America was met with stiff resistance. Many of our citizens had lost faith in government and rejected its policies at home and its involvement in Vietnam.

Amidst all of the turmoil of the sixties, I was puzzled to find my brother enlisting in the Marines. Why would a young African American male who could not fully exercise the rights and privileges guaranteed him under the constitution sign up for the military? Why sign on to a war against foreigners when there was a cultural war to be won here at home? After completing Boot camp and advanced training, EJ arrived home for thirty days leave prior to departing for Vietnam. From that time forth, I never questioned his reasons for enlisting. When he arrived in Vietnam, we kept in touch through letters until my last letter was returned unanswered.

Corporal Edward Wade Jr. was killed in Quang Tin Province, in the Republic of South Vietnam, on September 10, 1969 by hostile artillery fire. He was a member of Kilo Company, 3rd Battalion, 4th Marines; Edward Jr. is buried in a local cemetery alongside his grandfather. Buried but not forgotten, just as his name is inscribed on the Memorial at the local Veterans Plaza. Countless others like him have their name in places of honor in numerous cities, towns, and hamlets. To all of the families and friends who have suffered a loss they are so much more than names etched in stone. Americans must protect America and each of us has a shared responsibility in making our country a better place. Enlisting in the Marines gave Edward Jr. an opportunity to defend his country and use the military as an avenue for change.

He held true to his beliefs and while I honor his service I question the need for his sacrifice. No matter how jingoistic our sons and daughters are, we should never send them off to war without questioning the need to send them. We should never succumb to apathy and complacency and allow political rhetoric to blind us from the truth.

Freedom requires a sacrifice but never should we pointlessly sacrifice our children. We must ensure the call to battle is for a just cause and not an economic opportunity embarked upon by disingenuous politicians. For selfish reasons, I never wanted my brother to enlist in the military. Now, many years later, I realize his unselfish reasons for volunteering. I miss that skinny bow-legged kid who never had the chance to experience life. This Veterans Day I salute him and so many others like him who gave all they had. There is a photo of Edward Jr. hanging on my wall with his medals and the flag that once draped his casket. I can see the inexperience of youth in his eyes though I can't look through those eyes and visualize what they have seen. I can only look inside the frame and wonder what if? Every day that picture reminds me of the sacrifice he made and each day I strive to prove myself worthy of his sacrifice."

At the time I wrote the article; I thought EJ had made the ultimate sacrifice, now I wondered if EJ had met a fate worse than death. Stressing out would not solve anything, I decided to take it one day at a time. Adversity and challenges were things I experienced for many years, and this would be another battle, a battle I intended to win. Vanessa told me she would put EJ's name on the prayer list at her church. I wasn't one for praying, but never doubted its power. I asked her why she prayed and she pulled out a short poem she carried in her purse, a poem titled "Why I Pray" by an unknown author:

Why I Pray

A homicidal and suicidal mother chose life today

Why I Pray

A young war weary soldier returned home today

Why I Pray

A disgruntled worker found help today

Why I Pray

A God in Heaven would not have it any other way

She gave me a hug and a kiss; I didn't ask any more questions. I loved Vanessa she was the answer to anyone's prayer. I was at max stress level and did what I always did to relieve stress, ran. I ran about two miles and went to a local gym to work out for an hour before I met my brothers at a local bowling alley. Bennie and I decided to tell the rest of the family about EJ. To Chris who was eleven when EJ left it all seemed surreal, he never really got to know his older brother. Of course, he remembered having another brother but it seemed so long ago. For Jason and Tommy the thought of EJ brought back a ton of memories, their oldest brother still alive. Bennie and I gave them the complete run down, and they were as baffled as we were. Jason asked what about mom and dad did you tell them? Tommy said if you haven't told them you should, they deserve to know. Tommy summed it up in a nutshell; they deserved to know. It was a Friday night we decided to bowl a few games, have a few beers, and tell our parents about EJ on Sunday when mom got home from church.

At six a.m. Sunday I was lying in bed when the telephone rang. It was dad he said "son, I think your mother is dead." His message was not a surprise; young men see visions and old men dream dreams. Through a dream, I was given a glimpse of the unknown. I fought my mother's gift for years, now it seemed inevitable I would accept it. Mom came to me in a dream and told me she was leaving.   I was lying there refusing to believe what I knew to be true.   She came into my dream to tell me good bye.

A conversation in a dream and I remembered every word.   I asked her what happened to EJ, she told me EJ would tell me and asked me to take care of him. I promised her I would, and she left. In my dream, she looked perfectly healthy and never told me why she was leaving. Although she didn't say it, I think it was because of EJ. I don't think she could have handled it when she saw him. Or maybe it was because of all the suffering she experienced over the years knowing what her son was going through.   Either way Adelia Wade was gone, and she could never be replaced.

Dad had called emergency medical services and EMS personnel had mom in an ambulance preparing her for a ride to the hospital. I got to the hospital a few minutes after talking to dad. There in a small area adjacent to the Emergency Room was my mom. I touched her; she was still warm, for some unknown reason I started to talk to her as if she were going to answer me. Dad said; she's gone son she can't hear you. She looked calm and peacefully at rest; I noticed dad holding her hand.   This is how it ends I thought. I didn't want her to leave this way, though the way she was leaving didn't matter because I never wanted her to leave. What would dad do now? Mom had been his soul mate for many years, I hoped this would not be one of those cases where one spouse died, and the other one followed shortly after.

Dad was doing okay until the morticians showed up; he began to tell me about the last time he and mom talked. Even though he knew she was leaving it still hurt, tears started to fall from his eyes. He always controlled his emotions; I had never seen him cry. I thought about how much he loved mom, they had been a team for a long time and now half the team was gone. Mom was gone, but he still had a strong support system. Chris, Tommy and Jason made no effort to hold back any emotions, they hurt and their tears showed it. Bennie and I hurt as much though we didn't shed any tears.

Pap was our teacher; we remembered his teachings. Tears were for women; I couldn't shed a tear even though I hurt as much as the rest of them. Dad followed mom's funeral instructions to the letter. She always told us to give her flowers while she lived so she could smell them. She didn't want any at her funeral although mourners left some beautiful ones. She requested no ceremony; friends and family were able to view her body for four hours at the funeral home. Later she was taken by hearse to Alabama where she was laid to rest next to the grandmother I never knew. In what seemed like no time at all someone I knew all my life was gone. My mom was a wonderful, loving and giving God-fearing woman who wanted to go home quietly in her final hour.

I thought I knew her well, but I guess there were some things about her I would never understand. I didn't know she was originally from Alabama, that her mother was buried there. Didn't know she had a younger sister who was raped and murdered as a teenager or that once she had a baby daughter. I never knew she experienced so much grief and heartache in her life not to mention the burden of knowing what her son was going through. Dad decided to tell us about some of the tragedies in mom's life only after her passing. He said she was ready to go; I could understand why. I only saw the bright and happy side of her never knowing about some of the burdens and the dark secrets she carried for years. There would be no attempt to tell EJ of mom's death. Trying to communicate with him would only have been a futile gesture. Tragically he could not mourn his mother's passing. We made no effort to see him; dealing with one tragedy at a time was enough. She requested only her husband and sons make the trip to Alabama to witness her internment. She was laid to rest in a small cemetery enclosed within a wrought iron fence within walking distance of a church. Dad pointed out headstones of relatives we would never know. We met family members who were all foreign and some who bore a remarkable resemblance to mom.

For some reason, we never met them; it puzzled me because Alabama was only a short distance from Ceeville. There must have been some shameful secrets or horrible memories that kept her away for so many years. I said before mom was a wonderful person, but there were some eventful happenings in her life she refused to share. I could never see death as a part of life, grudgingly accepting it only because there was no other choice. Every time he came into our family he not only took a loved one, he took a piece of me. He took a piece of my heart and a piece of my soul. When it was my time to die I wondered if there would be anything left to take except a lifeless body with no heart and no soul. If there was a heaven and I made it there, what would I have to give; what would I have to share when I got there. God didn't have to explain things to me; I learned long ago that I and every other man lacked the intellectual capacity to question or understand God. Regardless of how intelligent we become we will never be able to fully comprehend God. His ways are truly the ways of God.

We got back to Ceeville and dropped dad off at home, the rest of us headed for the "300" which had become our favorite watering hole. It was a hangout for old schoolers; we met there on a regular basis. After a few beers, I suddenly thought about Pap. What would he think about the little boys he left behind? I looked around the table at Jason who as much as Bennie hated it was a seasoned cop; Chris and Tommy were experienced carpenters and construction workers. Bennie and I had retired from one career and embarked upon another one. Time was moving on, and we were moving with it, no longer the young boys Pap left behind. Soon we would be moving up to take our dad's place and then Pap's place. Death doesn't give you an opportunity to be selective; you're given a short time to live and time without end to die.

With mom gone dad, made the decision to retire. His home was paid for; he had earned a factory pension and was eligible to draw Social Security. And besides he no longer had kids to support, he could start to enjoy his life without having to work. Between his peach seed hobby and chores around the house, he had more than enough to keep him busy. Maybe now he would have the time to teach me his craft.

We made several visits to see EJ; his doctor had suggested no more than two people visit at any one time. The first time Vanessa saw him I had to take her out. She was unable to contain her sadness completely overwhelmed with emotion. She remembered the old EJ and seeing him in his current state was more than she could handle. My God what in the world happened to him? I'm sorry, but I could not look at him without crying. She kept apologizing, but I knew exactly what she was going through. She held my hand tightly; I could feel her trembling.

Mom was gone and impossible as it was EJ was getting worse. He would crouch in a corner and not look up even when the nurses tapped him on his back. I thanked God he had given me Vanessa, I don't know what I would have done without her. My life was spinning out of control; she was the one that kept me stable. It had been nearly four months since our first visit to Camp Lejeune and to add to the confusion Bennie, and I were being called back to Camp Lejeune to give statements before EJ's Board of Inquiry. Bennie and I were in a small room waiting to go into another room to give our statements.

Bennie went in first and after about ten minutes the walls seemed to be shaking. I could hear Bennie on the other side of the wall as clear as if he were directly in front of me. "That's bullshit, I don't give a damn what any other Motherfucker says. My Goddamn brother was not a coward" and you, you son of a bitch you better not tell me he was a deserter. The Lieutenant taking his statement came out of the room looking like a broken man, a few minutes later Peterson went in. Shortly thereafter Peterson came out and asked me to come into the room. He said Marines I understand how highly charged this situation is, but I have to ask you to bear with us. No one in any shape or form is saying or implying your brother was a coward or a deserter. Let me state that for the record before I say anything else.

You both were and still are professional Marines; you know that in a Board of Inquiry there are certain questions that have to be asked and sometimes they can put a burr under your ass. Sergeant Major I am not criticizing your actions, I only ask as a professional you understand my position. I want both of you to know regardless of what your experiences were in the Corps this is not and will not become a witch hunt. I'm also a professional Marine; Lieutenant Stevens is a little new at this, although he's trying to do a good job. Now if either one of you is uncomfortable with him taking your statement I will be happy to take it, it's up to you. No sir, I said, I think we're okay with the Lieutenant; Bennie nodded. Well gentlemen he said, I think we'll take about a thirty minute break and resume. Can I get you a cup of coffee? No sir I said, we're fine.

Look Bennie you need to calm the fuck down what the hell did he say to you. Bobby I knew where he was going, I wasn't going to let him take me there, so I headed him off before he could get there. Look you're the calm motherfucker maybe you should go in first. Yeah, I think that's a good idea, and if you hear me yelling like you were, we're getting the heck out of here. After giving our statements and heading out, I noticed another guy in the adjacent waiting room. He stood up when Bennie was giving the Lieutenant hell, and now he was following Stevens. I saw him earlier at the motel, now I wondered if he knew EJ. Peterson met us before we left and personally thanked us for our cooperation. Bennie said I don't trust that motherfucker either.

We went back to our rooms and started packing our bags when there was a rap on the door. I figured it was Peterson when I opened the door there stood the guy I saw earlier at the board. He told me his name was John Gates and asked if I were related to Eddie Wade. I told him both of us were his brothers. He asked if we would like to go off base and grab a beer there was something he wanted to talk to us about. He seemed a bit edgy and nervous. We agreed to meet him off base in an hour at a club called the Sand Trap. The Sand Trap was only a few miles away; John was sitting at the bar he stood up when we walked in. I'm here for your brother's Board of Inquiry. We went through boot camp and ITS[60] before we got separated. I met him again in Vietnam we were assigned to the same platoon. I don't know if he ever told you about me they called me "Ridge Runner." Your brother gave me that nickname in boot camp. What's going on you do know your brother was killed in Vietnam. We thought he was, but he's alive. He took a step backward and said what! No one ever told me he was still alive.

---

[60] Infantry Training School

But how can that be I was there when he got hit, there was nothing left. I mean I was looking at him just before the artillery shells came in. He can't be alive, are you sure? He's alive I said it was as much of a shock to us as it is to you. Were you with him when he died asked Bennie? Yeah, I was, we were returning from patrol when we came under artillery fire. Eddie was one of us there is no way in hell that we would have left him behind if he were still alive.

We went back and searched the area; I found his dog tag in his boot it was all that was left of him. There were body pieces strewn throughout the area; we took back everything we could find. You were in the Corps you know Marines would never leave another Marine behind. You know we would never have left Eddie behind. Even if you hated someone's guts you never left them behind. Did you hate his guts asked Bennie? No way, Eddie, was a good guy one of the best in the Company. Look you may think I'm an old country son-of-a-bitch but what I'm telling you is the truth, and you can verify what I'm saying with any other guy from the platoon.

I told John that wasn't what we were saying, and we were not making any judgments, we just wanted to find out the truth as much as he did. He said I found out who you guys were and were told not to have any contact with you. Nevertheless I had to find out if Eddie were somehow still alive, why else would there be a Board of Inquiry being held over twenty years later. John had a few more beers with us and told us about some of he and EJ's adventures in Vietnam. He freely called himself a redneck but said he was tight with EJ because they were both Southern boys. I immediately understood what he was saying. Black or white people from the South identify strongly with other people from the South.

He had a certain air of honesty about him, and I believed what he told us. If he were a bigot, he had no reason to conceal it. I thanked him for his honesty and for being a friend to EJ. There is always that ten percent that leave you wondering but most Marines have a bond that transcends personal biases. I don't know about Bennie, but I left there feeling less apprehensive than when I came. I was more optimistic and trusting, trust, something I never allowed myself to have. EJ's fate was not in my hands; I could only give him my trust, my love and support. John left the bar and Bennie said, "Do you trust that bastard." Yeah, Bennie I trust him and believe he told the truth. Well I don't trust any of those cocksuckers. Bennie had always been somewhat of a pessimist, and now he was more of a cynic than I was.

A fruit fly[61] came into the bar and spoke to us as he passed. I returned his greeting Bennie only grunted. He said that homo looks like the one whose ass I beat with a belt. Around 1978 Bennie and I were home on leave and went to a local bar looking for Chris. Two fruit flies sitting at a table behind us kept laughing and giggling. Some guy called "June Bug" came into the bar. He saw us and told us he saw Chris at a local motel with two fags taking him into a room. He said it jokingly with a smile until he saw the expression on our faces. Man I'm just trying to tell you about your brother ask those two sitting behind you, they will tell you. We got up and walked over to their table and asked them what happened to Chris. One of them immediately went on the defensive and pulled out a straight razor, their favorite weapon of destruction. Without hesitation, Bennie busted a beer bottle across his face and had his foot on his neck before he could make another move. His friend was much more cooperative when I stuck a 38 in his face.

---

[61] Slang term for homosexual

He told us he didn't know what happened he just saw his two friends leaving the club with Chris, who was drunk. He gave us a description of the vehicle they were driving. We got to the motel and spotted the car. We kicked the door open, there were Chris and the two homos naked in bed. We were wearing heavy leather belts and commenced to beat the shit out of all three of them with a belt buckle. After about fifteen minutes of the belt one of the homos told us he had slipped Chris a Mickey but they didn't do anything to him. He started begging for mercy, we did show mercy we only beat the crap out of him we didn't kill him.

They picked the wrong guy to engage in their perverted practices, and their bodies had the bloody belt buckle bruises to prove it. Unfortunately, Chris had those same bruises; he was pissed at me and Bennie for a long time. Bennie and I weren't homophobes we just didn't have the sensitivities and compassion others had, besides we didn't like fruit flies. We finished our beers and headed back to the hotel. I got home, and Vanessa wanted to know how things went. I told her about Bennie's explosion and the guy we met who personally knew EJ.

What did he tell you? He told us EJ was a good Marine and that no one would have purposely left him behind. He swore to us he saw EJ killed and that he was the one that found his dog tags when they went back to search the area. Did you believe him? I did there was something about him that made me believe he was telling the truth. During the next few months, Peterson was true to his word and kept us up to date on the progress of the board. It was never anything new but at least he was keeping us in the loop. About two weeks after his last call, he contacted me and told me he was coming to see us. He would not give me anything over the phone but over the weekend he would see Bennie and me.

J. Wesley Gold

Around 0800 on a Saturday morning Bennie and I were at my house having breakfast when there was a knock on the door. I opened the door; there was Peterson, good morning he said. I invited him in and offered him some breakfast. Surprising us all, he accepted the offer. He said I really would like a good breakfast. He took a seat at the table and Vanessa started to fix him a plate. We didn't mention anything about why he was there until he finished his breakfast, and we went into the living room. Vanessa stayed in the kitchen; Peterson invited her into the living room.

He wanted everyone to hear what he had to say. First of all I want to thank you for your cooperation and your support in this difficult situation. The board has concluded its findings. EJ has been returned to an active duty status and will receive full pay and allowances for all the years he was in a KIA status. He will be kept at the hospital until he's physically qualified for release from active duty and retired. Hopefully one day soon he'll be released to your care. I can't discuss anything about the board only what I've already told you and to tell you that all records of the board have been sealed. After all, you've been through I felt I had an obligation to tell you in person. I don't mind telling you this was the conclusion I wanted. Marines, Mrs. Wade again thanks for all your help. You'll be contacted when Eddie has progressed enough to be released. He gave me all the paperwork to prove EJ was still alive which could circumvent problems in the future.

Bennie said sir; we owe you a debt of gratitude. We don't know how to thank you. There is no need to try gentlemen we're all Marines we take care of our own. He shook my hand and then Bennie's I honestly felt he was as relieved as I was. Having those documents sealed meant no one would ever know EJ's story. I'm sure there would be news media coming around once the story got out but now there was no story to be told. His story may have been one worthy of telling now it would become an unsolved mystery. This horrific chapter in EJ's life was coming to an end though I suspected the next chapter would be just as daunting.

I called Tommy, Chris and Jason and asked them to meet us at dad's house. We had good news and wanted to share it. Vanessa grabbed me and gave me a big hug; Bennie even hugged me which was a rarity for him. My faith in the Marine Corps was upheld everyone involved with EJ had gone out of their way to do the right thing. For once my trust in something was justified.

Progress for EJ was slow. A year went by before he progressed to the point where there was a possibility of him being released and sent home. He would always need constant care. He was talking some; I'm not sure he recognized us; at least he wasn't crouching in a corner. When we visited him he would sit at the table watching us and everything we did studying our faces. More than two people could visit now; he especially seemed to like it when we brought children. The doctors could not tell us if he couldn't speak or didn't want to talk. There did not seem to be anything wrong with his speech mechanism.

Gradually week by week he progressed to the point where he seemed to recognize us, he seemed to enjoy our company. Improvements were slow but steadily EJ started to talk more and something else, he began to laugh. Having EJ transferred to a Veterans Administration nursing home in Ceeville was now becoming a possibility. Maybe one day he could come to live with one of us. He was making good progress and hopefully there would be no more setbacks. He looked much better; he had gained weight his teeth had been fixed, and he had a fresh haircut. Yet EJ would have problems for the rest of his life. Mom always told us there was nothing better than a praying mother and I don't think her prayers ended at the grave. I believed those prayers beyond the grave were helping EJ. It was my dad's birthday, Vanessa, and I joined him on a visit to EJ. Dad was talking to EJ, and he seemed to be engaged in the conversation with him. Dad was showing him a picture of his granddad, and it slipped out of his hand. When he bent over to pick it up the chain he was wearing around his neck came out of his shirt and exposed something attached to it. It was an angel carved from a peach seed; a peach seed dad carved for mom years earlier.

EJ saw it; his tired eyes began to sparkle, he moved closer to dad holding out his hand. He wanted to touch it, dad pulled his wheelchair closer. EJ held it in his hands and softly stroked it back and forth covering every ridge and cut and then he stopped. He looked at dad and began to stroke his face, looking at him for a long time. He knew; he knew this was his dad tears started to fall from his eyes; he stretched out his mangled and crippled arms for a hug from his dad. Dad moved closer, and EJ's arms encircled him.

They were both crying, as I watched in awe. Vanessa, two nurses in the room and strangers visiting other patients were crying. I never witnessed a miracle in my life. I was sure I was witnessing one now. The miracle of seeing a father and son reunited after so many years and a relationship reborn. Dad took the angel off his neck and placed it around EJ's neck. This was their moment I got up, took Vanessa by the hand and left the room.

There was little conversation on the way home everyone was in a happy yet pensive mood. No one knew what happened or what it meant. Setbacks occur too often; we didn't want to take a chance on setting our hopes to high. We wanted to think about what happened and enjoy it if only for a short time. A small peach seed had given us a ton of hope. Maybe it was the catalyst needed to bring back his memory or maybe not. Either way it was like a small candle light now illuminated our path on a dark night. We dropped dad off at home; Vanessa and I decided to go out to dinner and celebrate a small victory for EJ. Vanessa wanted shrimp and lobster; I ordered an appetizer knowing I would eat most of her meal anyway. She wasn't a big eater, and I was always happy to help her out. Do you think EJ is going to be okay, she asked? I don't think he will ever be the EJ we knew, but I think he'll be okay. He has a long road to travel. Will you ever tell him about your mother? Not for a long time and only if he progressives to a level where he'll understand what I'm telling him. I feel so sorry for EJ I just can't help it every time I think about him and what he's been through I want to cry.

God has to have a special place reserved for him. I know you don't have much faith in God. No, I do, I have total faith in God. Then why don't you go to church with me Sunday, your brothers go? I don't know I don't know if I'm ready for church yet. Well you'll know when you are, and I'll be ready to take you with me. I didn't know if I would ever be ready for church that bothered me. I didn't understand why my opinions about government policies, politics, and religion were so different from my family. Maybe it was because of the negative vibes I got from my country's history of hypocrisy. Or from less than sincere people like Reverend Winters, the fake "Buckwheat" and the missionaries in Japan.

Some friends and I were standing on the street in Naha, Japan along came two fellows spreading the word of Christ. I listened rather intently until I found out where they were from. They told me they were from South Africa. This was during the apartheid era; these guys were in another country spreading the good news of Jesus Christ. You're from South Africa I said, and you're here attempting to tell me about Christianity. You're from South Africa, and you're here in Japan telling me about the teachings of Jesus. Why don't you go home and preach the teachings of Jesus to your white racist government?

But sir he said, that's not all of us. I didn't give him a chance to say anything else I turned and left. Maybe the guy wasn't guilty of what I was accusing him of. But as far as I was concerned, it was guilt by association. There were good people in the world I knew that, and maybe if I stopped being such a cynic I could find more of them. I didn't want to think about those guys I didn't know who was right or wrong, for now it felt good just to be home. My family was nearby, and it was good running into people from years past. Some recognized you, and there was that awkward moment when you tried to figure out who they were without asking their name. And at times it worked in reverse.

Ceeville had grown significantly and was no longer the small town I grew up in. Unfortunately, too many of its residents still had a small town mentality which at times can be synonymous with small minds, narrow minds that resist progress. Here there was too much emphasis placed on Civil War Reenactments, restoring Confederate forts and showcasing Hillbilly Balls. White Southerners were the only people I knew who could not disassociate themselves from a racist past. People who regularly celebrated losing; I could never figure that one out.

They had to know every civil war reenactment helped to preserve the legacy of hate that created a bigger divide between black and white. They passed it off as heritage not hate, but I knew differently. They could claim the Civil War was about states' rights and not slavery but I wasn't buying it. I knew it was all about states' rights to have slavery. Still I was thankful there were no more "colored" and "whites" restroom signs around. I had grown to love cities like San Diego, Atlanta and Virginia Beach, yet Ceeville provided something they couldn't, a sense of family and history.

With all of its good memories and bad, Ceeville was my link to things past. It was where my dad taught me to drive a tractor, where my mom taught me to make "T" Cakes and where I ate bologna and cheese sandwiches at Mr. Ipp's grocery with my brothers. Where I met my wife, and it was the place where the people I loved most called home. Civilian life was a big adjustment from military life. Being able to work eight hours a day and go home took some getting used to. Not having to worry if every task were completed or if a safe were secured. There were a lot of former military personnel working at the VA. Although it was an eight-hour operation after work everyone went in different directions. Unlike the military where you worked, ate and lived in the same community. I missed the after work functions I was used to. I loved my family, but I sometimes missed the camaraderie of the Corps.

Although as I said earlier the military is a young man's game, I was glad, I moved on. I took off-duty education courses while I was on active duty and decided to complete my degree. I enrolled in a local college and started to attend classes. I attended a satellite college on the nearby military base with active duty soldiers, retirees and dependents. The students were older than the average college student, and it was a lot easier to attend classes where you didn't feel like an old man in the class. I had acquired a great deal of knowledge in the military and class work came easy for me. Taking college classes made me aware of how the world had changed in a few decades. My school system was integrated all the way to the college level. Black History was being taught as part of the regular school curriculum. With so many different nationalities in the class, I got a much broader perspective than I ever would have going to mediocre segregated schools. My professors were black, white and everything in between. I thought the world was changing then I remembered my trip to the Post Office.

I went for my hiring interview and got there early, the Postmaster's secretary told me he would be in shortly. I took a seat in the waiting area in front of her desk. While waiting a white couple came in and took a seat. When the Postmaster arrived the secretary told the white couple "the Postmaster can see you now." The young couple politely told the secretary I was first. I got up stood directly in front of her desk and said "you do see me don't you? I mean I'm not invisible am I?" She acknowledged that she did see me; I went into the Postmasters office. I had a few choice words for this individual; I held back because I needed a job wondering if someday I could live in a world where race didn't play a part. The actions of that young couple, however, told me that, in fact, the world was changing.

9 IT'S A GIRL

Vanessa and I liked to catch a movie on Friday night as part of our regular routine. It made us feel like kids again eating popcorn and sneaking a kiss. The movie house downtown had long been abandoned, now theaters were located in nearby malls with giant screens, Dolby sound, and multiple movies playing simultaneously. We watched the movie from the top seat I don't know why. I guess subconsciously we could not get away from the Roxy and its balcony. On Saturday, I got up early, mowed the lawn, trimmed the hedges, and washed cars. I usually finished my chores around noon and stretched out on the couch with a cold beer to watch TV. I heard Vanessa outside talking to the mailman and minutes later she came through the door shuffling letters. Vanessa said you've got a letter. Is it from the President again or one of his flunkies I asked? Don't know she said there is no return address. I asked her to open it, she started reading it.

She was standing up pulled out a kitchen stool sat down and continued to read. You'll want to read this. Not wanting to leave my beer I said I'll read it later. No, you'll want to read it now. Whose it from? She didn't answer just handed me the letter. Talk about getting a Saturday morning shock, it was from my first wife whom I had not seen or heard from in over twenty years. Dear Bobby she wrote, I know this letter will come as a complete surprise to you. You may still hate me for what I did, but this is about something more important than you and me. I'm sick, and there is a good chance that I will not be alive by the time you get this letter. You have a daughter; I haven't told you all these years because I was too self-conscious and afraid of what you would think of me. When you left me the guy, I had an affair with left me too. He found out I was pregnant and didn't want anything to do with me. He told me it wasn't his baby, and if I played around on my husband I was probably playing around on him. I don't know why but I decided to name my daughter after you and not him. After she was born I took him to court seeking child support and as it turns out he was right, it was not his daughter, the blood test proved it.

I know you may not think much of me, but you, and he were the only ones I slept with. I'm sorry; I didn't have courage or faith enough to tell you she was your daughter. She's a grown woman now, but she still needs her father. You're a good person; I know you will treat her like the daughter she is. You don't know how I've suffered all through these years over a foolish mistake. My only regrets are that I never gave you a chance to know your daughter, and you never gave me a chance to say I'm sorry.

I've carried that guilt with me for a number of years and hope that you can eventually forgive me. Please contact your daughter. She's out of college and working as a nurse, she needs her family. I have included her address and telephone number in Atlanta. Her name is Bobbie Wade. I pray you love your daughter and forgive me....... Renita. I didn't know what to think I was stunned and sat there holding the letter not knowing what to believe. My mind raced back over twenty years to the last time I saw Renita. Why would she do this to me was she trying to play me for a fool a second time? Finally, I wadded the letter up and dropped it in the trash can. Vanessa promptly pulled it out. Don't think about this right now she said, drink your beer later you can decide what you're going to do. I only have one question to ask, did you give her a chance to tell you she was sorry? No, no I didn't. Well honey, you've already made one mistake, please think about this before you make another one. Vanessa we don't know anything about this girl. We know she is your daughter. No, we don't it's just what someone told me in a letter. It's more than a letter Bobby it's a dying declaration, think about it! Why is life so complicated with unexpected twists and turns? I wasn't asking for much all I wanted was a quiet Saturday afternoon to drink beer and watch football. I wasn't the one who ruined my first marriage, but now I was being forced to accept the fact that my actions denied me a relationship with my only child. I didn't think of myself as a bad person but what she said was true. I had never given her the opportunity to say I'm sorry. To make matters worse I never gave it a second thought before today. Vanessa said honey I'm going over to help mom out with some things, stretch out on the couch and relax. I'll be back in a little bit.

About thirty minutes after Vanessa left Bennie and Tommy were coming through my door. What's up said Tommy? Nothing! Hell said Bennie; something must be up, or Vanessa would not have told us to come over. Did Vanessa tell you that? She sure did what's up? I went into the kitchen got the letter and gave it to Tommy. Let Bennie read it when you're through. They both read it, Bennie said well you know you were pretty cold.

Pretty cold, you said I did the right thing. Yeah, but that was a long time ago. What about your daughter said Tommy? Tommy how do I know that's my daughter. Well if you're not sure a DNA test will let you know. But I don't think you'll have to do that because Renita knew about DNA tests too. Bennie said it doesn't matter about any damn DNA test. When I see her, I'll know if she's your daughter. And besides I don't know of anybody who would lie about something like that on their death bed. Look I don't know if she's dying and don't know if her child is my child.

Before I make any decisions there are some things, I need to find out. Well there is one thing I know said Tommy. Vanessa sounded excited when she called me on the phone. She hadn't told me anything, but I could hear the excitement in her voice. And right now I would say Vanessa is making plans for her daughter. What? You heard me. You know what big brother said Tommy. You might have made some mistakes in your life, but I think you made up for a lot of them when you married Vanessa. She's for real, and I'm proud to have her as a sister. Well what about me? Yeah, I'm proud to have you as a brother too sometimes. So make this one of those times. He's right said Bennie, don't make us look bad.

You're getting a daughter without having to change the shitty diapers. On the serious side, I think having a daughter would be the best thing that could happen to you. Life doesn't always throw bad eggs your way sometimes it gives you a few good ones. I know we've got a lot of things going on right now, but this may be something you can tag as a win. Besides me and Tommy are already here, call over some 5-Up players and let's beat some ass. Fire your grill up so we can cook some hamburgers and drink up all your beer. I called a few friends and minutes later we had enough players to make up several teams. Tommy said, "Bennie before we get started tell us a good lie; I mean story." Hey, I never tell a lie but I do have a good story. Now I wasn't there but the guy who told this story swore it was true.

It had been a slow day at the Horseshoe Club, "Boss Man" the Zebra working the counter was ready for last call. He had only five customers who were all somewhat inebriated. Two horses named Mr. Wee Wee and Jim Bob sitting at one end of the bar. Two mules Grady and Foot Stomper sitting at the opposite end of the bar and a one-eyed Jack Ass named Ziggy sitting in the center. Last call said, "Boss Man" anybody want another round? Give us, another round said Ziggy, two red horse beers for Jim Bob and Mr. Wee Wee, two wild mule beers for Grady and Foot Stomper and I'll have another crazy donkey. Horses are light weight beer drinkers and after a few hours of drinking they began to get loud and indirectly insult the mules. Mr. Wee Wee talking to Jim Bob said man, I met this fine young filly at the feed store the other day. She asked, "Are you the one I saw pulling a wagon loaded with kids in the Christmas Parade?" I said, "hell no," looking in the direction of Foot Stomper and Grady, you must have me mistaken with one of your mule friends. I told her I'm a thoroughbred baby Mr. Wee Wee does not pull wagons; I eat corn for dinner, not hay. Jim Bob said speaking of pulling I saw old Foot Stomper out in the field pulling a plow. That plow must have strained him because he let out a fart that sounded like one of Custer's Cannons.

They couldn't stop the laughter, Jim Bob said the reason they fart so loud is because they have really big butt holes. Foot Stomper said you two guys are full of crap, thoroughbred my foot you two nags earn your hay by running that dirt track at Smokey's. He decided to flip the script and play their game, he said Grady did you hear what happened to Jim Bob? No, what happened? Well it seems his neighbor had a mare named Molly who came in heat and her owner wanted old Jim Bob to provide some stud work. When Molly was brought to Jim Bob's place his owner said Jim Bob can't breed her. He told Molly's owner you own me a lot of money, we can't conduct any business until you pay me. Jim Bob had been patiently listening to the conversation.

As they were about to leave Molly swished her tail a couple of times in front of Jim Bob, when he smelled her pleasure zone he broke down. He fell on his knees and said no, no, God no, please boss, please, please, please don't let her go, he'll pay you; he'll pay you. He was worse than a dog begging for a biscuit. Not wanting to be outdone Jim Bob said man you know that shit would never happen to Big Jim, I put the "S" in stud. Horses are always ready for a fight, and they were okay with taking on the mules until Foot Stomper stood up. Jim

Bob said, "damn" you're a big son of a gun I'll bet you can tear up some hay. Mr. Wee Wee said we didn't mean anything man we didn't know you guys were mules, we thought you were Jack Asses. What the hell do you mean by that asked Ziggy? Mr. Wee Wee said oh, I'm sorry, Mr. Jack I didn't mean to offend you. My names not Jack said Ziggy. Oh, I'm sorry, Mr. Ass. What's wrong with you stupid horses my name is Ziggy, are you trying to piss me off? You guys think you're funny it wouldn't be so funny if I came over there and ass-kicked you. Oh yeah, said Jim Bob and get your one good eye messed up.

By this time the mules were feeling pretty good and Grady still seated at the bar said, "Don't talk about Ziggy like that." Anyway he could be your daddy. Hell he's not my daddy said Jim Bob, not that one eyed hee haw. Foot Stomper now completely under the influence of his beer said yeah or he could be your momma. How in the hell could I be his momma asked Ziggy? Foot Stomper apologized and said sorry, Ziggy those damn horses have me screwed up. Ziggy said all of you have gotten on my last nerve; I'm about to tear up some shit in here. Finally, Boss Man fearing his place might be broken up picked up his shotgun and racked it. He said stop acting like animals; I just had a new water trough built and put fresh straw on the floor. You horses and you mules it's time to go, as they staggered towards the door Boss Man said hold up. Pointing to Ziggy still seated at the bar he said take your ass with you.

Laughing Tommy said hell Bennie I thought you said that was a true story. Come on Tommy you know any story that starts out with "this is a true story" is probably a lie. But what the hell it was a funny lie. Jason brought his son Jabari with him; I wanted to give him a few tips on playing the game. Jabari remembered a joke he heard at school and said hey, Uncle Bobby did you here this one. The devil called God and asked him to transfer some of the Niggas from Hell to Heaven. God said why would I want to do that? The devil said

212

because they are causing chaos down here. God said, well what have they done now? The devil said you would not believe it; they done put the fire out. Look I said that might be funny but you know I'm not into Nigga jokes. Yeah, I know said Jabari you guys don't like them, but I thought it was funny. I mean it's not like there is anybody here you guys were laughing. We're here said Jason and I've told you about those "Nigga" jokes. Bennie said aw what the hell leave him alone maybe we're living in the past. Nigger doesn't mean what it used to. I'm not sure but to me Nigger will always mean Nigger.

Having said that I thought about what I overheard in a bowling alley. There was a group of black and white teenagers hanging out. One white kid asked a black kid if he knew another white kid and he said "bet that's my nigga" and they all laughed. They all laughed, and I knew I would never see that word the way they saw it. They would never have my degrading experiences with it and never have to carry the baggage from it. Maybe it was my generation stuck in the past and refusing to forget the pain and disgust caused by a single word "nigger." But hey, I said it's no big deal let's get that grill going. These guys proved one thing; there is nothing like family, and if my daughter's mother were gone she needed a family. My leisurely retirement cruise was suddenly starting to take on the feel of a run-a-way roller coaster. EJ coming back from the dead, mom dying, and now out of nowhere I find out I may have a daughter. My life was turning into a soap opera, and I hated soap operas. One question lingered in my head, after the way our relationship ended why would Renita name her daughter Bobbi?

For the moment, I put my problems on the back burner and relaxed enjoying a day off with family and friends. It felt good to be home, it felt even better just being alive. After a few rounds of beer and several games of 5-Up, I was completely relaxed. It was Saturday and all of my problems could wait until Monday. When I got up on Sunday Vanessa was already out of bed getting dressed for church. I said Vanessa when you talked to Tommy yesterday he said you sounded excited. Were you excited? Yes, I was, and you should be too. We're getting a daughter. She's a grown woman Vanessa. I know she's a grown woman, but still a young woman who needs parents. I love you Vanessa. She turned gave me a wink and said I love you too Bobby Wade. Do you want me to fix your breakfast before I leave? No thanks you know I'm a master chef. Yeah, that's why I asked.

Monday rolled around, and it seemed the day would never end. I got home and would have sworn I had been at work at least twelve hours. Vanessa was out and left me a note to call Doctor Cooper. I called and was told EJ was making a remarkable recovery since our last visit, if his progress continued he would soon be released to the care of a nursing facility closer to home. I told Doctor Cooper EJ wasn't going to any nursing facility, he was coming home.

While I was in the mood to take care of business, I took out paper and pen and decided to write my daughter. I had no idea what I would say; nothing I could say would make up for all those missed years. I wrote dear Bobbi, your mother recently told me about you; something I'm sure was hard for her to do. I'm sure she did it only because of her love for you. I'm sorry! Sorry for not giving your mother the opportunity to tell me about you earlier. Sorry for all the years I haven't been a part of your life. Sorry that you haven't had the father and family you rightfully deserved. Although I am not going to linger on things that happened in the past. It's the future I'm concerned with, and I hope that future includes you. There are so many things I want to say to you, so many things I want to tell you. I can't say them in a letter; I have to tell you face to face. I don't know how you feel about this situation. You're my only child; I want to know you and understand the feeling may not be mutual. I only ask that you give yourself a chance to

214

know me. If I don't hear from you remember, my door will always be open. I couldn't think of anything else to say, I sealed the letter and dropped it off at the Post Office before I had a chance to change my mind. Now the ball was in her court, it was up to her to make the next move. I never thought about having a child of my own, now it was a very pleasing thought. Vanessa would love having a daughter as much as I would.

Three days later I got home from work and there on the kitchen counter was a letter from Bobbi. How in the world did this happen I thought. This could not possibly be a reply to my letter. The Post Office was good but not that good. I picked up the letter; there was something familiar about the smell of the envelope. I sniffed it again before I opened it. Dear dad she wrote, I have been thinking about you since mom told me who you were. Trying to build up the courage to write you and then I find out you have been doing the same thing. Thank God you have a wife with courage enough for both of us. It was a wonderful letter; I could not wait to write you back. The first thing I want to do is thank Vanessa for writing such a warm heartfelt letter. She immediately made me feel like part of the family.

I've wanted a dad for as long as I can remember, now I have one. After mom passed I felt as though I had no one else, and now all of that has changed. Vanessa told me you didn't have any other children and that somehow made me feel extra special. I can't wait to meet you, Vanessa, and the rest of the family. I feel as though I know all of you. I have so much to say and so many questions to ask there is no way I can do that in this letter. Thank God I now have a mom, a dad and tons of relatives. I can't wait to meet all of you. You've brought joy to my heart; I'll call and let you know when I'll be able to visit, kiss Vanessa for me, love Bobbi.

With my letter in hand, I found Vanessa outside sweeping off the patio. You wrote her I asked? Well I couldn't wait for you to write her. We looked at each other; I moved toward her put my arms around her pulled her into me and kissed her. I didn't say anything else I left her on the patio holding her broom and wondering about the nut she married.

I called dad and asked what he was doing, he said nothing why don't you come over. Okay, I said feel like drinking a beer. Bennie was pulling up when I got there, Jason, Chris and Tommy were already inside. Everyone grabbed a beer; I put the rest in the fridge. I told them I got a call from the hospital and was told EJ is doing much better. Good enough where there might be the possibility of him being released. Dad said he can stay with me; I'll take care of him. Chris said dad I think he may be too much for you. He's going to need a lot of care. Chris is right I said, I'll take care of him. He needs a place that's handicapped accessible, why don't we build him a place? Now you're talking said Tommy; Bobby has a big lot we can build EJ a place in the back of his house and connect the two.

Dad said no EJ will never be able to live alone. Why don't you build an addition to Bobby's house, I think he would like that better. That way he will never be alone. Chris and Tommy were great carpenters; they built an addition to my house that could have passed for part of the original. EJ had what was essentially a luxurious mother-in-law apartment. Throughout the house doors were made wider, rails added, and outdoor ramps built. He could leave his room and go out onto a nice deck and take in some fresh air. It was ready for EJ and a motorized wheel chair.

Vanessa picked out the furniture and added a woman's touch right
down to the cushions on the couch. It turned out to be a family
project with dad and everyone else giving him some things to remind
him of home. When EJ was ready, his new home would be ready
for him.

I spoke to Bobbi at least once a week, and Vanessa talked to her
at least three times a week (it's a woman thing) and this weekend she
was coming for a visit. She would leave Atlanta early Saturday
morning and arrive in Ceeville around noon. I had a lot of
anticipation and excitement and thought about having a drink to
calm me down. I passed on it, deciding that a drunk wasn't the first
impression I wanted my daughter to have.

We decided against having her meet everyone at once, rather we
would let her get to know me and Vanessa before we took her
around and let everyone else meet her. Bobbi arrived; it was like
seeing her mother walk through the door. She had some of my
features, but she was definitely her mother's child. She was about
five feet four inches and weighed somewhere around a hundred and
fifteen pounds with my mother's eyes. She wore a short stylish hair
style and looked like a high schooler rather than someone who
graduated college. She hugged us both and went directly into telling
us all about herself. She was bubbly with a perky personality,
someone easy to get to know.

I didn't know her although she had a familiar smell, like the letter
she sent me and like her mother. She spent a couple of hours with
me and Vanessa, I asked her if she were ready to meet the rest of the
family. Ready when you are she said. Are you ready Vanessa I
asked? No, I'm going to let you two go, I'm going to stay here and
get dinner ready. We went from house to house; I introduced her
to the family; everyone was excited to see her. She met her
Granddad and his dog a small Jack Russell Terrier he called

"Blackjack," a present Jason gave him after mom died something to keep him company. Blackjack was the perfect companion and dad treated him more like a person than a dog. Dad had a screened in front porch, and on the porch Blackjack had a custom built dog house made by Chris. No one ever got to see dad without getting past him first. Tommy stuck a cigarette in his mouth and took a picture. Dad had it framed and told everyone Blackjack smoked more than he did. In between visiting relatives, I got to know a lot about my daughter. She didn't appear to have a lot of secrets; her life was an open book.

I knew that one day she would ask me what happened between me and her mom. And when that day came I would tell her the full story, not just what her mom did wrong, but what I did wrong. That day would come later; today I just wanted us to get to know each other. We had a wonderful weekend. Vanessa and I hated to see her leave. She told us now she wasn't a stranger; she would see us often. I met her on the first day and began to miss her on the second day. Maybe someday she would leave Atlanta and move to Ceeville. I knew this probably would never happen. She was young and had her own life to live, Ceeville couldn't compare with the bright lights of Atlanta.

EJ continued to improve mentally, physical improvements would come very slow if at all. Doctor Cooper told me he was speaking clearly and could be easily understood. The next time I saw him he was speaking clearly. Problem was he was speaking Vietnamese. I couldn't understand him, and he was trying his best to make me understand. He became frustrated because I couldn't understand him. His medication was doing a good job of controlling his fear; he was so eager to talk to me he was pulling my arm. EJ became so agitated he had to be sedated; I could understand his frustration finally being able to speak and not being understood. Thank God this didn't last long, a couple of months later EJ was speaking English. He continued to have a problem with focusing and at times his thought patterns appeared to be scrambled for lack of a better term. It was as though he had to say to himself speak English, not Vietnamese; it was frustrating to everyone and frustrated him most of all. Six months from that visit EJ was being released; he was coming home. EJ came home; his mental state continued to improve all the while his physical state was deteriorating. It felt great having him home, a nurse took care of him during the day and Vanessa and I took care of him at night. His brothers came by to visit him every weekend, and of course dad came around several times during the week, he and EJ were constant companions.

Vanessa came to me and said you know I want to take EJ to church with me this weekend. Do you mind if I take him? No, I said do you mind if I go with you? She grabbed me kissed me once hugged me and then kissed me several times. The story of EJ's ordeal had gotten out; the local newspaper had requested an interview which we always refused. There were people who would come to my house to see EJ. If he thought, they were there to gawk he pretended he didn't remember them. Others he seemed genuinely glad to see.

Dad spread the word Vanessa was taking EJ to Mount Nebo. We got there early; the church was already packed. The pastor acknowledged EJ and surprised us by preaching an old sermon titled "The Prodigal Son." It was a wonderful sermon; it was good seeing so many people who were honestly glad to see EJ. It felt good to be back in church. I still had mixed emotions but was glad to be there with Vanessa my family and friends.

Our lives were returning to normal. Whenever EJ felt up to it, we ate dinner, played games and watched old movies together. When he got well enough to ask about mom, I told him the entire story even the parts she never told me. He asked me a lot of questions about her and other things that occurred during his absence; he had a mournful expression on his face though he didn't cry; he sorrowfully accepted his mother's passing.

10 HAIL AND FAREWELL

EJ had been home for several months and one day he started telling me his story, a story of pain and heartbreak. He said: on the last day I was with my unit, I remembered being bombarded with artillery fire. There was a loud noise, a bright light, and then I was floating through the air. Before I hit the ground everything started to go black, the next thing I remember I woke up in a bamboo hut with a thatched roof. I had been captured by the enemy; I don't know how they found me alive. My boots, belt and utility jacket, were gone. There was a tremendous burning sensation coming from my back. My hands and feet were tied together bound with rope tight enough to restrict my blood flow, causing numbness in my limbs.

Every part of me either ached or burned, for about a week I had trouble staying awake. The hut was built over bamboo plants; some were purposely cut off near ground level. They were left in strategic places to prevent me from getting into any position that was comfortable. I never got an opportunity to exercise other than when I cleaned my hut, or emptied my toilet which was nothing more than a one gallon bucket. They seldom gave me an opportunity to wash, my muscles started to deteriorate. When my ropes were untied, I had trouble standing up and using my arms and legs. On some days, I received neither food nor water. I had never been a big man and each day I felt myself shrinking, getting smaller and smaller. My diet consisted mostly of rice, if they didn't feel like untying my ropes it was placed on the ground. I ate it out of a bowl the way a dog eats its food. Other times I was given bread and some type of bland soup that tasted like boiled cabbage, or other vegetables unknown to me. Sometimes foul-smelling meat or fish was dumped in my cage. I was hungry enough to eat it but couldn't keep it down.

Other times I didn't even try and on those days my food was dumped on the floor of my cage to attract insects. I had no protection from biting mosquitoes and ferocious ants. My captors kicked me with their boots, beat me with their fists and caned me with bamboo poles. When they tired, of the fun and games they tied me in excruciating positions with rope. No human being should ever be degraded in such a manner. Beaten and interrogated for what, I didn't know anything; I was only a Corporal. I later learned it wasn't to extract information from me; its purpose was to have me denounce my country and fellow Marines. They used race as a propaganda tool by telling me, "You, you soul brother why you here? You not free. Why you hate us? America hates you."

They wanted me to publicly denounce my country and admit that I was fighting for an imperialist nation. They wanted me to acknowledge we were bombing women and children and attacking a small nation that wanted peace. When they asked, "why no one come looking for you?" It made me think, why hadn't someone came? I wondered how I wound up in hell, and why no one cared. How could they have left me behind? The beatings and torture went on forever, when they couldn't think of anything more humiliating for me they urinated on me. Because of the horrendous beatings, lack of food and shameful living conditions, I got really sick and delusional. They gave me enough medicine to keep me alive, not enough to heal me. I was in a zombie like state and thought I was going to die a miserable death locked inside a cage. I didn't know how much longer I would be able to use my deformed hands and the head injuries were causing me to lose memory. I didn't want to forget who I was, and I didn't want the world to forget. I found a rusty P-38[62] underneath the grass of my cage. I risked losing what blood I had left to cut my name into my arm. I can forgive them for crippling my body. I can never forgive them for crippling my mind. I tried to be a good Marine and followed the Code of Conduct. I remembered Pap's teaching and tried to hold back the tears. But they broke me; some nights all I could do was cry and pray.

I had given up hope and prayed for death. When I thought my prayer was being answered some incredible things happened. I was lying in my hut sick, cold and wet and I saw mom. She was standing over me, and it wasn't a dream, she was crying and reached down to kiss my cheek. I held her hand, she told me God was not ready for me to die, that she was praying for me, and then she was gone. Shortly after that a young Vietnamese girl who had been one of my guards risked her life to save mine.

When the Vietnamese soldiers left camp, during the day she would loosen my ropes and try to relieve me of some of my pain. She tried to communicate with me; I couldn't understand her. One day I woke up, and she was inside my prison, she didn't have her weapon. She stretched out her hand and placed something underneath the mat I was sitting on. She left, and I reached under my mat to see what she had placed under it. It was something I would never have expected an enemy to give me, a copy of "The New Testament." The same miniature type I carried before I was captured.

Later she brought me a piece of fruit, a mango, I devoured it eating every part of it including the seeds and the stem. As often as she could, she brought me fruit and bits of meat. A terrible part of

---

[62] Small folding can opener sometimes called a "John Wayne" used to open "C" Rations

my ordeal was that I had been completely isolated. I saw no other prisoners and could not communicate with anyone. I spoke little Vietnamese and wished I had taken the time to learn their language before I was captured. I only knew the crap every Marine and soldier learns bookoo, boom boom, and poon tang. My Vietnamese captors spoke broken English at best. This angel of mercy was my only link to humanity.

When my mind began to lapse into forgetfulness, and my body was so crippled I couldn't try to escape, they no longer tied me up or secured my hut. They knew I was dying and didn't deserve their attention. They broke camp pulled out and left me to die. It was then that my guardian angel pulled me from my prison and from death's door. I had no way of knowing what year it was or how long I had been there. I'm not even sure the war was over when they abandoned camp and left me to die.

She literally pulled me from my cage because I was too weak to assist her. The pain was so great I cried, when she tried to get me out I resisted, I wanted to die. I was covered with sores and scabs; every part of me was in pain. With the aid of two more women, she got me out of my prison and took me to an orphanage ran by her mother and two sisters. Ironically an orphanage supported by American soldiers. She bathed me, and I can't describe how painful it was. She cut off my hair which contained God knows what and put medicine on my sores. She started the slow process of bringing me back to life. After countless nights of sleeping on the ground, I slept in a bed. At first I couldn't adjust to it; I was so wracked with pain I had trouble sleeping. I was given morphine and for the first time in a long time I could sleep. I slept but was tortured by nightmarish dreams that nearly drove me insane. I couldn't tell if I were conscious or unconscious. I don't know how long I was bedridden unable to walk and care for myself. Linh was the name of the angel who saved my life and unofficially she took me as her husband. Her name was Nguyen Tan Linh, and it was because of her humanity, I was able to survive. She was an enemy, someone who held my life in her hands and someone who became the love of my life. I spent years at the orphanage helping her care for abandoned children, many of them Amerasians and other orphans whose parents were killed in the war. Others were kids no one wanted. When Vietnamese officials would, come through inspecting the facilities, I would hide so afraid I became paralyzed. I couldn't walk or talk only crouch in a closet corner. I could not control it that same fear paralyzed me when I arrived back in my country. I don't know how to explain it but sometimes I don't know where I'm at, and it frightens me because I can't control the fear.

Linh taught me her language and her culture; she gave me a totally different image of Vietnam. She was a loving, compassionate, person beautiful on the inside and outside. She defied her own family to care for and love me, loving me to the day she died. And if she had not died I, would have died in Vietnam with her. I was the enemy who at one time would have killed her yet she forgave me.

I forgot about my past and made no effort to reconnect with it. My life was with Linh, and I will love her forever. Many in her country would have branded her a collaborator, many in mine would have branded me a traitor. She died as a result of wounds she received in the war. After her death, her relatives took me to the American Embassy, I was returned to my country. I was taken to Kadena Air Force Base and hospitalized. I never had any type of identification; they identified me by the name I had cut into my arm a long time ago. You're the only person I will ever tell this story; no one else will ever know. Everyone will have an opinion, but I don't care they can have any opinion they want. I came home because of the grace of God, my mother's prayers and the love of a good and forgiving woman. I thought a lot about the last conversation we had, and I hope you never felt guilty. I joined the military because it was something I wanted to do, and believe it or not after all that has happened to me I'm not sorry; I joined. You were proud of me once; don't change your mind about me now, I will always be EJ. This is a great country. I realize that now more than ever and so do you, though you may not admit it to yourself.

Mrs. Castleberry was wrong when she told me my country hated me; she was my country and she loved me. Mom was right when she told you not to be bitter to learn to forgive and forget. You were wrong about those missionaries in Japan. I looked at him and said EJ I never told anyone about those missionaries, how do you know about them? How do you know that EJ? He was out on his deck sitting in his wheelchair he pushed himself up and stepped out.

Astonished I said you can walk! He said yes, and I won't need this anymore. I looked closely at him; he was standing erect; his hands were normal, and so was the rest of his body. He looked remarkably like the young kid he was when he left home. I've got to go Bobby; it's time for me to leave. Where are you going? He didn't answer; he stepped off the deck and walked into the yard. There standing in front of him with an outstretched hand was a lady I had never seen before; he reached out took hold of her hand, and they faded away. I woke up with a jolt; I couldn't believe I was dreaming. I moved so quickly I woke up Vanessa as I jumped out of bed and ran towards EJ's room. He wasn't in his room; I looked towards his deck, there he was sitting in his wheelchair.

I walked up to him and called his name; he didn't respond. I checked his pulse; there was none, and he wasn't breathing. His mutilated and mangled body sat motionless within his chair. EJ had made it back to his family to die. Is he okay, asked Vanessa? No, only his body is here his soul has moved on. After a lifetime of pain and suffering on earth, he had moved to a higher plane. Death is seldom a welcomed visitor. Yet I smiled knowing EJ now had a healthy body and eternal youth, truly he was in a better place.

His death for me brought about a time for soul searching. Through all of his trials, EJ loved his country and fellow man. His ideals never wavered and on some things neither had mine. I realized as close as EJ, and I was, there was still a great ideological divide between us. In some areas, things had changed very little in this country and as long as greed and opportunity existed chances are they never would. I blamed that greed and opportunity for having taken a brother from me. No matter how hard I tried, I could not justify his death.

For over twenty years, I took an oath that said I would support and defend the Constitution of the United States, seldom considering what that meant. It meant America is my country and I put my life on the line to defend her. It means I have a moral and ethical obligation to ensure my country upholds the ideals adopted in the Constitution. Not only for the top 5 percent who have riches beyond one's dream, but for the bottom 5 percent struggling to pay their bills and feed their children. It means I should question why poor citizens were given draft notices, and affluent ones were given deferments. It means I should ask why a true patriot would not put his life on the line and defend his country. Rather than use political and family connections to garner a deferment and have someone else defend it.

It means I have a responsibility to ensure America honors her commitment to blind justice for all, and not turn a blind eye for others. It means I should challenge her when incarceration is given more consideration than education, for some of her citizens. It means I should never allow America to stop being the land of opportunity and promise, never allow her to stop being the greatest nation on earth. I will always be the first in line to commend my country for a praiseworthy accomplishment and the first in line to criticize her when she forgoes the opportunity. My country wasn't perfect; there were things I disagreed with. Having visited numerous foreign countries I knew there were very few that allowed me the freedoms I enjoyed here. Looking back, I saw my country had made great strides in the area of civil rights, struggling to ensure the same freedoms for all its citizens during my lifetime. Changes brought about by the voracity and determination of ordinary citizens. Citizens willing to be beaten and killed in the pursuit of "equal opportunity, freedom, and justice for all." And by the efforts of extraordinary politicians who chose "moral principles over profit."

I couldn't live the rest of my life being cold and unyielding, blaming everyone for mistakes made by some in the past. I couldn't overcome all the ills of society it was beyond my scope. My job was to try and make America better starting with myself. I kicked a junkie out because I was more concerned with myself than doing the right thing, trying to save her life. At times, I was too critical of myself and those I came in contact with, setting unrealistic standards for me and other people. My daughter had grown up without me because of my stubborn unforgiving nature. My mom told me to learn to forgive and forget. I had learned to forgive but learning to forget would be much harder.

Over the years, I learned to stop putting people and things into collective groups. I strived to judge each and every one by their actions and merits, though I had not abandoned all skepticism. I understand a certain amount of skepticism is healthy for Americans and America. My stalwart hatred towards hypocrisy had not changed.

I still believed the extremist views of religious zealots and self-serving politicians pose our greatest threat to a civil society. These threats are just as dangerous, destructive and real as any conceived by a terrorist group.

Dad always said some people get older and wiser; others just get older. I thanked God I was the one becoming older and wiser with a greater appreciation for all things human. I now knew all scriptures in the bible written by man were penned through divine intervention of God. Simply declaring myself a non-Christian didn't give me a free pass. God's rules are rules for Christians and non-Christians alike. After many years, I understood what my mom told me, "only God is perfect."

History had repeated itself and here we were preparing to bury my brother again after so many years. My brother who had died was reborn and died a second time. For a brief moment, I had my older brother back, now I was able to answer the question of what if. I now knew he would have been the same person he always was. Someone with a high regard for family, friends and country. I was still bitter and sorry for the appalling things that happened to him in his life. But, pleased to know he was someone who overcame adversity without malice. This time for me things were different. I accepted his death without the rage and turmoil I had experienced earlier. I felt calm even peaceful knowing he was no longer suffering.

EJ left a will and instructions for his funeral. He did not want his old grave site disturbed and requested burial in a nearby Veterans Cemetery, only his headstone was removed. Some of his requests were unusual, but I was determined to follow his wishes. After my wedding, all my uniforms were cleaned and stored away. I never intended to wear them again for any occasion. I wasn't going to join any veteran's organization or march in any parades. My years of wearing a uniform were over. Nothing had given me greater pride than to serve my country and serve with Marines, now it was time to move forward. Now because of EJ's request, I was wearing Dress Blues seated within the pews of Mount Nebo. The crowd was so large the front doors were opened, and people lined the walkway all the way out into the parking lot. Reverend Winters was no longer around, a new pastor, Reverend Bingham had replaced him, and. Somehow it gave me a sense of comfort.

EJ like his mother had requested a short and simple funeral. The service was almost over as the musicians prepared to play a special song he requested. "We shall Overcome," I hadn't heard the song in a number of years. EJ called it his song; that's the song he told me; that's the song I want to take me out. I understood the song and knew why he and every child of the sixties loved it. He knew exactly what he wanted, how he wanted it played, as if he were listening to it. For me, it was a song that brought back good and bad memories. I witnessed the civil rights marches, heard the song for many years and understood its passionate plea for justice, its yearning for change and its cry for hope. But why did he forego the traditional song sung by legendary gospel artists, for this instrumental version from a jazz musician? Sister Leola Beaumont the piano player took her seat in front of the keys. A young Marine with a clarinet in hand stood a few feet away. They were in position to play Larry Golding's rendition of "We Shall Overcome." Every Marine in attendance rose from his seat, placed his cover over his heart, looked directly at EJ's casket and stood in silence. After a few notes, I knew why he chose this particular cut. It was beautiful, a sweet, haunting, rendition that captured the spirit and mesmerized the soul.

It was the music of life that for a brief moment held death at bay. It filled the chapel and took you to a place where times were hard but simple, when everything could be made whole with a kiss on the cheek or a pat on the head, when a big brother was the best friend you ever had. My eyes were fixed on the flag that draped his casket. He told me once I was proud of him, and pleaded for me to overlook what he had become.

There was no need for pleading. I would always be proud of him. My heart ached, but I would not break, I would not cry. In a whisper, I heard my grandfather's voice telling me be strong. Tears are for women and a man should give them a shoulder to cry on. His voice faded, and I felt the gentle hand of my mother wiping the tears streaming down my face. Tears for my grandfather, tears for my mother and tears for my brother, it's all right she said; it's all right.

He knew, yeah, he knew, this one would get me!

J. Wesley Gold

Epilogue

While this story is one of fiction, the horrors of war are very real. Our sons and daughters are returning from Iraq and Afghanistan with physical and mental scars that will never heal. We owe these warriors a debt of gratitude for willingly putting their lives on the line in defense of American's freedom. I understand the necessity of going to war. I also recognize the obligation to fight for peace. We must ensure the drumbeat for war is justified. I honor those dedicated men and women and abhor those political leaders who see them as little more than expendable pawns in a chess game. We owe them something better.

J. Wesley Gold

ABOUT THE AUTHOR

J. Wesley Gold was born in Chapsmanboro, Tennessee, one of fifteen siblings. He was raised by his mother following the early death of his father. He received his secondary education at Burt High School Clarksville, Tennessee and completed his undergraduate studies at various colleges. A military veteran who currently spends his time gardening, writing, and enjoying the works of other writers. He lives in Clarksville with his wife and grandson.

J. Wesley Gold

Peace is costly, but it is worth the expense.

---African Proverb

44209886R00149

Made in the USA
Charleston, SC
17 July 2015